WHO WATCHETH

Also by Helene Tursten

WHO WATCHETH

HELENE TURSTEN

Translation by Marlaine Delargy

First published in Swedish under the title *Den som vakar i mörkret*
Copyright © 2010 by Helene Tursten
Published in agreement with H. Samuelsson-Tursten AB, Sunne, and
Leonhardt & Høier Literary Agency, Copenhagen

English translation copyright © 2016 by Marlaine Delargy

First English translation published in 2016 by
Soho Press
853 Broadway
New York, NY 10003

Library of Congress Cataloging-in-Publication Data

Tursten, Helene | Delargy, Marlaine, translator.
Who watcheth / Helene Tursten ; translated by Marlaine Delargey.
Other titles: Den som vakar i mhorkret. English
ISBN 978-1-61695-404-8
eISBN 978-1-61695-405-5

1. Murder—Sweden—Ghoteborg—Investigation—Fiction. 2. Police—
Sweden—Ghoteborg—Fiction. I. Title

PT9876.3.U55 D4613 2016 839.73'74—dc23
2016019150

Printed in the United States of America

10 9 8 7 6 5 4 3 2 1

To Johan Fälemark and Hillevi Råberg
with grateful thanks for all your help on the
crossover between literature and film

WHO WATCHETH

With me they are safe. I protect them from evil. That is part of the agreement. They love me. And of course I love them, every single one of them. They need me. Their loneliness is immense. I am there for them. I enable them to feel safe and secure. I will show love to a thousand generations of those who love me and keep my commandments.

I am the one who watcheth in the darkness. I am the Guardian.

THIN VEILS OF mist lingered in the glow of the street lamps, but soon they would disperse completely. The gusts of wind were getting stronger all the time, carrying the first drops of rain. Dampness clung to her face as she leaned forward, fighting her way across the parking lot. Nobody was out and about without good reason; even the dog owners in the area seemed to have abandoned the idea of a last walk. The neighborhood was dark and silent; most people had already gone to bed. Only Bosse Gunnarsson's kitchen window showed a warm, inviting light. He was sitting at the table with a sudoku puzzle as usual, his reading glasses slipping down his nose.

Her own house lay in darkness, but she would soon change that. Switch on the lamps, make a cup of tea, fix herself an egg and caviar sandwich. Light some candles on the coffee table. Wrap herself in a thick, soft blanket and watch the late news. Then off to bed, she promised herself.

She reached into the mailbox: nothing but bills and flyers. She continued toward the door, searching in her purse for the key. As she was about to insert it in the lock, she noticed a rapid movement in the darkness by the shed. Suddenly someone was right behind her. An iron grip around her chest pressed her close to her attacker's torso, forcing the breath out of her body. She was paralyzed by the man's strength and by the acrid stench emanating from him. Only when she realized what he was doing did she manage to offer some resistance. The man was using his free hand to try to loop something around her neck but was having difficulty getting it over her head—not because he was so much shorter than her, but because she was struggling, twisting from side to side as she tried to free herself from his grip. He growled and hissed something unintelligible but managed to hang on to her. After a brief battle he had the noose where he wanted it. Instinctively she reached up and slid one hand under the twine. The attack itself had been so sudden that she hadn't had time to scream. She tried to call for help, but the only sound that came out was a faint whimper; the noose had already been drawn too tight. She felt him loosen his hold on her body so he could put more force into the act of strangulation. Even if she could manage to keep her hand between her throat and the twine, she was getting hardly any air. The darkness flickered before her eyes, and she realized that she would soon lose consciousness.

She managed to slip her other hand into her pocket and rummaged around feverishly. Paper tissues, a box of painkillers, her cigarette lighter . . . Wasn't it there? It must be there! She panicked even more, her movements growing clumsy. Was it in the wrong pocket? The pain in her throat was unbearable. She couldn't breathe.

All at once she felt the car key against her fingertips. She managed to find the little cylinder attached to the key ring and grasped it with trembling fingers. Her thumb slipped on her first attempt, but she could feel the button. Summoning up the last reserves of her strength, she pressed it again.

The screech of the attack alarm sliced through the silent neighborhood. She felt her attacker stiffen, and for a few vital seconds he lost concentration. She lifted one foot and kicked backward as hard as she could. The heel of her leather boot caught him just below the knee. He doubled over and groaned, loosening his grip for a fraction of a second. At the same time, she heard Bosse Gunnarsson open his door and yell:

"What the hell is going on out there? I'm calling the cops!"

Then the presence behind her was gone. She heard the crack of the gate as he flung it open and disappeared in the direction of the parking lot.

"Hey, stop right there! What are you doing?"

Bosse's voice again. Thank God for Bosse. She sank to the ground, trying to call for help, but all that emerged was a pathetic croak.

She had survived. She was alive!

Panic had locked her hand around the slim cylinder in a vise-like grip. She couldn't bring herself to let go of the object that had saved her life.

The screech of the alarm stopped abruptly as the darkness closed around her.

UNDER NORMAL CIRCUMSTANCES Irene Huss was not a morning person, but there were days when she seriously considered trying to become one. Mornings like this, for example. The air was crystal clear, with a hint of crispness left over from the chill of the night. Above the horizon an amazing sunrise filled the sky with intense shades of gold. Could there be a more perfect start to the day?

She drew her robe more tightly around her body as she paused on the top step and inhaled deeply. The moisture from last night's rain intensified the smells. The garden looked as if it had just woken up feeling refreshed. The luxuriant asters glowed deep red in the cast-iron urns on either side of the steps, a final defiant protest against the inexorable approach of the fall.

She padded down to the low gate in her slippers, leaned over and took the newspaper out of the mailbox on the fence. As she turned to go back indoors, she stopped dead. It took a few seconds before she realized that the small garden seat that normally stood between the two kitchen windows had been moved and was now in the middle of the flower bed beneath one window. The newly planted rose bushes were badly damaged: several branches were broken. Annoyed, Irene picked up the seat and put it back against the wall. Strange—it had been there yesterday evening, hadn't it?

• • •

"I THINK SO," Krister said when she asked him a little later.

He was standing at the stove cooking eggs, with crisply fried bacon and halved tomatoes piled on a plate beside him. As far as Irene was concerned, preparing such a hearty breakfast was a total waste of time. Three cups of black coffee and a couple of cheese sandwiches had been her standard start to the day for decades, but now her husband had decided that this was unacceptable. Perhaps it was, but it suited her. When she wondered how fried eggs and bacon could be regarded as healthy in view of the bad cholesterol involved, he had waved away the argument: "GI foods! A whole world of dieters can't be wrong!" To tell the truth, Krister was the one who needed to lose weight, not Irene.

He put a plate of GI breakfast in front of her. As usual she could only manage to push the food around. At times like these she was seriously tempted to turn vegan, like Jenny. Their daughter had stuck to her principles for almost ten years and was now in Amsterdam, training to be a chef specializing in vegan dishes. Jenny was following in her father's footsteps, but perhaps not exactly the way Krister had expected.

"But you have to admit it's weird, the seat being moved," Irene persisted.

"Oh, it's probably just Viktor and his pals fooling around."

"Why would Viktor . . . You could be right."

The boy next door was ten years old, and he and his friends were always running around the neighborhood. As far as Irene could tell, they all seemed to get along with everyone, and she hadn't heard of them getting into any serious trouble. She found it difficult to imagine why they would have picked up a seat and thrown it into the rose bed; it seemed completely pointless. The kitchen window was so low that Viktor could easily look through it if he wanted to; he wouldn't even need to stand on tiptoe.

She shook her head and poured her third cup of coffee.

THE FOLLOWING MORNING Irene woke at seven, despite the fact that it was Saturday, and she didn't have to go to work. Krister had worked late at the restaurant the previous night, and the soft, regular breathing from the bed beside her suggested that he would remain deeply asleep for quite some time. She crept out of the warmth of the covers. When she had finished in the bathroom she put on her running gear, automatically reaching for her knee brace. Her knee was too painful if she didn't use it these days. *I'm starting to fall apart*, she thought gloomily.

She opened the door and jogged down the steps, then stopped and stared straight ahead. Slowly she turned around.

The glorious asters had been torn out of their urns and lay strewn all over the lawn.

"VIKTOR WOULD NEVER do such a thing!"

Malin, who was Irene's neighbor and Viktor's mother, folded her arms and looked deeply insulted. Irene tried to adopt a conciliatory tone.

"To be honest I don't think he would either, but . . ." she began.

"So why have you come here accusing him, then?" Malin snapped.

This was not good for neighborly relations, Irene realized. Nor did it constitute a successful interrogation, her professional side noted.

"I'm not accusing him, I just wanted to eliminate the possibility and ask him if he knew anything," Irene tried to explain.

"Fucking police abuse!" Malin yelled as she slammed the door.

Police abuse? Presumably she meant abuse of power. To a certain extent Irene could understand why Malin was upset, but if she was so sure of her son's innocence, why was she reacting so strongly?

As if in response to Irene's train of thought, Viktor came ambling along the street. He opened the gate and grinned at her.

"Hi!"

"Hi, Viktor. Listen, I just came to ask your mom something, but she got real mad at me."

Viktor's grin disappeared and he looked anxiously at her. Irene gave him an encouraging smile. "The thing is, someone's being doing weird stuff in our garden. They've moved a seat and pulled up some flowers. I just wanted to ask if you know anything about it."

The boy shook his head; he looked genuinely surprised.

Irene looked him in the eye and smiled again. His expression was still a little uncertain, but he returned the smile. A guilty ten-year-old wouldn't look that way.

Viktor wasn't behind the vandalism.

So who was?

My beloved is having a party. I don't like that. Lead her not into temptation, but deliver her from evil. She must be removed from the destructive influence. Behold, I shall send an angel before you to guard you along the way and to bring you into the place that I have prepared. I will take care of you, my darling. We will be forever united in our love.

I am here for her. She knows that I am watching over her. We are united by our love. For ever and ever. Amen. Two men and two women. They are sitting at the table, eating. And drinking. So much alcohol.

Now the other couple has left, and he is still there. They have kissed each other and . . . more. Even though she has switched off most of the lights, I can see more than enough. She has let down her hair. He has started to undress her. Her large breasts are . . . disgusting. She is revealing her true self. The façade has fallen away. She looks like a witch. A troll.

Thou shall not suffer a sorceress to live.

DOGS WERE NOT allowed in the churchyard, but nature called; Egon had to go out. Just a quick walk. At this time of night it was unlikely there would be anyone to complain if she didn't pick up after him. He was small, so he wouldn't produce too much, and the asthma made it difficult for her to bend down.

She was lucky enough to find a parking spot right by the gates. Puffing and blowing, she clambered out of the Škoda. She put Egon on the leash before letting him out, then she entered the churchyard, dragging the dachshund along behind her. He wanted to stop and check out all the interesting smells.

"Come along, Egon! We haven't got time for all that!"

She carried on grumbling at the dog, who was becoming increasingly reluctant to cooperate. In the end he sat down, and with a little twist of his head he managed to slip out of the worn, stretched collar.

Free at last! Egon took off across the grass as fast as his short legs could carry him. Sniffing with pleasure, he buried his nose in the wet leaves, inhaling all the pheromones left behind by some unknown beauty. He could have spent hours there if it hadn't been for his mistress. He could hear her heavy tread lumbering across the grass, and even though he was trying to ignore her shrill voice, he couldn't misinterpret the tone: she wasn't happy. In fact, she sounded angry. As she approached with the leash at the ready, Egon realized it was best to stay out of reach for a while. Resolutely he plunged deeper in among the rhododendrons. His mistress's voice grew even more shrill, but she couldn't reach him.

Another smell began to penetrate through the strong scent. At first Egon stood still for a few seconds, unsure of what to do, but then curiosity took over. He had to find out what that strange smell was. He put his nose to the ground and started to follow the trail. Safely hidden behind the bushes, he moved along by the wall. At the point where the rhododendrons came to an end, he tracked down the source of those peculiar odors. He was slobbering with excitement. He started biting at the thick plastic enveloping the smelly object. He forgot to remain alert, and suddenly he felt the collar slip over his head. But instead of shouting at him and telling him off, his mistress was staring at the bundle wrapped in plastic. She started to make little screeching noises that hurt his ears. Egon crouched down. His sensitive nose had picked up another smell, overriding the interesting package. An acrid stench was emanating from every pore of his mistress's body: fear. She was terrified.

I am sitting here with the photograph of her in front of me. Ostensibly so innocent and beautiful, but I have seen through her. A liar. She, too, has broken our agreement. I saw it with my own eyes. The lusts of the flesh. It is unforgivable. I have to make an example of her. No one is permitted to act this way against me and against God's commandments. When it comes to this crime, there can be only one consequence: death. For I shall visit the sins of the fathers on the children to the third and fourth generations, when I am hated.

I am the Punisher.

By the time Irene Huss and her colleague DI Fredrik Stridh arrived, the scene had been cordoned off and uniformed officers had been posted to keep back any curious onlookers. Several patrol cars were on site, along with the CSI van. The lights pulsating in the darkness gave the faces of the onlookers a creepy bluish pallor at regular intervals. Bearing in mind that it was freezing and almost nine o'clock, it was strange to see so many people in the churchyard. Then again, after many years as an investigator with the Violent Crimes Unit, Irene knew that homicide always attracted sensationalists. Personally, she could have thought of many more appealing pursuits, and if Jonny Blom and his entire family hadn't been struck down by the flu, she wouldn't have been there. When the call came in about the discovery in the churchyard, Fredrik had contacted Irene and asked if she could come along in Jonny's absence. On Monday Fredrik was going back to the Organized Crime Unit, and someone else would have to take over the case; why not Irene? With a sigh she had said yes. Krister was working all weekend, so she was home alone anyway.

Irene and Fredrik showed their IDs to the uniformed officers guarding the scene, lifted the police tape and made their way over to the brightly lit spot where the body had been found. The flourishing rhododendrons partially obscured the onlookers' view. The powerful spotlights illuminated the large package on the ground by the wall. The body itself was just visible through the transparent builders' plastic in which it was wrapped.

They nodded to Svante Malm and his team.

"What can you tell us so far?" Irene asked.

Svante shook his head apologetically. "There's nothing here but the body. We're sending it to the path lab shortly, so we can take a closer look at the ground, but I'm not optimistic. There's all kinds of crap lying around that people have thrown into the bushes, and something tells me that our killer has been careful. Just look at the way the body has been wrapped."

Irene had to agree with him. The entire package was held together by long strips of brown electrical tape. She knew from past experience that there was no point in trying to trace the tape; it was sold in vast quantities all over the country. All over the world, in fact. Their only hope was that the perpetrator had left traces of himself on the packaging or on the body.

'I've spoken to the lab, and they're happy for us to unwrap the body there," Svante said.

"In that case we'll come with you," Irene decided.

IRENE AND FREDRIK gave the recently appointed CSI Matti Berggren a ride to the lab. He told them he'd spent two years working at the National Forensics Laboratory in Linköping. Irene guessed he was around twenty-five, but he was probably a few years older than he looked. Fredrik had been about the same age when he joined the unit. That was ten years ago, and he had developed into an excellent investigator. It was just a shame that the Organized Crime Unit had also spotted his potential.

"Why are you sighing?" Fredrik asked.

"Am I? I guess I was thinking about a cozy evening on the sofa with a glass of wine and something delicious to eat. An early night. That kind of thing. It is my weekend off, you know."

"In another life, Irene. In another life," Fredrik countered, his tone serious.

The complaint was really for young Matti's benefit, but he didn't seem particularly impressed. Instead he gazed out of the window with interest as they drove past the Scandinavium Arena. The evening's event was over, and thousands of people were pouring out of the building.

THEY WERE IN luck, partly because the forensic pathology lab was pretty quiet and partly because Morten Jensen was on duty. Irene and Fredrik knew him well; he had worked there for several years.

He seemed more than happy to have some company.

"Things can get a little dead around here on a Saturday night," he said.

Matti Berggren raised one eyebrow a fraction but smiled politely. Presumably he wasn't too sure whether the pathologist was joking. Irene always found dealing with Morten Jensen quite liberating. He was much more easygoing than his boss, Professor Yvonne Stridner. Then again, so were most people, in Irene's opinion. The overwhelming majority of police officers in Göteborg would agree with her. Fortunately the risk of running into Yvonne Stridner this evening was minimal. Professors are never on call overnight, and they certainly don't work weekends. Morten Jensen wouldn't normally have been around either, but there was a terrible shortage of doctors in forensic pathology.

Matti took samples from the outside of the plastic, paying particular attention to a dark brown patch about the size of the palm of a hand they saw when they turned the body over. There were similar patches in other places, too, though they were smaller.

"Some kind of thin oil . . . probably engine oil," he murmured to himself. He looked satisfied as he pushed the cotton bud into the sterile sample bottle. He then carefully removed each piece of tape, placing them in separate glass containers. "Tape can carry a great deal of information; traces the perp would never have thought of can adhere to it."

He appeared to be highly competent and conscientious. There was some talk of Svante Malm retiring next year; this young man could well prove a worthy successor.

Matti gently began to open up the plastic covering the body.

"There's a lot of water on the inside," he noted.

When the victim was fully exposed, they could see that they were dealing with a middle-aged woman. The entire body was wet. The moisture had remained inside the plastic rather than evaporating, thanks to the perpetrator's meticulous use of tape. The shoulder-length hair lay plastered to the skull, but it was possible to see that it was bleached blonde. The woman was short and plump.

"Strangled," Jensen said.

His voice had lost any hint of humor. He pointed to a nasty dark purple mark around the victim's neck. The noose had been pulled so tight that only the ends were visible at the nape, knotted into large loops to provide a better grip. Irene recognized the material; it was exactly the same as her blue nylon clothesline at home.

Jensen measured the woman's height: five foot two. He checked the temperature of the body, and made a note of the hypostasis and the degree of rigor mortis.

He then entered the data, along with the outdoor temperature for the past twenty-four hours, into his computer and made a rapid mental calculation before stating that she had been dead for a maximum of forty-eight hours. And she had probably died a bit more recently than that, but no more than five hours.

"So she was killed between forty-three and forty-eight hours ago—between five o'clock and ten o'clock on Thursday evening," Irene said after glancing up at the clock. "That's quite a big window."

"I know, but I can't be any more specific. There are still too many unknown factors. The hypostasis indicates her position was changed four to twelve hours after death, from lying on her stomach to lying on her back. The hypostasis on the front of the body has faded. Tomorrow I'll do a more detailed examination and send off a range of samples. I'm afraid it will be a few days before we get around to the actual autopsy," Jensen said apologetically.

Irene realized she would have to be satisfied with that. At least they had been given some useful information; the main priority now was to establish the woman's identity. Fredrik would open a missing persons report in the system right away, and they would meet on Sunday. It was important to maintain momentum in the early stages of an investigation.

FREDRIK HAD FOUND her almost right away. Ingela Svensson, forty-six years old, divorced, lived alone. The florist's store at Frölunda torg had contacted the police when she didn't turn up for work on Friday morning. Ingela was a dedicated florist, and she had had a lot of orders for a funeral on Saturday. The woman who owned the store had been beside herself with worry when she called. According to her, Ingela was reliable; she never took time off without good reason, and certainly wouldn't disappear without a word.

Ingela Svensson's sister in Kungälv was contacted on Friday afternoon, while they were still thinking in terms of a missing person. She had said exactly the same thing: Ingela wouldn't just disappear. Besides, she had just met a new man—a guy from Borås who seemed to be good for her. The sister had been delighted; apparently Ingela's marriage had been nothing to cheer about.

New and ex-partners are always of interest in a

disappearance or a homicide investigation. A quick check on Ingela's former husband revealed that he had remarried two years ago, and could be eliminated from their inquiries right away since the family lived in Marbella, Spain, where he had set up a business selling property to sun-seeking Scandinavians.

It was with a heavy heart that Irene called Ingela's sister in Kungälv early on Sunday morning. The woman broke down when she realized it was probably Ingela who had been found murdered in the churchyard the previous evening.

A few hours later her husband drove her to Göteborg, and she was able to carry out the formal identification. Irene asked the couple to accompany her to police HQ for a preliminary interview.

INGELA SVENSSON'S SISTER, Christina Mogren, gave them the name of the guy in Borås: Leif Karlberg. The Mogrens had been introduced to him the previous weekend, when Ingela had invited them over to meet the new man in her life. He had made a very good impression on both of them. According to Christina, her sister had met Karlberg on a weekend trip to Prague three months earlier, and love had begun to blossom soon after. When Ingela got home she had dared to hope that something might come of the relationship, even though she had sworn she was done with men. She had visited him several times in Borås, and he had been to stay with her in Göteborg. Everything seemed to be going very well, and for the first time since her divorce, it looked as though Ingela was head over heels in love.

"It can't be him. He and Ingela were crazy about each other. He seemed so . . . nice!" Christina said.

Over the years Irene had met quite a few killers who had been described in similar terms by those around them, but she didn't mention this to Ingela's sister. Suddenly Christina's husband spoke up.

"Did she ever find out where that flower came from?"

Christina thought for a moment, then shook her head. "No. Well, not as far as I know."

"Did someone send Ingela flowers?" Irene asked.

"One flower. A big white chrysanthemum, and an envelope with something written on it that didn't make any sense."

"Can you remember what it said?"

"No, but she did say there was no name on the envelope, just a few scribbled numbers and letters."

"It seems a bit strange to send a flower to someone who works in a florist's," Irene said.

"That's exactly what Ingela said."

"When did she receive this flower?"

Christina and her husband tried to work it out.

"We usually call each other on Mondays or Tuesdays, and sometimes toward the end of the week. We've done that ever since we left home. We've always been very close." Christina's eyes filled with tears as she realized what she had said. She wiped her eyes with a tissue and swallowed hard. "She must have called me last Tuesday. We couldn't talk for long, because I had to take Tobbe to his hockey game. She told me a flower had been hanging on her apartment door when she got home from work the previous evening—so that would have been on Monday. When she unwrapped it there was just the single chrysanthemum and a crumpled envelope. At first she thought it was Leif, but when she called and thanked him for the flower, he had no idea what she was talking about."

Irene wondered whether this flower was important. Experience told her that any deviation from the norm was usually relevant.

"So this flower hadn't been delivered by a store or a courier?" she asked, just to clarify things.

"No, Ingela said it was wrapped in newspaper."

"Do you know what she did with it?"

"What she did with . . . well, I suppose she put it in water. Although I don't know for sure—we didn't have time to discuss it."

"Have you brought the keys to her apartment?"

"Yes. I guess we're not allowed to go there until you've . . ."

"Yes. We need to take a look around first. I'll make sure the keys are returned to you as soon as possible," Irene said, getting to her feet to indicate that the conversation was over.

THE RUN-DOWN FORMER workers' quarter of Majorna used to be a disgrace, but a regeneration program had transformed the area into a very attractive place to live. The inner courtyards of the apartment blocks were particularly appealing, lending a cozy charm all of their own.

Ingela Svensson had a two-room apartment on Såggatan. Before they went inside, the officers put on latex gloves, along with protective shoe covers and caps. Even though it was on the ground floor, the place was light and airy. The traffic on Karl Johansgatan and Oscarsleden hummed faintly. The living room faced the street, while the kitchen and bedroom overlooked the small courtyard. It was idyllic, with a beautiful chestnut tree and beds containing a variety of roses that were still in bloom.

There were no signs of a struggle in Ingela's home. A double closet contained her shoes and outerwear, along with a smart purse in which Irene found Ingela's cell phone, wallet and makeup items. There were no keys in the purse, nor in the pockets of any of her coats, which suggested she had taken them with her when she went out and encountered her killer. Why take just the keys and not the purse? Presumably she hadn't thought she was going to be out for long.

A door off the hallway led to a compact bathroom, recently renovated, from the look of it, with black and white tiles. The living room had a personal feel, with older pieces of furniture mixed with IKEA's standard offering. Next to an open copy of *Amelia* magazine stood a wineglass with a little drop of red still shimmering in the bottom.

The bedroom was quite small, with a white shaggy rug and fine, delicate curtains. The pale grey walls and closet doors provided an air of serenity. Irene was interrupted by the sound of Fredrik's voice from the kitchen.

"Come and take a look at this."

He was standing just inside the door, pointing to the cupboard under the sink, which was wide open.

"Empty. No trash can," Irene said immediately. She looked around the kitchen, with its smooth, shiny cupboard doors. There was a table and four chairs over by the window. The place could do with an upgrade, but everything was spotless. The only jarring note came from the open door and the empty cupboard.

"She took out the trash," Irene concluded.

"Where? And where's the trash can?" Fredrik wondered.

"Let's take a look."

They removed their protective clothing before leaving the apartment. A short flight of steps led down to the back door, and through the glass they could see the imposing trunk of the majestic chestnut tree and its lower branches swaying gently in the breeze. The hinges squeaked as they pushed open the door and emerged into the cobbled courtyard. They walked over to the passageway and saw a row of garbage cans.

"Let's see if she threw anything away," Fredrik said.

They lifted the lids to check if there was a trash can among the garbage, then they searched the whole area, but they couldn't find a thing that seemed to be connected to Ingela Svensson.

"So where is it?" Irene asked.

Fredrik pointed up at the wall, where a large handwritten notice informed them: *Glass, wood, plastic, chemicals and other items that cannot be placed in these garbage cans must be placed in the appropriate containers at the recycling station.* There was a map showing the location of the nearest station.

"Maybe she went there," he said.

The recycling station was located in a corner of a large parking lot. It looked and smelled the way most of those places do. They started searching. People had dumped stuff if they didn't know what to do with it: there were a couple of old bedside lamps, a broken food mixer, a kitchen chair in pieces, and a few sodden banana boxes. Peering into the containers to see if anything might have belonged to Ingela Svensson was a far from pleasant task. Irene felt like giving up and leaving it to forensics.

"This is depressing." She sighed.

"Sure, but we are kind of in luck—according to the notice the containers won't be emptied until Tuesday," Fredrik pointed out.

They called CSI, who promised to come out as soon as possible. While they were waiting, Irene and Fredrik continued to search, but there was no sign of a trash can.

"It's probably buried under tons of crap. If it's here at all," Irene said.

Fredrik didn't reply; he was gazing pensively at a row of plastic igloos designated for glass in one corner of the recycling station. He searched all around them but came up with nothing more than an empty paper carrier bag. Then he crossed to the other side of the fence surrounding the containers, and peered into the lilac bushes growing close beside it. He lifted up the lowest branches and shone his flashlight into the undergrowth.

"Yes!" he shouted.

Irene hurried over as he triumphantly lifted the branches higher. Buried in the vegetation lay a grey bucket.

"There are some wine bottles in it. She'd had a party over

the weekend, remember? That's why she came here: to get rid of the empties." Fredrik looked around, assessing the location. "This could well be the scene of the murder. He followed her and strangled her here, then threw the bucket into the bushes. Presumably he was too stressed to think about hiding it properly. The important thing was to move the body before someone turned up."

He couldn't suppress the excitement in his voice. Finding the scene of the crime usually means a breakthrough in a homicide investigation. This time they had been lucky; they were still at an early stage.

"Yes, she finished work at six, so she wouldn't have gotten here much earlier than seven," Irene speculated out loud.

She was carefully walking around one of the igloos when suddenly a faint glimmer caught her eye over by the fence. As she moved closer, she could see it was a bunch of keys, with the initials IS on the enameled key ring. She didn't touch it but pointed it out to Fredrik.

"That makes it even more likely that she was killed here!" he exclaimed.

"The killer must have had a vehicle in order to move the body. It would be easy to drive nearly all the way to this spot," Irene went on.

"No chance of any tire tracks," Fredrik said.

He was right; the whole area was covered in tarmac. Their hopes were pinned on the bushes where the bucket had been hidden, and on the area around the igloos where the attack had presumably taken place.

IRENE WENT BACK to Ingela's apartment, leaving Fredrik to keep an eye on the scene until the CSIs arrived. They didn't want people trampling around until they had secured all possible evidence.

She put on her protective gear once more. Even if the killer had attacked Ingela at the recycling station, there could be other clues in the apartment.

It was worth noting that one thing was definitely missing: the white chrysanthemum. Ingela had probably thrown away both the flower and the envelope with its incomprehensible combination of numbers and letters. It was a shame, but it just meant they would have to go through the trash cans in the passageway more carefully. Irene hoped they hadn't been emptied since last Tuesday either.

Ingela Svensson had kept a tidy home. Everything was neatly arranged in cupboards and drawers, and nothing seemed to be out of the ordinary. In the pantry Irene found three unopened boxes of white wine and a box of red. There was also half a bottle of Grönstedts cognac, plus several bottles of medium-priced red wine. Nothing strange about that, apart from the fact that it seemed like rather a lot of wine for a woman on her own.

Irene had almost given up hope of finding something interesting when she suddenly realized there was another trash can she hadn't checked—in the bathroom. She flipped open the lid and peered inside. A few cotton wool pads that had obviously been used to remove makeup, a flattened toothpaste tube, an empty toilet paper roll. And a photograph. Cautiously she picked it out.

Ingela was smiling and raising her glass to the man who was sitting beside her on the sofa. The glow of the candles on the coffee table was reflected in her eyes, and she looked very happy. The man was facing her, with his back to the camera. He was wearing a pale jacket, and Irene could see a hint of a white shirt collar. He had the beginnings of a bald patch at the top of his head.

The picture had been shot through the living-room window. The photographer had been standing on Såggatan.

The date in the bottom right-hand corner showed it had been taken on the Saturday evening, the weekend before the dog found the body in the churchyard. Five days before Ingela was murdered.

THEY MANAGED TO get a hold of Leif Karlberg at about four o'clock in the afternoon. He explained that he had been to a football game with his youngest son. He didn't seem to know what had happened to Ingela Svensson—either that or he was a very good actor.

"We need to speak to you," Irene said.

"About what?"

The surprise in his voice sounded genuine. Irene decided not to tell him anything over the phone.

"Would it be possible for you to come over to police HQ in Göteborg today?"

"No, I've got the boys this weekend, so unfortunately I have to stay in Borås."

Irene thought fast. Best to get this out of the way, as soon as possible.

"In that case we'll come to you."

There was a long silence before Leif Karlberg spoke again. This time he was obviously worried. "Has something happened? Why is it so urgent?"

"I'll explain everything when I see you," Irene said.

LEIF KARLBERG LIVED in Sandared, and neither Fredrik nor Irene had any idea where that was. Irene had been to the zoo in Borås twice, and Fredrik had gone on a date there once, but neither the girl nor the town had made much of an impression on him. However, thanks to their GPS they had no trouble in finding Leif Karlberg's address

Irene rang the bell, and the door opened before the chime had faded away.

"Hi—I saw you walking over from the parking lot. Come in," Leif Karlberg said.

No point in trying to blend in with the surroundings, Irene thought with a certain amount of resignation. As usual they might as well have had a big illuminated sign above their heads saying COP!

According to their information on Karlberg, he was forty-four years old and divorced with two sons. He was an electrician and ran his own business with his brother. The previous year he had been caught speeding and had lost his license for two months. Otherwise he was clean. He was medium height, with the beginnings of a paunch. His face was quite round, with warm blue-grey eyes and a pleasant smile. His sandy-colored hair was thinning on top. "Ordinary" just about summed up Leif Karlberg.

He showed the two officers into the living room and invited them to sit down. Before they had time to settle he asked anxiously, "What's this about? I called my parents and my brother. I even spoke to my ex-wife. Nothing had happened, and none of them had any ideas, so . . ."

"Did you call Ingela?" Fredrik interrupted him.

"Ingela? No—why?"

Karlberg was staring at them, his eyes darting from one to the other like a spectator at a tennis match.

"Oh my God . . . Ingela. Is this about Ingela? What's happened?"

"When did you last speak to her?" Irene asked calmly, as if she hadn't heard his questions.

"On Wednes—no, Thursday."

"Did you call her?"

"No, she called me."

"What did she want?"

Leif Karlberg took a deep breath and swallowed hard before he answered.

"Someone had put a photograph in her mailbox. It . . . Well, the whole thing really started last Monday."

He fell silent, thinking back. Irene and Fredrik kept quiet, letting the silence work for them. After a moment Karlberg went on:

"We met up last weekend. Ingela wanted me to meet her sister and brother-in-law. We had a really good time . . . it was great. Then she called me on Monday to say thank you for the lovely flower. I didn't know what she was talking about—I hadn't sent her a flower. I thought she might be kind of drop-ping a hint, maybe she thought I should have sent her something . . . but when she realized it wasn't from me, she thought it was really weird. And it was just one flower, not a bouquet. There was an envelope, too, with something written on it, but she couldn't work out what it meant."

Karlberg had shuffled forward to the edge of the sofa. He rested his elbows on his knees, and was gesticulating anima-tedly as he talked. He was keen to talk, and seemed to be trying hard to remember every detail. Irene was more and more con-vinced that he had no idea what had happened to Ingela.

"Did she give you any details about what was on the enve-lope?"

"She just said it was written with a felt-tip pen, and that it was messy and illegible. Oh—she did say it was letters and numbers."

"So you had this conversation about the flower and the envelope on Monday evening," Irene said, just for clarifica-tion.

"Yes."

"And what time did she call you on Thursday?"

"At about seven. The boys and I had just gotten back from training; they were tired and hungry, so I didn't have much time to talk to her. I was in the kitchen making pancakes when she called my cell phone."

"What did she say?"

"She'd received a photograph. Nothing in writing this time, just a picture."

"Did she say what was in the photograph?"

"Yes . . . it was a picture of us. Last Saturday. Someone had taken it through her living-room window; she lives on the ground floor."

"Were her sister and brother-in-law in the photograph?" Irene asked, even though she already knew the answer.

"No, it was just the two of us. She said we were sitting on the sofa."

"How did she feel about this business of the flower and the photograph?"

"How did . . . Why don't you ask her?"

For the first time he sounded slightly irritated, but that could just as easily be attributed to nerves.

"I'd like to know how you perceived her reaction," Irene said.

"She thought it was weird. I tried to joke with her, said that whoever had sent her the flower must have taken the photograph, but she got kind of mad at me. I guess she found it a little creepy."

"But you had football practice on Thursday evening, so you couldn't go over to Göteborg to see her?"

"That's right. The boys are with me this week. We change over on Mondays. I pick them up from day care, then they stay with me until the following Monday. I don't want them to meet Ingela yet; it's best for both them and her. She doesn't have kids of her own, and they need time to get used to the idea. Their mother might have found herself a new boyfriend before we'd even split up, but I think you have to be a little more careful with children's feelings. And then—"

"Do you work full-time?" Irene interrupted him.

"Yes. And more. When the boys are with their mother, I work as many hours as I can, often late into the evening. But when they're with me I always finish at three-thirty on the dot. I pick them up from day care, then fix dinner. On Mondays and Thursdays they have football; I train the junior team."

"Where are your sons at the moment?" Irene asked.

"They're with their grandma . . . my mother. We're having dinner there tonight, so I asked her to come and pick them up before you arrived. I was a little worried because the police wanted to speak to me. But it has something to do with Ingela, doesn't it? Please . . . what's happened?"

They told him. His reaction seemed entirely genuine, and Irene was sure his alibi would hold when they checked it out.

Leif Karlberg had not murdered Ingela Svensson.

IT WAS DARK by the time Irene pulled into her parking spot. It warmed her heart to see Krister's old Volvo in the next space. He was home. It was almost eight o'clock, so there was a good chance dinner would be ready. The thought cheered her up as she realized how hungry she was.

She opened the front door and took a deep breath, trying to guess what delicious meal her husband had come up with.

Nothing.

Just to be on the safe side she sniffed the air a few times, but all she could smell was dust and the morning's leftover coffee sitting in the machine. The light above the table was on, but the kitchen was empty. The table hadn't been laid. From the floor above she could hear a TV weather forecaster outlining the prospects for tomorrow. Irene took off her coat and went upstairs.

Krister was sitting in one of the armchairs, snoring away. Next to him on the table was an open can of beer. Nothing else—no plate, no crumbs from a sandwich. He had simply drunk the cold beer straight out of the can.

Irene went over and kissed him gently on the forehead. He gave a start and opened his eyes, gazing up at her in confusion.

"Krister, honey, are you sick?" Irene asked with a reassuring smile.

"Sick? No, I'm just so goddamn tired," he replied.

He sounded as if he was about to go straight back to sleep.

"Would you like something to eat?" Irene ventured.

"No. I just want to sleep." He sighed heavily and struggled out of the chair.

Irene was worried. Was he heading for a burnout again? A few years ago he had taken an extended break from work; since then he had been more careful, working less and taking steps to cut down on the stress. She thought things had been going well, but right now he looked exhausted.

"This has nothing to do with burnout," he said, as if reading her mind. "Two of our chefs called in sick this weekend, and I couldn't find anyone to cover. Needless to say the restaurant was fully booked. I can't carry on like this."

Irene knew they had to talk about this, but she didn't really know what to say.

"Listen . . . I'll make an omelet. And there's salad . . . bread and cheese . . . a couple of slices of ham . . . You stay there, I'll fix something."

He gazed at her, a tired smile playing around one corner of his mouth.

"You, make an omelet? I don't think so. I'll do that—you fix the rest."

Irene knew she was a terrible cook, but Krister only had himself to blame. He had spoiled her. She crept into his arms, feeling safe and warm as she inhaled the smell of him.

"You're the best," she said, licking his ear.

"Careful—I might just forget about the food and get interested in something else!"

"One thing at a time," Irene said, kissing him on the nose.

They cooked dinner together. The omelet smelled wonderful; it was filled with onions, ham and cheese. There was a salad of tomatoes, black olives and thinly sliced red onions sitting on the table along with a piece of Brie and several slices of toast. The kitchen was beginning to smell exactly the way it should.

At that moment the telephone rang. Irene's first instinct was to ignore it, but then she thought it could be one of their daughters. She went into the hallway to take the call.

"Hi, it's Malin."

Irene recognized her neighbor's voice. Perhaps Viktor's mother wanted to apologize for her behavior the previous day. Before Irene had time to speak, Malin continued.

"Håkan and I just got home. We parked the car, and as we were walking toward the house, we saw someone coming out of your gate. He or she headed in our direction, but then they saw us, turned around and hurried off the other way."

What was going on? Was Malin trying to lay the blame on some ghostly figure hanging around the area, instead of tackling Viktor and his pals? At the same time Irene remembered her conversation with Viktor and her conviction that he wasn't the one who had damaged her garden.

"When was this?"

"Just now."

"I'll go outside and take a look, then I'll call you back," Irene said quickly.

Before Krister had time to ask what was going on, she was out of the front door without even pulling on her jacket.

Malin and Håkan had walked from the parking lot toward their house, so the person they had seen must have gone off in the opposite direction. Irene broke into a run, moving as fast as she could. She was a good sprinter, but she was wearing ordinary loafers, not proper running shoes. Two blocks along there was a bigger parking lot with several spaces for visitors.

She heard the sound of a car engine starting. She reached the lot just in time to see two taillights disappearing in the direction of Stora Fiskebäcksvägen.

"Shit!" she yelled.

She made her way back home at a more leisurely pace, giving herself time to catch her breath and to think. The car that had driven off didn't necessarily belong to whoever Malin said she had seen coming out of Irene's garden; the driver could have been visiting a friend who lived nearby.

But if there had been someone in their garden, who was it? And what were they doing there? Had this person done more damage? If so, why?

Too many questions, all requiring an answer. Irene decided to unravel the mystery systematically; she had to start in the right place. Resolutely she went inside and ate the omelet, which had gone cold on her plate. She told Krister what Malin had said, then she fetched a powerful flashlight.

"I'm leaving this to the police," Krister said with a big yawn. "I'm going to bed."

Irene gave him a kiss on passing as she headed out into the darkness.

THIS TIME THE Prowler, as she had begun to think of their visitor, hadn't destroyed anything. Or perhaps he hadn't had time. The only proof that someone had been in the garden were the imprints of two toecaps in the soil under the kitchen window.

When Irene had removed the seat from the flower bed, she had weeded and raked both beds, and fresh marks were clearly visible in the smoothed-down earth. Only the front part of the sole could be seen, so it was impossible to determine the shoe size.

But one thing was certain: someone had stood there looking in through the kitchen window. It was the window above the counter, not the one by the table. The Prowler had been out there under cover of darkness, watching them as they prepared dinner and sat down to eat. But something had startled him, made him decide to leave.

Neither Malin nor Håkan was able to provide a clear description of the person they had seen. Dark clothes, a bulky jacket with the hood pulled up. They had no idea of age or sex, although Malin thought the figure had been quite powerfully built and not very tall. Håkan wasn't so sure.

"I'd guess it's a young guy," he said. "Maybe he's checking out different places, planning a break-in."

"But then he wouldn't leave traces behind like he's done in Irene's garden," Malin objected.

"It doesn't seem like the smartest thing to do. We'll just have to be more careful about locking doors and closing windows," Irene said. "And maybe we should start keeping an eye on each other's houses and gardens."

"Neighborhood Watch! I'll put up some posters," Malin said determinedly.

It wasn't such a bad idea. Irene had nothing better to suggest, so she nodded in agreement.

"And perhaps you might even stop suspecting Viktor," Malin said sharply.

"I stopped suspecting him as soon as I'd spoken to him," Irene replied.

He drove out your enemies before you and said: destroy them!

That is what I did. My beloved is at peace now; she has been redeemed from sin.

This one is faithful. She comes home when she is supposed to, she does not behave foolishly. Behold, I am close to you. Now she is starting to make dinner. Aha—it's one of those soups that you drink from a cup. You only need to add hot water. Convenient for one person. We will share more lavish dinners. Romantic dinners. We are happy together. Because she is mine. Only mine. Even if we are not yet formally married, we are one in our hearts. Both she and I respect that. Remember this: thou shall not covet thy neighbor's wife.

And she thinks I don't know about the wine in the pantry. She has poured herself a glass. I will allow this for the moment if she has had a particularly stressful day at work, but I cannot tolerate alcohol abuse. It must change. He will not pardon your transgression, for my name is in Him. Drinking is most definitely a transgression. Under my loving control, she will learn to abstain from all alcohol.

But now she is pouring herself another glass of wine.

Superintendent Efva Thylqvist walked into the conference room with DI Tommy Persson following close behind. According to the rumors there was something going on between those two, but no one knew for sure. Irene thought the gossip was probably true, but she had no real proof, except for the fact that the guy who had been her best friend for the last twenty-five years hardly spoke to her these days, unless it had to do with work. He was never unpleasant, just very correct.

She and Tommy had become friends during their initial training in Ulriksdal. In those days there had been no training facilities outside the capital, so they had had to travel from Göteborg to Stockholm. They had found each other right away. Over the years they had maintained a strong friendship, probably because they had never been anything but friends. They had both married and had children, and the two families had spent a great deal of time together, joining forces for major celebrations and vacations. They were godparents to each other's children. Everything had been fine until Tommy and his wife, Agneta, split up.

After the divorce Irene had tried to keep their friendship going on a personal as well as a professional level, but Tommy had withdrawn. Neither Irene nor Krister had any idea why. Over the past year Irene thought she could guess at the reason behind the change: Superintendent Efva Thylqvist. Tommy wasn't stupid and knew Irene well, so naturally he was aware of her views on their new chief. Most men found Thylqvist sexy, with her neat figure, curves in all the right places, her pretty face and her thick auburn hair. She could be immensely charming when it suited her. If there was a man around she made every effort to appear competent, attractive and pleasant. When she was dealing with women, however, she didn't try as hard to keep up the façade. If Tommy was having an affair with Thylqvist, it was hardly surprising that he preferred not to have personal conversations with Irene. He was probably afraid of giving himself away, so he had chosen to keep his distance. Irene suspected that Tommy had put himself in a very tricky situation.

She mourned the loss of their close friendship, but there wasn't much she could do about it. Tommy's withdrawal made her feel much more lonely, both at work and privately.

Her thoughts were interrupted as the superintendent began to debrief the staff, a practice they had come to refer to as "morning prayer" over the years.

"Good morning. Does everyone have a cup of coffee? I understand you've had a busy weekend with what the press is calling the Package Killing. Fredrik and Jonny were on duty; Fredrik has returned to the Organized Crime Unit, so perhaps you could run us through the key points, Jonny?"

Efva Thylqvist smiled encouragingly at Jonny Blom, who had to admit that he had been sick all weekend and that Irene had stepped in. Thylqvist gave Irene no more than a brief nod.

Irene ran through the information she already had, ending with, "Matti Berggren at the lab has promised to get in touch as soon as he has time to summarize his findings. We can probably check with Morten Jensen to see if he's taken a closer look at the body yet, though he did say it could be several days before he gets around to the autopsy. I'll give him a call later."

"What about Leif Karlberg's alibi?" Thylqvist asked.

"I've already spoken to our colleagues in Borås, and they've promised to help out."

"Door-to-door inquiries in Ingela Svensson's apartment block?"

"Already organized—they're starting this morning."

"The garbage cans? And the containers at the recycling center?"

"Forensics is on it. We're lucky—nothing has been emptied since Tuesday," Irene replied.

The superintendent made no further comment on Irene's report; instead she said, "Okay—Jonny, I'd like you to take this investigation, working alongside Irene. The rest of you carry on with your current cases for the time being."

Everyone in the room looked very surprised. They might have been short-staffed as usual, but two investigators on a fresh homicide was cutting things to the bone. It also seemed unusually stupid to put the person who knew nothing about the case in charge.

"As soon as we have more to go on, we'll invest more resources," Tommy said quickly.

He's covering her back, Irene thought angrily.

As if he could read her mind, Tommy continued, "I suggest we meet again later this afternoon, see where we are."

"I'm in a meeting from three to five, but you're more than capable of dealing with this," Efva Thylqvist said.

There was an acidity in her tone that escaped no one. Irene was well aware that Thylqvist couldn't bear it when someone said or did something that could be interpreted as questioning her authority. *Self-esteem issues*, Irene thought spitefully.

WHEN SHE CALLED pathology she was informed that Morten Jensen was away until Wednesday, and was scheduled to carry out the autopsy on Ingela Svensson on that day.

Which meant they wouldn't get his report until the end of the week at the earliest.

M ATTI B ERGGREN LOOKED to be in top form when Irene visited the lab just before lunch.

"Anything interesting for me?" she asked.

"Are you kidding? I've got plenty!" he said with a smile.

"Seriously?" Once again, Irene was impressed.

"Absolutely. I'm coming up for a meeting this afternoon, so we can go through everything then."

"Great! Come around three, and I'll provide coffee and cake."

"W OW ! I S IT your birthday or something?" Jonny said, rubbing his hands when he saw the plate of delicious-smelling pastries on the table.

"No, I've invited Matti in to give us his report on what he's found. Plus I think we could do with something to cheer us up on a miserable Monday," Irene said.

"Do you know if we got anywhere with the door-to-door?" asked Tommy, who was already sitting down with a steaming cup of coffee in front of him.

"Yes—a girl met Ingela Svensson on her way out with the trash can. They live in the same part of the block, so she's sure it was Ingela. The girl parked her bicycle in the passageway and went up to her apartment. She can't remember seeing anyone else standing near the door. We'll talk to her again," Irene said.

"Good. So if he was watching the main door, he must have been hiding," Tommy said.

Sara Persson walked into the room; she was a classic beautiful blonde, slim and toned with blue eyes. Matti Berggren halted in the doorway and stared at her. A faint smile spread across his face, and his brown eyes began to sparkle. Sara said hi but didn't appear to notice his reaction. Perhaps Irene was the only one who had detected it.

When the pastries had been picked over, Matti began his report.

"The plastic in which the body was wrapped is ordinary builders' plastic; it can be bought everywhere. The same applies to the brown tape. I found some stains on the back of the plastic; they seem to be some kind of thin oil. Not cooking oil—it's more like a fine-grade engine oil."

Jonny interrupted him:

"So it could well be that the body was lying on its back on the ground after it had been packaged."

He made quotation marks in the air around the final word.

"Exactly. The killer washed the victim with some kind of soap, then rinsed the body with water. So Ingela Svensson was lying on the plastic when he sluiced away all traces from the body. No blood or semen is visible on the plastic, only water, but we've taken samples to find out what kind of soap we're looking at, and whether there are any microscopic traces of our perp."

"So you didn't get much from the inside of the packaging," Jonny clarified.

"Not so far; we'll see what the samples tell us. But the tape was a lot more useful. People don't think about the fact that just about everything sticks to tape."

He looked very pleased with himself; Irene remembered he had said something similar when they unwrapped the body.

"So what did you find?" Jonny said impatiently.

Matti refused to let himself be pressured, and continued calmly, "Gravel. Grit. Dust. Grease. Cat hairs. From a short-haired domestic cat. Black. At least the hairs we found were black."

"So we've got plenty of evidence against the cat if we can just track it down," Jonny quipped.

"That's your job," Matti said with a smile.

"Did you find anything at the recycling center?" Tommy asked.

"Yes. The keys belonged to Ingela Svensson. We also found several strands of blonde hair that came from her, right next to the igloos. We found her fingerprints on the paper carrier bag that was lying there, and footprints on the edge of the grass, right next to where the bucket of empty bottles was hidden under the bushes. The footprints aren't very clear, but it's obvious that they were made by a heavy boot or shoe. Although of course we don't know if they're connected to the murder."

Irene offered him the last remaining pastry, which he accepted with enthusiasm. She had bought one for the superintendent just to be on the safe side, in case her meeting had been postponed. It was unlikely that she would have taken it, but she would have been annoyed if there hadn't been one for her.

THE WITNESS WHO had bumped into Ingela Svensson on the night of the murder was a young woman with a sallow complexion. A lilac woolen hat was pulled down on her greasy, dyed-black hair. She sported large silver rings in her lower lip and in one nostril. Her face was completely free of makeup, apart from a slash of bright red lipstick on the small mouth. She reminded Irene of a geisha, apart from the piercings. However, her clothing was as far from a geisha's as possible: a chunky knit black cardigan, black harem pants, a man's shirt in pale lilac and worn sandals. A brief association with the hippie fashion of her childhood flitted through Irene's mind, possibly evoked by the guitar hanging on the wall and the fact that they were sitting on mattresses on the floor. The coffee table was made up of a wooden pallet and a thick sheet of glass. On top of the table stood a large ceramic dish with a dark, silver-grey glaze with small flashes of bright red and yellow. In one corner of the room stood a statue in various shades of blue; it was almost the height of a man, but Irene wasn't sure what it was meant to be.

The young woman's name was Ida Bernth. The creation in the corner made more sense when Ida explained that she was studying ceramics at the School of Design and Crafts at the university. She sat there twisting her thin fingers as Irene wondered how such graceful hands could produce such alarmingly large works of art.

"Tell me what happened on Thursday evening when you bumped into Ingela Svensson," Irene began.

"I was just about to park my bike, so I was standing outside with my key in my hand when she . . . when Ingela opened the door."

"Did she say anything?"

"We both said hi, then she said it was time to get rid of the body."

A macabre comment, to say the least, from someone who would be murdered just minutes later.

"She said 'it's time to get rid of the body'?"

"Yes—she meant all the empty bottles. She had a bucket full, and a paper carrier bag."

That was why Ingela had taken the bucket to the recycling center. She must have been collecting empty bottles for a long time; they couldn't all have come from the weekend. Unless she was a big drinker. An alcoholic, even?

"Did Ingela seem the same as usual, as far as you could tell?"

"Yes . . . she laughed. She seemed a little embarrassed."

"Why do you think she was embarrassed?"

"I guess she thought it didn't look so good, having so many empty bottles!"

Irene felt a pang of guilt as she remembered all the bags full of empty beer cans sitting in the laundry room back home. Krister would sometimes point at them and say: "Our retirement plan." Given the state of world economics right now, he could well be right. Then again, maybe it was high time to take the cans in and reclaim the deposit. She couldn't possibly deal with them all at once, though; people would think she and Krister were alcoholics. Maybe that was how Ingela Svensson had felt when she met Ida in the doorway.

"Did you and Ingela know each other well?"

"No. I've only been living here since July. We usually just say hi."

"Did you notice anyone standing near the door, or out on the street?"

Ida shook her head. "I didn't see anyone. I've thought about it over and over again, but I don't remember seeing anyone nearby."

"Could there have been a car you didn't recognize parked somewhere close to the apartment block?"

"I wouldn't have noticed. Cars aren't really my thing."

The last sentence provoked the shadow of a smile around the little red geisha mouth.

As usual it was impossible to find a parking space near police HQ. The entire area was one gigantic construction site. And of course Irene had left her umbrella at home. She ran from the car to the main door, but she still got soaked. As she traveled up in the elevator, she started to shiver in her wet clothes. A big cup of hot coffee was exactly what she needed to bring her body temperature back up, but she would have to hurry if she was going to have time to take off her coat and dash to the coffee machine before morning prayer. As she rounded the corner of the corridor leading to her office, she almost collided with Hannu Rauhala.

"Hi—don't be long!" he said, carrying on past her.

Before she had time to ask what was so urgent, she heard him say over his shoulder:

"They've found another one."

Another one? Another body wrapped in plastic? Another homicide? Irene felt an icy chill crawl across her scalp and down the back of her neck. This wasn't good news. In the worst-case scenario they could be dealing with a serial killer, or a copycat. If it was a copycat who had been inspired by Ingela's murder, they would soon know. The way the body had been wrapped was very particular, and no details had been released to the press. Irene headed to the meeting room with a heavy heart and no coffee.

"Last man on board is a woman. Nice of you to join us," Superintendent Thylqvist said in a voice dripping with sarcasm.

Irene merely nodded to the others, barely looking at her chief. She couldn't deal with Thylqvist today.

"A paperboy called at six thirty-two this morning. He had found a package wrapped in plastic and thought it looked as if it contained a body. Apparently he had cut through Frölunda churchyard on his way home. So the body was discovered just under an hour ago. I'd like Jonny and Irene to get over there right away, and keep in touch with Hannu. Hannu—you stay here and deal with any calls about missing persons, and check on anyone who's been reported missing over the past few days. We don't know how long this person has been dead; the body could have been dumped before Ingela Svensson's."

Thylqvist had a point. What if this body had been lying there for some time? The icy chill over Irene's neck and shoulders wouldn't go away.

FRÖLUNDA CHURCHYARD WAS at the top of a hill. It was comparatively small, and they could see the crime scene from some distance away, in spite of the fact that it was still pouring. The CSIs had rigged up floodlights, and several patrol cars were parked nearby, their blue lights flashing. The churchyard looked far from well tended, and gave the impression that it was no longer used.

The body, wrapped in plastic, was lying on top of an old grave that was surrounded by a sparse, unclipped coniferous hedge. Decades of wind and rain had made the inscription on the headstone nearly illegible, but Irene could just about make out the name Johan and the year 1893.

The killer tried to hide the body we found on Saturday, but he hasn't bothered this time. *This is a later murder*, Irene thought, *if it's the same perp*.

Judging by the packaging, it was. The thick builders' plastic was tightly wound around the body several times, firmly secured with wide brown tape.

"We'll do the same as last time and take the whole package over to the lab," Jonny said.

EVERYONE'S LUCK RUNS out at some point. The chances of avoiding Yvonne Stridner had been slim. Even though Irene knew that Morten Jensen would be away until the following day, she had nurtured a faint hope that they might be dealing with another pathologist rather than his boss. But no—it was the distinguished professor herself who met them when they arrived.

"Another victim within three days! Now you really do have to bring in all available resources," she said, fixing Jonny with a beady stare.

Even he shrank in the face of an onslaught from Stridner, but he did manage to say:

"Five days. Ingela Svensson was murdered last Thursday, but we didn't find her until Saturday, so that's five—"

Yvonne Stridner interrupted him with a loud snort.

"That's the worse excuse I've heard in my entire life! And I've heard plenty."

For once Jonny had the sense not to respond. Or perhaps he couldn't think of anything to say. Irene didn't really care, as long as he kept quiet.

"I'll look at the body right away. After lunch I have a part-time forensic medicine course with a group of surgeons."

The final sentence was almost drowned out by the tip-tap of Stridner's high-heeled pumps as she marched away from them. *She certainly knows how to walk in heels*, Irene thought with a stab of envy. Personally she had never mastered the art, since she measured six feet without shoes.

Yvonne Stridner stopped and glanced at her diamond-encrusted Rolex. "I shall be starting in exactly fifteen minutes. You need to have taken all external samples by then."

At that moment the outside door opened and a rain-sodden figure appeared. Irene was just about to say hello when Stridner's harsh tones got there first:

"You're too early. The course doesn't start until after lunch."

Matti Berggren looked a little confused, but after a couple of seconds he broke into a warm smile.

"Forgive me—I'm new, and I haven't had time to introduce myself yet, Professor Stridner. Of course I know who you are, but there's no reason why you should know me."

He strode forward, holding out his hand. Small puddles formed on the floor behind him, and his shoes squelched with every step. There was no mistaking the fact that his feet were soaking wet. Stridner's body language softened a fraction as they shook hands.

"Mattias Berggren, forensic technician," Matti said, still smiling.

Stridner capitulated and returned the smile. "How nice to meet a polite technician."

Matti kept that smile in place, gazing at her with his brown eyes, but as the professor turned to lead the way into the autopsy suite, he winked at Irene and Jonny.

The process of opening up the plastic was a repeat of Saturday night. Matti took samples and placed them in various containers. There were oil stains on the back of this package, too. When Matti spotted them, Irene noticed that his face lit up. Stridner was running out of patience, trying to hurry him along, but he merely smiled at her yet again and carried on with his work, calmly and methodically.

The difference from Saturday was of course the contents of the package. The body was just as wet as Ingela Svensson's had been, and it was a woman, but she bore no resemblance to Ingela. There was a long vertical scar running down her belly that looked quite old. She was probably a similar age to the previous victim, and had the same purple-red mark around her neck. The murder had left behind the blue nylon cord this time too, deeply embedded in the soft tissue, with only the ends visible, knotted into loops as before.

Stridner stepped forward. "I'll take it from here." She studied the body closely from top to toe. Then she looked more carefully at certain places, all without touching. Only then did she begin to feel the woman's stiff limbs.

"Fully developed rigor mortis. It was pretty cold overnight, around seven degrees. That slows the process down somewhat, but I would say she was killed yesterday evening."

"When?" Jonny dared to ask.

"I have to do a number of tests before I can answer that, but probably not before six. I can't be any more precise at the moment."

"When will we know for sure?" Jonny persisted.

"When I've finished. Perhaps you could leave me in peace to get on with my work. That will speed things up significantly," Stridner said, glaring at Jonny.

They had no choice but to leave. The only person who looked reasonably satisfied was Matti. As the door closed behind them he said, "I found oil!"

"Cool. Call Norsk Hydro," Jonny said.

Matti ignored the feeble joke. "It's probably the same oil we found on the plastic Ingela Svensson's body was wrapped in, and these marks were on the back, as before."

"Did you find anything else on the back of the packaging?" Irene asked.

"Sure. Gravel and grit from the locations where the bodies were found, but there was something else that didn't come from there. Swarf—tiny particles of metal. They were in the oil and on the outside of the plastic Ingela was wrapped in, so I knew what to look for. I found the same thing on the plastic and the tape today."

"So apart from the usual dust and dirt, there are patches of oil and swarf on the floor in the place where he washes his victims and wraps them up," Irene said thoughtfully.

"That's right. A garage or workshop would be my guess," Matti said.

"ELISABETH LINDBERG. FORTY-SEVEN years old. Divorced, lives alone. A nurse in the emergency room at Sahlgrenska Hospital. She was supposed to be on a night shift but didn't turn up. Reported missing by her boss; she'd tried to get hold of her, but without success. Apparently she has a son at college in Umeå. Her boss has a spare key to Lindberg's apartment; we can pick it up from the ER."

Hannu Rauhala finished his report and looked at his colleagues. Irene nodded.

"Description?" Thylqvist said.

"Five seven, slim. Short auburn hair, long, thin face. Grey-blue eyes. Scar from a C-section on her stomach."

"Sounds like the victim we saw this morning; she had a long scar on the lower part of her belly," Irene said.

"There must be lots of women who've had a C-section," Jonny said. "Maybe our little nurse just got tired of the crap weather and took off to Rio with her secret lover."

"Nice try, but she sounds a lot like the woman in the churchyard. We'll check her out," Irene said.

Jonny sighed loudly at the thought of having to go out into the rain once again.

"I can come with you if Jonny takes over here," Hannu offered.

All three of them thought that was an excellent idea. Just

as Irene and Hannu were about to leave, Matti called to tell them he'd found cat hairs stuck to the tape from the new package. They looked as if they came from the same cat, but he would have to do further tests before he could be sure.

"It's obvious—the hairs come from the copycat," Jonny said with a grin.

"WHERE DID SHE live?" Irene asked when they were in the car.

"Kobbegårdsvägen."

"Not very far from where she was found."

"Just under a kilometer," Hannu said.

"Although Ingela Svensson lived on Såggatan; it's a little farther from there to the western churchyard . . ."

She left the sentence hanging in the air, because she wasn't sure how far it actually was. Hannu didn't disappoint her.

"One point two five kilometers from Ingela's front door to the place where she was found."

"As the crow flies?"

"No—the shortest route by car."

"He dumps them in graveyards. Why?"

"They're usually deserted at night?"

"Yes, but could it mean something else?"

Hannu thought for a little while before asking, "Something religious?"

Irene couldn't quite put it into words, but she didn't believe the killer had chosen to leave his victims in churchyards by chance.

"It was just something that struck me, but you're probably right. He knows he's likely to be undisturbed while he's getting rid of his victims, so a churchyard is a good choice from his point of view."

Irene's cell phone rang; it was Jonny.

"I've gotten a hold of Elisabeth Lindberg's passport photo.

It's four years old, but it looks like the lady we have in the mortuary."

THE HOSPITAL CORRIDOR and waiting room were a hive of activity, but department supervisor Ellen Ström had closed the door of the room in which they were sitting. It was small and cramped, with two desks, computers and a printer. Irene and Hannu were sitting on stools made of stainless steel; they could feel the cold metal through the seat of their pants.

"I'm sorry to tell you that we have reason to believe the body we've found is that of Elisabeth Lindberg. She was murdered," Irene began.

"I hope . . . I hope not. I just can't believe it—it's terrible. Could it be someone else?" Ellen Ström said quietly.

"Unfortunately every indication is that it's Elisabeth," Irene replied.

Ellen nodded and swallowed hard. She had gone very pale, and her eyes filled with tears.

"How long has she worked here?" Irene went on.

"The same length of time as me—almost ten years. We've been friends since we started training, and we both applied for posts here when we qualified," Ellen explained, her voice breaking.

"So you know her well. Could you possibly come with us to identify the body? Her son is traveling down from Umeå, but he won't be here until this evening. It would be very helpful if we could be certain of the victim's identity as soon as possible," Irene said.

"Of course."

Ellen wiped her eyes and tried to pull herself together. She bent down, unlocked the bottom drawer of her desk and took out her purse. She handed Irene a bunch of keys.

"We have keys to each other's apartments so that we can water the plants and so on if one of us is away. Elisabeth is from

Jönköping and I don't have any living relatives left in Göteborg, so we're . . . best friends." Her voice broke again on the final words.

"I realize this is very difficult for you, but perhaps we could ask you a couple of questions, just to save time?" Irene said.

"That's fine," Ellen said, sitting up a little straighter. She pressed her lips together in an attempt to hide the fact that they were trembling.

"Was Elisabeth seeing anyone—did she have a boyfriend?"

"No. She'd had enough of men. Her divorce was very messy. Her ex-husband was a director of some huge pharmaceutical company. He earned plenty of money, but he started drinking. He became an alcoholic and lost his job. He went to pieces, and Elisabeth just couldn't cope. He never accepted the divorce; he persecuted her and Tobias for years. Every time he got drunk he called them up or arrived on the doorstep, either crying or threatening them."

Hannu quickly asked, "Did he ever carry out his threats?"

"Not as far as I know—you'd have to ask Tobias."

"Where's her ex now?"

"In Högsbo Hospital. He's in a coma; he got into a drunken brawl last year. He sustained serious trauma to his skull, and they didn't think he would survive. But he did, and now he's lying there like a cabbage," Ellen replied with a grimace.

It was obvious that she didn't feel too sorry for Elisabeth's ex.

"So there's no new man in her life?" Irene tried again.

"Again, not as far as I know. I'm sure she would have told me. We're such close friends . . ."

The tears began to pour down Ellen's cheeks. She wiped them away with her hands. Irene nodded sympathetically to show that she knew how difficult it was for her to talk about her murdered friend. And the dreadful ordeal of identifying the body lay before her.

• • •

A VOICE CAME from behind one of the closed doors in the corridor of the forensic pathology department. A young man in a white coat slipped out of the room. Before the door closed he took a cell phone out of his breast pocket and pressed it to his ear. Irene heard him whisper: "I'm in a forensics class, I can't come now." She could also hear Professor Stridner's dulcet tones: ". . . algor mortis . . . change in . . . a gradual decline until . . . the ambient temperature . . . several hours . . ." Irene had no idea what she was talking about; she was just relieved that Stridner was otherwise occupied. At the same time, she felt a wave of sympathy for the surgeons being educated in the finer points of forensic medicine; it was unlikely to be a restful experience, given what she knew of Professor Stridner.

She found a technician she already knew and asked him to accompany them to the cold room. He pulled out one of the drawers and showed them the victim's face. Ellen Ström identified the body as Elisabeth Lindberg.

THE APARTMENT ON Kobbegården was in a three-story block with a grey stone façade. The area had been developed in the 1970s, and the mature trees lent warmth and charm. The ground-floor apartments each had a small garden. Elisabeth Lindberg's place had three rooms, with a large west-facing window and glass patio doors, through which Irene could see a glorious rose bed and blue-painted garden furniture on the terrace. There was a six-foot fence separating her garden from the neighbors' plot, and a row of flourishing jasmine bushes gave her some privacy from the building opposite.

The double closet in the hallway contained coats and jackets, some protected by plastic bags. At the bottom were stacks of shoe boxes, neatly marked with a description of the contents: "Black high-heeled pumps" and "White sandals," Irene read. *This is a very tidy woman*, she thought as an image of the chaos in her own closet flashed through her mind. On the shelf she saw several purses. She went through them, but none contained a cell phone, wallet or keys. The purse Elisabeth had been using when she was killed obviously wasn't here. Perhaps she had just slipped whatever she needed into the pockets of her coat; however, something about the orderliness of the apartment told Irene that Elisabeth Lindberg wasn't the type to stuff things in her pockets.

The living room was furnished with a modern leather suite grouped around a glass coffee table, a thick brightly colored rug and a large flat-screen TV. In front of the TV was an inviting armchair with a footstool. The bedroom was nothing out of the ordinary: a wide bed with a matching bedside table, a chest of drawers that looked like an antique to Irene's untrained eye and two matching chairs with embroidered cushions. On top of the chest of drawers was a selection of framed photographs of the same boy at different ages. The latest showed a serious dark-haired young man wearing his student cap. No doubt this was Tobias; there was a certain resemblance to Elisabeth.

One wall was entirely taken up by closets. Methodically Irene went through them, but she found nothing unusual. One closet contained running clothes and several pairs of running shoes, with a list of results taped to the inside of the door. Elisabeth had done well in the Göteborg half marathon and similar competitions on a number of occasions.

The kitchen cupboards had shiny white doors; there was an oval table with thin stainless-steel legs, and four Myran chairs. In the pantry she saw an open bottle of red wine, and there were a couple of beers in the refrigerator, plus a plastic box containing what looked like the remains of a chicken casserole. It smelled quite fresh. Otherwise the refrigerator was virtually empty.

The smaller room was Elisabeth's study. The walls were covered with overstuffed bookshelves. In every room there were well-tended house plants, and the tiny garden was also pristine; there wasn't a weed in sight in either of the flower beds, and the postage-stamp-sized lawn had been cut very recently. Large baskets overflowing with flowering plants hung from hooks attached to the underside of the balcony. They were still flourishing in spite of the increasing cold of the past few days. Elisabeth Lindberg had definitely had green fingers. Just like Ingela Svensson.

"They both lived alone," Irene mused.

"Yes. And they both lived on the ground floor." Hannu was on the same page right away. Presumably he had been thinking along the same lines.

"Divorced, between forty and fifty years old. Both interested in plants and flowers—in fact, that was Ingela's job," Irene said.

They both pondered in silence for a little while, then Irene said, "They've actually got quite a lot in common. My first instinct is to find out whether Elisabeth Lindberg knew Ingela's new boyfriend in Borås."

"I'll check it out," Hannu said, nodding in the direction of the computer on the desk in Elisabeth's study.

"My second thought is to find out whether Ingela and Elisabeth knew each other. Elisabeth might have bought plants in the store where Ingela worked, for example."

Irene found Elisabeth's address book in one of the desk drawers. Hannu went through her computer, and established that there were no links to any dating websites. The same had applied to Ingela Svensson, and neither of them were on Facebook or other social media platforms.

There was no indication that Elisabeth had ever had contact with Leif Karlberg, or that the two homicide victims had known each other. Elisabeth's meticulous accounts on the computer revealed that she had bought most of her plants at Högsbo garden center; she didn't appear to have visited the florist's store in the Frölunda torg shopping mall over the past three years, which was how far back her accounts went.

Her address book contained very few names.

"She seems to have lived a quiet life," Hannu said.

"With not a man in sight. Her only interests seem to have been running and plants. She didn't have many friends either: Ellen Ström and a dozen or so others. That's another similarity with Ingela Svensson: she didn't have a wide circle of acquaintances either."

Irene's gaze fell on a polished-glass letter rack on the desk; it held a number of letters, postcards and notes. She took out the entire bundle and started to go through it. A small envelope with something odd written on it caught her eyes. Someone had scrawled *2 Ey. 20.5* with a thick felt-tip pen.

When she opened the envelope she saw that it contained a photograph. She shook it out onto the desk. It landed facedown, and she carefully flipped it over.

Elisabeth was standing next to the leather sofa in the living room, with a coffeepot in her hand. She was smiling down at a visitor who was sitting on the sofa. He was looking at her and holding up his coffee cup. He looked happy, too; it seemed as if mother and son got along well. It was a nice picture of an ordinary, everyday situation. There was nothing unusual or threatening about it. Except that the photographer had been standing in the little patch of garden outside the living-room window when he or she took the picture.

They had found a similar photograph of Ingela Svensson, where someone had stood outside and taken the picture through the window. It could hardly be a coincidence.

Irene studied the image for a little while before she spoke:

"I think this is a lead. The killer took the picture and wrote something on the envelope—although I can't really make out what it says. Can you?"

Hannu shook his head.

"We need to try to work out what he means . . . two Ey twenty point five . . . I haven't got a clue what that is," Irene said.

Hannu frowned in concentration, then shrugged apologetically.

"Me neither."

Irene suddenly had an idea. She went into the kitchen and opened the cupboard under the sink. The trash can was a neat version, hanging on the inside of the door.

It was lying on top; she didn't even need to root through the garbage. Elisabeth must have received it in the last couple of days, because the white chrysanthemum still looked pretty fresh.

"It's definitely him," she said.

Hannu had followed her into the kitchen. "Mmm. Tomorrow I'll do a search on the computer at work. He might have attacked someone before. Without killing them," he said.

It's a well-known fact as far as investigators are concerned that "he who steals an egg will steal an ox"; the proverb may refer to thieves, but it can apply to most types of criminals. The majority of those convicted of homicide with a sexual motive have had contact with the police in the past, usually for exposure, accessing child pornography or other sex-related online offenses, harassment, rape, attempted rape and so on. There was a good chance that the man they were looking for already had a record.

"Good idea. I'm off to Landvetter to pick up Tobias Lindberg; his plane lands in an hour or so," Irene said.

Before she left she made a final attempt to find Elisabeth's purse, but it definitely wasn't in the apartment. It ought to contain her diary, wallet, keys and other useful information. They had found her cell phone charging on top of the chest of drawers in the bedroom.

Bearing in mind how empty the refrigerator was, Irene wondered if Elisabeth had gone shopping but failed to return to the apartment. She hadn't been due to start work until ten. Perhaps she had gone to the store earlier in the evening and come home in the dark. Since it had been pouring rain, it was unlikely that there had been anyone around to see if something had happened in the parking lot.

"We need to check out which of the cars in the parking lot is hers. Her purse and wallet are missing. I think she'd been shopping when he took her," Irene said.

"I'll find out what car she drove," Hannu replied.

IRENE RECOGNIZED TOBIAS Lindberg from the photographs in his mother's apartment. He looked pale and strained as he emerged into the arrivals hall. Irene felt sorry for him. In the car she explained that Ellen Ström had identified his mother's body, and he broke down in tears. When Irene asked where he wanted to go, he replied firmly that he would like to go straight to the mortuary to see her. Irene called and asked if it was okay to come in so late, and the security guard said they could come whenever they liked. For the second time that day, Irene headed for the forensic pathology unit.

IT WAS LATE by the time she set off for home. Darkness had fallen, but at least it had stopped raining. Tobias was staying with a friend on Linnégatan until the police had finished going through his mother's apartment. Irene had given him a ride to his friend's place, and they had agreed that she would meet him there the following day, so they could talk in peace. Right now he was too upset, and she was too tired.

On the way she stopped by the apartment in Guldheden. She had meant to do it over the weekend but hadn't had time because she had been called in to replace Jonny. After her mother's death almost a year ago, they had sublet the place, but now their excellent tenant had moved to Stockholm. Irene and Krister didn't know whether to look for another tenant or not; the housing association had made it clear that they weren't very keen on sublets. They had seriously discussed the possibility of moving into the apartment themselves—selling their house and relocating into the city. Why not? The twins no longer lived at home, and Sammie was dead. They had also talked about getting another dog but had agreed that it wasn't fair on the animal; it would have to spend far too much time alone. But sometimes Irene thought the house seemed empty and soulless without the sound of claws clicking on the floor. It was difficult for two people who worked too hard to fill a house with life and warmth. It would be much easier with two reception rooms and a bedroom. Another advantage was that they would need only one car since they could both cycle to work, or share a ride. And the rent was low; their living costs would drop by a couple thousand a month. The only thing that made them hesitate was that they would lose their little garden. Neither of them was what you would call a keen gardener, but they did enjoy pottering around, planting baskets and containers and flower beds. They did have the cottage outside Sunne, of course, but that had two disadvantages: it was in the middle of the forest with no possibility of a garden, and it was in Värmland. Driving a few hundred kilometers every time you wanted to feel grass beneath your feet was impractical, to say the least.

Irene put her key in the lock and opened the door of the apartment where she had spent the first eighteen years of her life. She switched on the light in the little hallway and went into the bathroom. She followed her normal routine, flushing the toilet and rinsing the sink. Then she went into the kitchen and turned on the faucet. The water came gushing out, clearing the system. Some of Gerd's furniture was still there, but their young tenant had taken everything that belonged to her. The place felt empty and desolate.

Was Gerd still here? Irene was surprised by the thought that suddenly popped into her head. Maybe it wasn't so strange. Her mother had lived here for forty-five years, after all. If Gerd was going to be anywhere, it was here.

Right now it felt perfectly natural for Irene to try to contact her. She switched off the overhead light and sat down in the middle of the floor in the empty bedroom. Through jiujitsu she had learned how to put herself into a meditative state; she closed her eyes and sought Mokuso. Slowly she sank down into meditation.

A cool touch on her forehead. Like a feather-light caress. A serenity that filled her from deep inside and spread throughout her body. Warmth. Security. She was a little girl again. Mommy was there, like a whisper in the room. A familiar scent of lavender soap and talcum powder. That gentle breath of wind on her forehead again.

Slowly the sense of Gerd's presence faded away. The scent of lavender disappeared. With an enormous effort of will Irene tried to hold onto the awareness of her mother by screwing her eyes more tightly shut, but eventually she was conscious of nothing but the faint smell of dust hovering in the air. When she opened her eyes she saw the familiar bedroom, illuminated by the glow of the street lamps. Until now Irene hadn't acknowledged just how much she missed her mother. The brief encounter brought consolation, but it also felt somehow final. Gerd had not stayed, and somewhere deep down Irene knew that she wouldn't be coming back. At least she had managed to leave a sense of solace with her only child, in the midst of the grief.

Irene's thoughts were interrupted by the sound of her cell phone. Last year Jenny had changed her old ringtone, "La Marseillaise," to Duffy's hit song "Mercy." Apart from the fact that she was still finding it difficult to realize that it was her phone, she quite liked it. It definitely felt more youthful than the French national anthem.

It was Krister, telling her he would be several hours late. One of the chefs was still off sick, so he'd had to take over his shift. And he was already feeling the strain, Irene thought anxiously.

• • •

BY THE TIME she pulled into the parking lot, the warm, positive feeling from the apartment had returned. Krister's space was empty, as expected. It had started drizzling again, but according to the forecast they were in for a period of warmer weather. However, it would be at least twenty-four hours before things changed. *He who waits for something good never waits in vain*, Irene thought. That had been one of her mother's favorite expressions. She had been a positive, optimistic person. *Perhaps I should try to develop that aspect of my own character*, Irene thought with a burst of self-criticism.

She automatically stuck her hand in the mailbox to see if there was any mail. She screamed as her fingertips touched something soft and sticky. She quickly withdrew her hand and held it up to the light. Blood. It looked as if she had blood on her fingers. She bent down and wiped it off on the grass, but her hand still felt sticky, and she rushed into the house to wash it. The water in the sink turned red; it was definitely blood. She scrubbed frantically with a nailbrush and rinsed her fingers over and over again. Then she went into the laundry room and dug out the big flashlight. She switched it on and went back out into the darkness. Cautiously she lifted the lid of the mailbox and shone the beam inside.

Behind the half-closed eyelids, the green irises glinted in the light. Blood covered the crushed skull like a dark, congealed beret. That was what Irene had dipped her fingers in.

There was a dead cat in the mailbox.

"SO YOU CAUGHT the copycat!" Jonny chortled.

No one else around the table even smiled, for which Irene was grateful. She wasn't in the mood for bad jokes.

The dead cat was lying in the middle of the table, encased in several plastic bags.

Irene had kept it in the shed overnight. Superintendent Efva Thylqvist contemplated the cadaver with distaste and said, "Why the hell have you brought a dead cat in here? We don't have the capacity to conduct an investigation."

Irene remained calm as she went through the incidents that had affected her family over the past few days.

"So a garden seat was moved, some flowers were destroyed, someone was looking in through your kitchen window—and now this dead cat in your mailbox. Where are you going with this? Do you feel like you're under threat? Or do you think it's got something to do with the case?" Thylqvist said.

Before Irene had time to respond, the superintendent pursed her lips and continued, "It sounds to me like the kind of thing boys get up to. Kids in the neighborhood messing around."

She turned to Jonny.

"Where are we with the investigation at the moment?"

Once again Jonny had to admit that he wasn't fully up to speed. Both Irene and Hannu had worked late the previous evening, so they hadn't had time to catch up. Instead Hannu began to report back on what they had found out so far; he also told them that he had managed to locate Elisabeth Lindberg's car after getting the make and registration number from the licensing authority.

It had been found in the parking lot with two bags from the ICA Maxi store in the trunk. It was a little Golf, so the bags were visible through the rear window. Forensics had opened the lock and examined the bags, which contained food and household items. Judging by the date on the items from the deli counter, it was clear Elisabeth had bought them the day she was killed.

"The refrigerator was almost empty. Her purse was missing, so we thought she'd gone to do some shopping before she went to work. It was Irene's idea," Hannu said, nodding in the direction of his colleague.

Thylqvist didn't appear to have heard the final comment. "Contact the store and see if we can find Lindberg in any of the images from their CCTV cameras to confirm the time she was there."

The superintendent looked pensive. No one broke the silence.

"It's beginning to look as if we're dealing with a serial killer here. We need to catch him before he kills again. Go back to that guy in Borås. Check our records to see who's on the loose. Talk to the woman who found the first victim and the paperboy who found the second. They might have remembered something that didn't register at the time. And talk to Elisabeth Lindberg's son again."

Her cell phone beeped. She pressed a few buttons and got to her feet. "I have to go. Report back to Tommy if anything interesting comes up."

With those words she left the room. In the silence that followed, Sara Persson cleared her throat and said, "I have a theory."

"What about?" Jonny said with an encouraging smile.

"The envelope: two Ey. twenty point five. It's kind of scrawled; I think it should say this." She got up and went over to the whiteboard, picked up a pen and wrote neatly:

2 Ex. 20:5.

"Of course. Why didn't we realize? That makes all the difference in the world," Jonny said, rolling his eyes.

"Actually, it does. Exodus, chapter twenty, verse five. According to the new translation of the Bible it says: 'For I am the Lord your God. I am a jealous God, and I shall visit the sins of the fathers on the children to the third and fourth generations when I am hated, but I will show goodness to thousands when you love Me and keep My commandments,'" Sara replied calmly.

She was reading from a piece of paper tucked inside her

notebook. Irene could see that it was an extract from a longer text, probably a computer printout.

"You're kidding me," Jonny said without conviction.

Irene was pretty sure that Sara had come up with the correct interpretation of the short message.

"How did you work it out?" Tommy asked.

A faint blush crept up Sara's cheeks. "I called in at the lab on my way here, just to see if Matti had found out anything else. He showed me the envelope. It took a while, but then it occurred to me that it could be a Bible quotation. I did go to confirmation classes, after all . . . So I Googled it, and that's what I found."

Called in at the lab . . . Perhaps Sara wasn't entirely immune to their new technician. However, Irene had to admit it was clever of her to make the connection. It hadn't even crossed her mind.

"We didn't find an envelope at Ingela Svensson's apartment, just the photograph," Irene pointed out.

"She probably threw it away, along with the flower—we didn't find that either," Tommy said. "We know that the garbage cans on Såggatan were emptied at lunchtime on Tuesday, so no doubt they're at the dump somewhere. She didn't receive the photograph until a few days later. As far as Elisabeth Lindberg is concerned, everything was left at the same time, possibly because the killer didn't want to run the risk of being seen outside his victim's front door on two occasions. But Ingela's envelope could have had the same thing written on it—or something similar."

"So what does this mean for the case? Should we be looking for an avenger from way back when?" Jonny wondered sarcastically.

"The sins of the fathers are visited on the children . . . Perhaps we should check out Ingela Svensson's and Elisabeth Lindberg's parents . . . see if they had anything in common," Tommy went on, ignoring Jonny's tone.

"This is about Ingela and Elisabeth. Not their parents," Hannu stated firmly.

Irene was inclined to agree with him. The attack to which both women had been subjected felt far too personal to be nothing more than revenge for something their fathers might have done. But of course they had to look into it. The consequences would be devastating if this turned out to be the clue that led them to the killer, and they had ignored it.

It took a few hours of intensive digging in every possible archive and database before they were able to exclude the possibility that there was something in the background of both victims' parents that could lie behind the homicides. Ingela's family came from Göteborg and northern Halland, while Elisabeth's relatives on both sides were from the area around Jönköping and Huskvarna. Both families had stayed put—apart from the odd emigrant to America at the beginning of the last century—and there wasn't the slightest indication that any of them had had any contact whatsoever, or had been in the same place even. Nor was there any evidence that the two women had ever met.

"There isn't a single point of contact." Irene sighed.

"The killer," Hannu said.

As usual, sensible Hannu had placed the focus exactly where it needed to be. Irene straightened up in her chair and looked at her colleagues.

"Okay. What do we know about him?"

"He photographs his victims through the windows of their apartment," Hannu began.

"Does he follow them for a period of time before he attacks?" Irene asked.

"Possibly. If he's a stalker, then definitely." Sara spoke up before anyone else had time to answer.

"What the hell do you know about stalkers?" Jonny sneered, raising an eyebrow.

Sara blushed, but refused to be cowed. "I've done some reading on the subject. And I was involved in a case that—"

"If we find anything to suggest we're dealing with a stalker, we'll get back to you, kiddo," said Superintendent Thylqvist as she walked in. She turned to Jonny. "Anything new?"

He quickly went over what they had found out during the course of the day, which to be honest wasn't a great deal.

Efva Thylqvist interrupted him. "The first body was found on Saturday. You haven't gotten very far with that either. Let's see some action, otherwise we'll have another package wrapped in plastic to deal with."

She could have put it more elegantly, but the message was clear: the chief wasn't happy. Presumably somebody higher up was on her case. Nobody pointed out that she was the one who had decided that only two inspectors from the Violent Crimes Unit should investigate the murder of Ingela Svensson. There were certain things you didn't mention to your boss if you wanted to maintain a positive atmosphere. At least the atmosphere was positive as long as Thylqvist wasn't around, Irene thought.

The intercom in the middle of the pale birch-wood table crackled into life: *"Call for DI Huss. Is she there?"* a female voice asked.

"Yes."

"Lars Holmberg wants to speak to you; shall I put him through to your office?"

"Please," Irene said, getting to her feet.

DI Lars Holmberg was one of the officers involved in the door-to-door inquiries in Kobbegården. Had they found out something interesting? Irene felt her pulse rate increase with anticipation.

"Hi, Irene. We've found a witness who says she saw a man

and a woman hugging in the parking lot outside Elisabeth Lindberg's apartment at around eight-thirty on the evening in question," Holmberg said, getting straight down to business.

"Hugging?"

"That's what she thought they were doing at the time, but she's been in London, so she didn't know her neighbor had been murdered. She was out of town yesterday. She only heard about Lindberg today, and then she made the connection with what she saw in the parking lot on Monday, and contacted us. Would you like to speak to her?"

"Absolutely. I'm seeing Elisabeth's son in less than an hour; do you know if this witness will be at home later?"

"Yes—she's a freelance journalist. She said she'd be working from home for a few days."

"Tell her I'll be there shortly after three," Irene said.

At last, a witness. But "hugging in the parking lot" sounded weird. Was there a man in the picture after all, a relationship they had missed? The only way to find the answer was to keep working on the case, with an open mind.

TOBIAS LINDBERG LOOKED as if he hadn't slept a wink all night. His eyes were red-rimmed, his face sunken, with a greyish pallor. His dark hair was greasy and uncombed. His gangly body was sprawled on a sofa that his friend had probably found in some secondhand store. The only decent piece of furniture was a long bookcase packed with rows of CDs and DVDs. Illegal downloads, Irene assumed. A large skull and crossbones flag hung on the wall above an array of computers, screens and other IT equipment.

Fate had dealt Tobias a rough hand. His father was in a coma, and his mother had been murdered. No siblings, no close relatives: unusual for one so young. It was fortunate that he had friends.

Irene impulsively went over and sat down in the armchair next to the sofa. She took his hand and said, "I really am very sorry for your loss. It's terrible to lose your mother. I know that from my own experience. But for her to fall victim to a murderer as well . . . It's just dreadful. I understand if you don't feel up to talking right now. We can wait."

He turned his head and looked at her. The naked pain in his eyes tore at her heart. He didn't withdraw his hand; Irene could feel it trembling.

"I want to . . . I have to . . . to talk. I'm going crazy!"

The last few words came out like a sob. Irene squeezed his hand.

"Okay, let's take it slowly. I can assure you that we're doing everything in our power to catch the person who killed your mother, but we don't have very much to go on—we need more information. That's why I need to ask you a few questions. Is that all right?"

He nodded and wiped his eyes with his free arm, not letting go of Irene's hand. She gave him an encouraging smile, and it was as if he suddenly became aware that they were holding hands. He pulled away and sat up straight. His bony knees were visible through his ripped jeans.

From past experience Irene knew that the best way to get someone to relax was to ask them to talk about themselves.

"What are you studying in Umeå?" she began.

"Psychology."

"Were you back in Göteborg over the summer break?"

"Yes, I've got a summer job down here. I worked there before I went to college."

"Doing what?"

"I help out in an assisted-living facility."

"Did you stay with your mother in the summer?"

"No, I stayed here with Ville. It's closer to work, and . . . well, Linnéstan is always Linnéstan, if you know what I mean."

"When did you go back up to Umeå?"

"Last Saturday evening. I flew because it takes, like, a whole day on the train. I worked on Saturday morning and caught the flight a few hours later."

Some of the tension had left his thin shoulders, but he was clenching his fists, and his hands wouldn't stop shaking.

The next question was a sensitive one, but it had to be asked.

"Do you know whether your mother had met anyone new—a boyfriend?"

"She hadn't."

There wasn't a trace of doubt in his voice.

"Nothing happened in the summer to suggest that might be the case?"

"No."

"Would she have told you if she was seeing someone?"

"Absolutely. We were very close . . . She was . . . fantastic." His voice was far from steady, but he tried to hide it by clearing his throat and straightening his shoulders. He was doing his best to help.

"Did she give any indication that someone might be following her, or watching her?"

Tobias started to shake his head, then stopped. A glimmer of uncertainty appeared in his sad eyes. "Not in the summer, but when we spoke on the phone . . . It was Monday . . . The day when she . . . the day when . . ."

His voice gave way and he swallowed hard. After a few seconds he was ready to go on. "She said someone had given her flowers. Or maybe it was one flower . . . Yes, it was one flower, and there was a photograph with it—a picture of Mom and me. How weird is that?"

"Did she say how the flower was delivered?"

"It was hanging on the front door when she got home after driving me to the airport on Saturday."

Which suggested that the killer had been watching Elisabeth over the weekend, and had seen her leave. The perpetrator seemed to be a person who had all the time in the world, and a great deal of patience. Sara had mentioned a stalker; maybe she was right.

"What time did you speak to your mother on Monday?"

"Just after seven-thirty. I called to tell her everything was fine with my new student apartment. The news had just started on TV, and she asked me to wait while she turned down the sound. Although I think she switched it off. She was going to go shopping before she started work, and she was in a hurry."

"How long did you talk?"

"Three or four minutes."

"And she said she was going shopping?"

"Yes."

"Do you know why she hadn't done her shopping earlier in the day?"

He shrugged his bony shoulders. "Maybe she had a slot booked in the laundry room or something . . . No, I remember! She'd been to the hairdresser's!"

Irene recalled the pretty red streaks glowing in Elisabeth's brown hair. They had shown up even though her hair was wet.

They carried on talking for a while, but it was as if all the air had gone out of Tobias, which was completely understandable. Irene thought he had been incredibly strong, and he had given her some very useful information. She had found out when the white flower had been delivered, Tobias had confirmed that there was no new man on the horizon and that his mother had left the apartment after seven-thirty to go shopping. Now it was time to see if the neighbor who had called in about the couple hugging in the parking lot could help to establish the time of the murder.

THE WITNESS'S NAME was Tove Josefsson, and she lived in the apartment above Elisabeth Lindberg. A couple of seconds after Irene had rung the bell, the door was flung wide open to reveal a smiling woman in her early forties. She was plump and looked like she had been hibernating since the 1970s: she was wearing a hand-dyed wine-red undershirt with a matching scarf wound around her frizzy blonde hair, and wide, dark purple pants made of a soft fabric. A blue stone glittered in her nose, and she wore red Crocs, which seemed to be the only item of her clothing dating from this century.

"Good afternoon—DI Irene Huss. Are you Tove Josefsson?"

"Oh . . . yes. I thought it would be the guy who was here earlier . . ."

The woman couldn't hide her disappointment. Her warm smile disappeared. Admittedly Lars Holmberg was a fine figure of a man, but Irene could have told Tove that he was married with three kids.

"May I come in?"

"Of course, forgive me. Would you like a coffee? I've just made some."

But not with me in mind, Irene thought. Tove Josefsson stepped aside to let her in. The apartment was identical to Elisabeth Lindberg's, although the style was very different. It was clear that Tove was a fan of Eastern decor. Candles in small colored glass bowls were everywhere, on low tables and shelves. The scent of incense was strong. As far as Irene was concerned, the aroma of freshly brewed coffee was much more appealing. Tove led the way into the living room, and a small mobile made of shells made a faint tinkling sound as they walked by.

"Please sit down," Tove said, pointing to a low divan covered in some kind of green brocade. Irene's knees complained as she crouched, but once she was settled she realized the divan was very comfortable, with well-stuffed cushions supporting her back. She took the opportunity to look around. The walls were adorned with photographs of exotic locations: a sunrise over a desert landscape, the interior of a Japanese temple, snow plains sparkling in the sunshine, an old, scarred lion yawning at the camera . . . The pictures were beautiful.

"Did you take all these photos?" Irene asked.

"Most of them. They were all taken on my travels, but sometimes I had a photographer with me. I travel a great deal."

"I believe that's why you didn't know what had happened to Elisabeth Lindberg."

"That's right. It's just dreadful! Poor Elisabeth—not to mention her son."

Tove's eyes widened, and Irene caught a glimpse of pure

fear. She also noticed the shudder that ran down the journalist's spine. Was she worried about her own safety? She was the right age, after all, and single.

A strand of hair had escaped from Tove's scarf, and she tucked it back in place.

"You're right; it's a terrible crime. Can you tell me what happened and what you saw on Monday evening?" Irene said.

"Of course. Hasse, the photographer, and I had just come back from South Africa. We were doing a piece on wine for a food magazine, and our plane landed at about seven. It took a while to load everything into the car, and it was pouring. I drove Hasse home, then came back here."

She paused for breath before continuing:

"My parking space is at the far end of the lot, so it's a pretty long walk. I had quite a lot of heavy luggage, so I decided to drive up to the main door. You're allowed to pick up and drop off, but not to park. As I drove past the parking lot I glanced over at my space for some reason—I have no idea why. I caught a glimpse of a man holding a woman. It was hard to see properly in the rain and the darkness, but it looked as if he was giving her a hug from behind—holding her in his arms and kind of . . . rocking her."

"Rocking her?"

"Yes . . . moving her gently from side to side. A tender moment, maybe."

Gooseflesh covered Irene's arms. She thought she knew the answer to her next question, but she needed to hear it from Tove herself.

"Was the woman moving? Did she seem to be trying to defend herself?"

"No—I might have reacted if that had been the case, but she seemed perfectly calm. Just kind of letting it happen."

Which meant that Elisabeth was already dead when Tove drove past, or at least unconscious.

As if she had read Irene's mind, Tove asked, "I've been wondering . . . Do you think I could have saved Elisabeth if I'd parked in my usual space?"

"Probably not. Can you tell me what time it was?"

"About eight-thirty."

"And how do you know it was Elisabeth you saw?"

"I don't know for sure, but I know where she parks her car, and this couple were standing right next to it. I helped her change a tire a few weeks ago; she had a puncture on the passenger side at the front." Tove smiled sadly at the memory.

"Did you know each other well?"

"No, not at all. She moved here last year, and I'm hardly ever home. We usually say hi if we meet on the way in or out. It was pure chance that I happened to be passing when she was about to change the tire. Her son was working and she needed the car, so I gave her a hand."

"Did you see anything of the man who was holding the woman?"

"Not really. As I said, it was hard to see in the dark and the rain, but he wasn't much taller than Elisabeth, and he was wearing a dark jacket and dark pants. Work clothes . . . that's it! He had reflective bands around the bottom of his sleeves and the legs of his pants. I remember seeing them catch the light—that's why I made the association with work clothes."

"Any idea of his hair color?"

Tove chewed her lower lip, concentrating hard. Eventually she said, "No—he had something on his head. A hat, maybe."

"Was he wearing glasses? Is there anything else you can remember?"

"I don't know. I only saw him from behind, but I got the impression he was strong." She held her hands apart to show that he was broad-shouldered.

"You mean fit?"

"Kind of . . . He was no flyweight, if I can put it like that. But he wasn't fat. Powerfully built, I'd say."

This could mean that the man was muscular thanks to a physically demanding job; he could be active within a particular sport, or he might just have a naturally athletic figure. He was probably very strong, given that Elisabeth had been pretty fit. Had she had time to offer any resistance? Perhaps the autopsy would tell them.

"How tall would you say he was?"

"Hmm . . . between five eight and six foot."

"Did you form any impression of his age?"

"I'd say he wasn't old, but he wasn't a teenager either. Between twenty and forty, maybe."

The killer was strong, average height, dressed in work clothes and a cap. Aged somewhere between twenty and forty. And he must have had a car in order to remove both bodies.

"Do you remember seeing a vehicle you didn't recognize anywhere near the spot where Elisabeth and this guy were standing?"

Tove shook her head slowly. "There are several spaces for visitors opposite where Elisabeth parks. If he'd left his car there, he would only need to carry her a few meters. I don't remember seeing an unfamiliar car, but I guess it must have been there. Otherwise he wouldn't have been able to take her away and . . . do what he did to her."

Irene saw the color drain from Tove's face.

"Is there a crazy person running around here? I mean . . . are the women who live here in danger?" she asked, looking Irene straight in the eye.

Irene did her best to sound reassuring. "Probably not, but we don't know very much at this stage. As you might be aware, we found a woman a few days ago who had fallen victim to the same perpetrator. She lived on Såggatan in Majorna, which is quite a way from here."

Tove nodded. "I went to London on Tuesday to discuss a major project, but I read about it online. She was found in the western churchyard, wrapped in plastic—just like Elisabeth. It's horrible!"

Irene merely nodded in response.

"How did he kill them?" Tove asked, her voice far from steady.

"We haven't even had the autopsy report on the first victim yet. It will be a few days before we know for sure."

They had deliberately kept the fact that the killer had strangled his victims with a length of thin nylon twine from the media. So far nothing had leaked out, but it was only a matter of time.

Irene got up, her knees creaking in protest once more. She gave Tove her card, just in case anything else came back to her.

IRENE'S CAR WAS in one of the visitors' spaces. Elisabeth's red Golf had been parked directly opposite. It had been taken to a workshop where a forensic examination would be carried out. Irene didn't expect anything to be found inside the car, but you never knew. The killer might have touched something.

Suddenly she realized how tired she was. She shuddered; the deserted parking lot was dark and creepy. Was he somewhere nearby? Was he watching her right now? The thought came from nowhere, but that didn't make it any less frightening. She got into her car as quickly as she could, and drove away.

"Package Killer brings terror to west side of city!" That's what the newspapers said today. Package Killer? They don't know what they're talking about! It is the only way. Our agreement is clear: I shall show goodness to thousands when you love Me and keep My commandments. When My commandments are broken, I must become the Punisher. Let Thy will be done.

KRISTER WAS ALREADY home, standing at the stove. The wonderful aroma of fresh herbs and saffron filled the air. As usual when he was cooking, he was wearing jeans and a T-shirt. Irene loved to see the movement of the muscles in his back and shoulders as he juggled pots and pans. Silently she crept up behind him, then she stood on tiptoe and kissed the back of his neck. She put her arms around him and slipped in front of him, kissed his throat, nibbled his earlobe and caressed his chest and stomach. Right now she thought he was the sexiest man on earth.

"Not now, okay?" he said curtly.

She immediately took a step back and stared at him. She was hurt, to say the least.

With an angry movement Krister threw the spoon into the pan of fish soup he had been stirring, splattering the golden yellow liquid all over the stove.

"Sorry, but I'm so fucking furious!" he snapped.

Irene's reaction changed to one of surprise. Krister was usually a model of even temperament, probably because he was conflict averse and kept his frustrations bottled up inside. There is a reason why people end up suffering from depression as a result of exhaustion. Irene had thought about this many times when Krister had been diagnosed with burnout, but over the past twelve months everything had seemed so much better.

Admittedly he had said several times that he was sick of his job and wanted to leave, but he hadn't mentioned it for a while.

"What's happened?"

"Some bastard broke into my locker and stole my wallet!" Krister said, waving the soup spoon around.

Irene fetched the paper-towel roll and started wiping splashes of soup off the cupboards and the stove. "When?" she asked.

"I don't know. During the day. I found the locker broken open when I was about to go home just after five. I was on the short day shift today."

"Have you blocked your cards?"

"Yes, I did that right away. But of course I don't know how long the thief had access to them before I found out they were gone. Shit!"

With a loud *plop* the spoon landed back in the pan. Irene sighed, tore off another sheet of paper towel and wiped down the stove once more.

THE FOLLOWING MORNING dawned clear and bright, and Irene felt as if the sunlight gave her a fresh burst of energy. She certainly needed it. Krister had been so angry about the theft of his wallet. Fortunately he had been carrying only the card for their household account. The bank had confirmed that the account had been emptied: a total of 8,950 kronor. He had reported the incident to the police, of course, but got the impression they weren't very interested. Krister was particularly upset at the thought that the thief could be someone who worked at the restaurant. He had asked around, but no one had seen anything unusual.

The kitchen staff's changing room was directly opposite the kitchen, which meant that not just anyone could walk in. Between the restaurant kitchen and the changing room was a hallway with a door that led to the back of the restaurant. Delivery vehicles parked in the loading bay outside the door, which wasn't always locked during the day, but there were usually people in the kitchen who would be aware of anyone coming or going.

Krister decided the best way to get in without being noticed was during the lunchtime rush, between twelve and one, when everyone was working flat out. It was possible that an outsider could slip into the changing room without being seen.

That was probably what had happened. The strange thing

was that none of the other lockers had been broken into—only Krister's. They were basic metal cubbies with simple locks. The owner's last name was on a piece of card slipped into a little holder on the door.

"It's a shame no one stuffed a body in my locker, because then I could have called you and something might have been done," Krister had said as they were eating the delicious fish soup.

He dipped his spoon in half-heartedly, with little appetite.

HANNU HAD GOTTEN a hold of two images from the CCTV cameras at the ICA store in Frölunda torg, both showing Elisabeth Lindberg. The first was taken at 7:57 P.M., and showed her entering the store pushing a cart. In the second she was at the deli counter; it was 8:06. She was wearing jeans and a light-colored trench coat. Over her shoulder was a large purse, which looked both expensive and new. Irene knew she hadn't seen it in the apartment. Presumably it was in the same place as Elisabeth Lindberg's and Ingela Svensson's clothes.

When Irene arrived in her office and switched on her computer, she found an email from Matti Berggren. She opened it and read:

Subject: cat (dead)

Appears to have been killed by a car as there are clearly visible tire marks on the head and upper body. No other signs of violence. A comparison of hairs from the subject and the cat hairs found on the tape used to secure the plastic around the two murder victims shows no match. The subject is a long-haired breed, but the hairs on the tape are from an ordinary black-and-white short-haired domestic cat. 2 white and 6 black hairs were found on the tape.

Sara came in just as Irene finished reading.

"Hi. We've found a case that could be his first," she said.

"His first?" Irene echoed.

"His first victim. Who is still alive."

Sara put down several sheets of paper in front of Irene and left the room. *She certainly doesn't waste time on small talk*, Irene thought.

The heading was attempted homicide, the date Monday, March 2. Almost exactly six months ago. A woman named Marie Carlsson had been found on the step of her terraced house. She had managed to set off her attack alarm, and a neighbor had heard it. His shouts scared off the perpetrator, and he called the police and an ambulance when he found Marie Carlsson unconscious. A noose was tightly drawn around her neck, but the neighbor managed to loosen it. Marie had forced one hand under the twine, which was probably what had saved her life. According to forensics it was a type of nylon twine often used for washing lines. However, there had been no loops at the ends. That was something he came up with before the two later attacks, Irene thought.

The notes included a transcript of an interview with the victim the following day. Marie Carlsson had gotten home late from work. She was a section manager at the ICA Maxi store in Frölunda torg.

Irene gave a start when she read where Marie worked. There it was again, that same ICA store. A remarkable coincidence, but she decided it didn't necessarily mean anything at this stage. She continued reading.

That day had been particularly difficult, because several members of the staff were out sick. The store closed at 9:00, but it had been getting on to 10:45 by the time Marie got home and put her key in the lock. Before she could open the door, she was attacked.

Marie Carlsson was forty-five years old and single. She lived in Högsbohöjd.

Though the attack had been investigated by another team, Irene remembered it, and knew how seriously the incident had been taken. So far they had gotten nowhere; the attacker had disappeared without a trace, apart from the noose with which he had tried to strangle Marie. But it was just ordinary nylon twine and therefore impossible to track down.

Irene jumped as the intercom crackled and she heard Sara's voice: *"I've asked Matti to compare the noose around Marie Carlsson's neck with the ones from our two murder victims."*

"Thanks," Irene said, but the intercom had already disconnected.

Irene stared at the sun-bleached print of Monet's *Impression, soleil levant* without really seeing it. It had been hanging on the wall when she started with the Unit, and it had blended into its surroundings with time. Even if it had been a new, more colorful work of art, she wouldn't have noticed it right now.

A victim who had survived.

This could be a breakthrough in the hunt for the Package Killer.

IRENE AND SARA got out of the car and set off toward the house where Marie Carlsson lived.

"Check out the windows. No more than four feet off the ground," Sara said.

They went through the little gate and walked up to the front door. Before Irene had time to ring the bell, they heard the sound of loud barking. *That's a big dog, and it seems to be doing its job*, she thought.

Irene pressed the bell firmly, which made the dog bark even louder. Then they heard a woman's voice give a brief command. The barking stopped, but Irene could hear the dog moving around just behind the door, emitting a low growl. When the door opened both Sara and Irene looked down at the woman's knees instead of at her face. She had a firm grip on the collar of the German shepherd who was responsible for all the noise.

"Inside, Hanko!" She gestured with her hand and let go of the collar.

The dog let out one more rumble from deep in his throat, but after a final appraising glance at the two officers, he turned and trotted away. He stopped in the kitchen doorway; from his body language Irene could see that he was alert but not aggressive. Sara seemed a little nervous of the large dog.

"Hi. Marie Carlsson," the woman said, holding out her hand.

Irene introduced herself and Sara, and Marie stepped back to let them in.

As she took their coats Marie said apologetically, "I'm sorry if Hanko scared you; he's actually very gentle, but he's a trained guard dog."

"Have you had him long?" Irene asked.

An expression that was difficult to interpret flitted across Marie's face.

"No," she said curtly. She led the way into the living room and asked them to sit down. On the table was a tray laid out with coffee cups and a plate of muffins.

"Coffee?"

"Tea, please," Sara said before Irene had time to answer.

It seemed as if she never drank coffee. A cop who drank only tea! *That girl is going to have problems*, Irene thought as she nodded and smiled to indicate that coffee was exactly what she wanted.

Marie Carlsson reminded her of Elisabeth Lindberg to a certain extent. She was almost as tall, slim, and her dark hair was cut into a bob with a few lighter streaks. Her makeup was subtle, but brought out her nut-brown eyes. She was wearing a boat-necked embroidered white tunic and skinny jeans.

Around her neck was a pale blue scarf. She looked fit without being too muscular.

Marie smiled at Sara. "I'll put the kettle on."

She went off into the kitchen, and Irene glanced around the living room. Modern but simple. Nothing that looked old or inherited. The color palette was red and grey, with the odd splash of cornflower blue. On the walls hung beautifully framed prints by Bengt Lindström. Irene had learned to recognize his distinct colors and contorted faces during a case many years earlier. In fact, one of his paintings had helped to solve the murder of one of the richest men in Göteborg.

Marie returned with a pot of coffee in one hand and a steaming mug in the other. She put the mug in front of Sara and said, "I'm sorry, I've only got tea bags."

"No problem," Sara replied as Marie poured two cups of coffee.

Hanko had settled down under the table, his head resting on Irene's feet. He must have been comfortable, because after a little while he started snoring. It was a restful sound; homicide and attempted homicide seemed far away.

"How long have you had Hanko?" Irene tried again.

There was a wariness in Marie's eyes, just as when Irene had asked her almost the same question a few minutes ago.

"Since the end of March. Almost six months."

"He's lovely. And you said he's trained as a guard dog?"

Marie sighed. "I know why you're here. The Package Killer. Two women about the same age as me. I presume they were strangled?" she said.

The fact that the killer carefully wrapped his victims had leaked out to the press, hence the Package Killer. Far too many people had seen the bodies; the security breach was inevitable. However, it wasn't public knowledge that both women had been strangled with a length of twine. Irene's expression gave nothing away.

"We're trying to gather as much material as we can, and we think it's possible that you were his first victim," she said.

Marie got to her feet, wrapping her arms tightly around her. Slowly she walked to the window overlooking the terrace and stared out. With her back to them she said, "The same thought occurred to me. And I have to tell you it doesn't feel good."

"I can understand that, but we would very much appreciate it if you could help us catch this guy."

Marie spun around. "You didn't get very far when it happened to me," she said bitterly.

"No. But now we have more leads, and we think we might be able to track him down, with your help."

Her arms still tightly wrapped around her body, Marie went back to the sofa and sank down, her expression resigned. She unwound her scarf to reveal an angry dark pink scar running around her neck, with a gap of about three inches at the front.

She pointed to the scar. "You have to understand how terrible this has been. Months have passed, and nothing has happened. I'm constantly wondering if he'll come back and finish . . . what he failed to accomplish last time."

Hanko was woken by his mistress's voice. He tilted his head to one side and looked inquiringly at her, then at the two visitors, before relaxing and resting his head on his comfortable cushion once more. Irene's feet were starting to go to sleep, but she didn't want to move them. Being around a dog again felt reassuring and familiar.

"You're a dog person," Marie said, looking at Irene.

"Yes. I've had dogs all my life, but we had to have Sammie, our last, put to sleep two years ago."

"It must be awful having to make the decision to . . ." Marie fell silent, then cleared her throat. "After the attack I got scared. I've always been so confident, so sure I could take care of myself, but suddenly I didn't dare sleep in my own house. I stayed with my sister or various friends at first, but then someone told me about Hanko. Since then I've had no problem sleeping here. The problem is I can't take him everywhere. That's when I get scared again. Sometimes I almost have a panic attack. I've never had a dog before; we're going to obedience classes to help us bond. To be honest I'm the one that needs training; Hanko already knows everything."

A little smile played around Marie's lips as she gazed proudly at her beloved dog. Irene decided it was time to broach the questions they had come to ask.

"Did you ever get the feeling that you were being watched in the period leading up to the attack?"

Marie shook her head.

"I was asked that before. No, I can't say I did."

Her voice was steady, but her eyes flickered. Irene had a feeling she wasn't telling the whole truth.

"No strange phone calls? Nobody sent you flowers or written messages?"

"No."

The answer was calm and confident; obviously nothing of that nature had happened. Irene decided to take a chance. After all, they had found two photographs taken through the victims' windows.

"There is evidence to suggest that the Package Killer's victims noticed someone watching them through the window at some stage before they were killed," she said.

She could feel Sara's surprise. Irene didn't look at her colleague; instead she kept her eyes fixed on Marie, who gave a start and looked terrified.

"Something like that might . . . might have happened. Once," she admitted after a while.

She fell silent, then appeared to make a decision.

"I mean, people are always passing by on the sidewalk outside the kitchen, and that's fine. I'm used to it. The backyard is next to a piece of land that was too small to build on. It's separated from my plot by a dense cypress hedge. One Saturday night . . . I remember it was February twenty-first . . . I had a friend here. She was sitting in the living room, and I was in the kitchen fixing us something to eat. Suddenly she called out: 'There's someone in your garden!' I rushed in here, but I couldn't see anything. I always have the outside light on when it's dark; I opened the door, and I could hear someone moving behind the hedge. I ran over there, but there was no sign of anyone."

"Did your friend notice what this person looked like?"

"No, she just saw a dark figure standing there."

"We need to talk to her. Could we have her name and address?" Irene asked.

Marie suddenly looked nervous and hesitant again, but then her resolve returned.

"She's my girlfriend. But she's married with two young kids. She's not ready to leave him yet. That's fine by me. I work long hours, and I don't like kids. Then again, I thought I didn't like dogs," she said, looking down at her sleeping companion.

"We really do need to speak to her," Irene said.

"Believe me, she won't want to speak to you. And she said she just saw a dark figure on the edge of the pool of light."

Marie's mouth set in a stubborn line, and Irene realized there was no point in trying to pressure her. Instead she asked, "Have you seen anyone in the garden since then?"

"No."

There was a brief silence, broken by Sara. "You said your girlfriend is married with children. How long had you been seeing each other before that evening?"

"We got together at the end of December last year, so about two months. That evening . . . It was actually the first time we'd met properly. She finds it difficult to get away, but she managed it somehow," Marie said with a wan smile.

"When you say properly, do you mean that's the first time you were intimate?" Sara went on.

"Yes."

"Could the man in the garden have seen you?"

"I guess so. We made love before dinner, maybe an hour before she saw him. And we . . . we started here in the living room before we went up to the bedroom. So yes, he might well have seen a few things."

The look she gave Sara and Irene was defiant, but at the same time she looked slightly amused. Perhaps she thought they were shocked.

"You didn't receive a photograph in the post later?" Sara continued, completely unmoved.

Marie looked genuinely surprised and glanced over at the window. She shook her head. "No—no photograph, or anything else. I'd almost forgotten our Peeping Tom. I didn't even think about him after the attack. I didn't connect it with . . ."

She fell silent and looked down at her hands, which seemed to be clenching and unclenching on their own accord.

Irene and Sara asked a few more questions about the attack itself, but nothing new emerged. Marie confirmed that her assailant had been very strong. She trained at the gym twice a week, but she had had no chance of escaping his grasp.

After being flatly refused contact details for Marie's girl-friend again, Irene decided to leave that aside for a while. "Is it okay if we take a look in the garden?"

"Sure," Marie said, getting to her feet.

With some difficulty she managed to open the door leading to the terrace and let them out, although she didn't accompany them. Hanko had woken up when everyone started moving, and he took the opportunity to slip outside. He went over to the cypress hedge and cocked his leg. Marie called him and he dashed back inside, happily wagging his tail.

"He's not usually allowed to pee in the garden, but sometimes . . ." Marie said apologetically.

Irene gave her an understanding smile. She had occasionally let Sammie go in the garden on the odd morning when nobody really felt like taking him for a walk.

Anyone could see that Marie Carlsson wasn't much of a gardener. The dense hedge and a sickly fruit tree were the only living things in sight. On the small stone terrace, two attractive blue ceramic pots contained something shriveled and unidentifiable.

"So where was this person standing?" Sara asked.

"Kind of in the middle of the garden, but a little to the left. Closer to the hedge. The outside light doesn't reach that far."

As it was midafternoon it was impossible to see where the pool of light would end, but it was easy to work out why the watcher had stuck to that side of the garden. There was a little gap at the end of the hedge. If he was seen he could slip back through to the small lot on the other side.

But was this person the Package Killer? They couldn't be certain. Marie hadn't received a photograph or a flower from the perpetrator before the attack. Were they looking at two different people? Then again, the noose around her neck had been exactly the same as the twine used to strangle both homicide victims.

If it was the same man, he had changed his MO after his initial failure. He had knotted the ends of the twine into loops and had added the flower and the photograph. Then there was the strange inscription on the envelope. Would he move on, change his MO again?

A short sequence of images flickered through Irene's mind: the garden seat in the rose bed, the uprooted asters, the dead cat in the mailbox, the footprints in the freshly raked earth. She couldn't prevent a shudder from running down her spine.

THERE WAS A delivery note on the drying rack with Krister's name on it; he had already signed it.

Irene heard his footsteps in the hallway and called out, "What did you order?"

"Nothing. I have no idea what it is."

"The sender is Expo Team APS, Denmark," Irene read out loud.

"I suppose it could be kitchen equipment, probably pans or knives—the kind of thing they send out as a bonus if you place a large order. The restaurant got new fans and worktops from a company in Denmark, but that must be at least six months ago. I placed the order, but I have no idea why anything would be sent here. How would they know my home address?"

Krister looked completely bewildered, but then he shrugged.

"We'll find out when we pick it up," he said.

IT WAS A large, heavy box. Krister sliced through the tape and opened the lid. There was a list of the contents on the top. When he glanced at it, Irene saw his expression change from anticipation to surprise.

"Is this a joke?" he exclaimed.

Irene moved closer and peered into the box. The first thing she saw was an enormous dildo. Underneath it was a black leather jockstrap, adorned with metal studs. Needless to say there was also a whip, and a lingerie set in see-through red nylon. At the bottom lay an inflatable doll and several DVDs. Judging by the covers they all involved sex with animals.

"Almost nine thousand kronor!" Krister said through gritted teeth.

Irene took the piece of paper and read it carefully. "The order was placed on the day your wallet went missing. The payment has been made from your account, and it matches the amount that had been withdrawn. It's the thief who ordered all this," she said, trying to reassure him.

Krister was still glaring at the contents of the box. "What do we do now?"

"Well, if there's nothing you want to keep, we send it back," Irene said with a teasing smile.

At first Krister looked furious, but then he smiled. "Maybe you'd like to hang on to the giant cock?" he said.

"Absolutely not! That has nothing to do with pleasure. Sixteen inches long and as thick as a rolling pin—it's an instrument of torture!"

"In that case I don't suppose I can tempt you with the whip . . ."

Krister took it out and swished it experimentally through the air. Both of them burst out laughing, and once they had started, they couldn't stop. Laughter was exactly the outlet they needed to shake off the unpleasant feeling evoked by the contents of the box. It was a while before they had regained their composure and were able to continue their conversation.

"We'll send it back, but I think we should photograph the box and the contents, and add the information to the report you put in about your wallet being stolen," Irene said, wiping the tears from her eyes.

"Okay, you're the cop," Krister said as he went to fetch his camera.

• • •

LATER THAT EVENING Jenny called from Amsterdam. She definitely wasn't in the mood for small talk.

"Guess what? I'm calling from a landline! Some idiot blocked my cell phone number." She was so angry that her voice was breaking.

Irene tried to calm her down. "Why would someone block your number?"

"I don't know, but that's what they've done!"

"It must be a misunderstanding. It's not easy to block someone else's cell phone number. The police can do it, but . . ."

"I called the operator. According to them, the request seems perfectly in order, but now I need someone to certify that I'm who I say I am, and that I don't want the number blocked."

"I'll fix it, honey," Irene said.

It was a long time since she had heard her daughter sound so upset. As far as Jenny was concerned, it was an absolute disaster if she didn't have full access to her phone 24/7, particularly as she was in a different country. Her entire social life would cease to function. Irene was well aware of this, and could understand Jenny's frustration. After a while she managed to convince Jenny that she would contact the operator and sort it out.

When the call was over, Irene was left with a feeling of anxiety. Krister had a terrible memory for numbers, and always kept a piece of paper with their daughters' cell phone numbers on it, in case he needed to reach them when he didn't have his own cell. Whoever had stolen Krister's wallet would be able to trace the girls' addresses through their cell phone numbers.

Krister had received a parcel containing lewd sex toys, and on the same day Jenny's number had been blocked. Added to the incidents of the garden seat in the rose bed, the footprints in the soil, the uprooted asters and the dead cat, a pattern was beginning to emerge.

Someone was trying to make life difficult for the Huss

family. The only person who had been spared so far was Katarina.

Irene called her daughter. Felipe answered; he was in a very good mood and happy to talk. It was obvious that he was really enjoying his course at Chalmers. The fact that there was a high level of unemployment among architects didn't seem to bother him at all; he was convinced that he would get a job when he qualified. Irene felt pretty sure that if there was anyone in his class who would find work, it was Felipe. She asked him to pass her over to Katarina, and after some small talk Irene told her about what had been going on recently.

"Are you sure it's all connected? You could just be having a run of bad luck," Katarina said.

"Sure, it's possible that there's no connection, but at the same time I can't help wondering why we're having a run of bad luck, as you put it."

"Shit happens!" Katarina said with a carefree laugh.

Maybe she was right, but why was everything happening at the same time? Something wasn't right. The first few incidents were annoying, but could be put down to kids playing around. The theft of the wallet, ordering the sex toys and blocking Jenny's number were of a completely different caliber, and not something a kid could reasonably be expected to achieve. And whoever it was had even managed to get to Jenny in Amsterdam.

Irene decided to discuss the latest developments with her colleagues the following day.

"WHAT MAKES YOU think we're dealing with a stalker?" Efva Thylvist asked.

"I've been thinking a lot about it. The idea struck me when we found out both homicide victims had received a photograph and a flower. The photos were taken through the women's windows, which means whoever took them was standing in the darkness outside, as if he were spying on them. That Bible quotation was a message to his victims. He expects them to understand what he means, but neither Ingela Svensson nor Elisabeth Lindberg knew what he was talking about. That's when I began to wonder if we could be looking at a stalker," Sara said.

The whole team was gathered in the conference room, and had just finished running through the progress made over the past few days in the hunt for the Package Killer. The obligatory mugs were in place, and Irene noticed that Sara was the only one who had tea in hers. She couldn't recall there ever having been anyone else in the Unit who had drunk only tea, although Superintendent Andersson had had some kind of gastritis toward the end of the '90s, and she seemed to remember he had stuck to tea for a while. Those had been particularly difficult weeks for his colleagues.

"Go on," Thylqvist said.

Sara took out a few sheets of paper that she had slipped into her A4 pad. Without actually looking at the document she began to speak:

"In this case we could be dealing with a delusional stalker, by which I mean someone who believes he has a connection with his victim. Or victims. He or she usually has several targets on the go at the same time, which fits in with our killer. The point is that the victims may not even know they are being stalked, or who the stalker is. The perp usually sees his victims only at a distance, or possibly in a picture. But that's enough. He or she begins to imagine some kind of relationship with the victim, usually a romance."

"But is this kind of stalker actually dangerous?" Thylqvist asked.

"To me it sounds like a harmless idiot living in a world of their own," Jonny chipped in.

"The stalker can become a danger if the oblivious victim does something that the stalker perceives as a threat to their relationship," Sara explained with a sideways glance at Jonny.

"Like what?" Thylqvist again.

"Like getting married. Moving in with a partner. Having a baby. Anything that jeopardizes the relationship he imagines he has with the victim."

"Since when did you become a profiler?" Jonny said with a snigger.

Everything fell into place as Irene listened to Sara. So many things would fit if they really were dealing with a stalker. And could a stalker be behind the worrying incidents that had affected her recently? When the time was right she would mention it to her colleagues, but right now they had to focus on the killer.

"I think Sara is on the right track," she said.

"Me, too," Tommy agreed.

Irene noticed that Tommy was sitting at the other end of the table, opposite Efva Thylqvist. They were as far away from each other as possible. Plus they hadn't arrived at the meeting together, which was unusual. *Trouble in paradise?* Irene thought, hiding a little smile.

"What makes you say that?" the superintendent asked.

Irene thought for a moment before she spoke. "Sara said the stalker can become a danger if the victim does something he perceives as a threat to their relationship. Marie Carlsson admitted that whoever was standing in her garden could have seen the foreplay between her and her girlfriend. If we think about the photographs the homicide victims receive, they look quite innocent—but if the stalker believed he had a relationship with Ingela and Elisabeth, then that changes things completely."

Irene got up, went over to the computer and found the photographs. An enlargement appeared on the whiteboard: First Ingela Svensson, sitting facing the window, the candlelight reflected in her sparkling eyes. She was smiling and holding a glass of wine, raised in a toast to the man sitting with his back to the photographer.

The second photo was similar: Elisabeth Lindberg was smiling down at her son, Tobias, who was sitting on the sofa waiting for her to fill up his coffee cup.

"The picture of Ingela cannot be misinterpreted. She's clearly in love with this man, and they are alone in the room. If the stalker thought that he and Ingela had a relationship, he would be furious."

"But what about the other photograph—the guy is Elisabeth's son!" Jonny objected.

"What if the stalker didn't know that? What if he'd seen Tobias there on only a couple of occasions? Tobias didn't live there, remember. He was staying with a friend. Maybe the killer thought Elisabeth had gotten herself a young lover," Irene replied.

"Sounds plausible," Tommy said.

There was a brief silence as everyone absorbed what they had just heard. A delusional stalker wasn't part of the victim's circle of acquaintances; he was a peripheral figure who wouldn't be easy to find.

"I've never been stalked," Jonny said.

"Thank God you're so ugly," Irene responded with a smile.

At first Jonny looked annoyed, but then he couldn't help smiling back. He and Irene had been colleagues for almost twenty years, and he could take a dig from her. Although of course she knew he would have his revenge. He always did, sooner or later.

"The victim is normally someone the stalker comes into contact with by pure chance. There are also many cases where the stalker has found out his victim's name by standing behind the victim in line at the bank, or something like that," Sara said.

"But surely it's not that easy to find out someone's address when you only have the name?" Tommy said.

"You can follow them, see where they live," Jonny pointed out.

"Anyone heard of eniro.se or hitta.se? There are a couple of other websites that do the same job," Sara said.

"Of course. You can see a little film clip of the house and the area where the person you're looking for lives. And it tells you when they were born. Talk about a total lack of integrity," Tommy said with a sigh.

MARIE CARLSSON HAD just put Hanko on the leash when she opened the door. She tucked a few black plastic bags in the pocket of her jeans with her spare hand.

"Hi—do you mind if we take Hanko for a walk? He's got a few tummy problems today," she said.

"No problem," Irene replied.

She had called an hour earlier to ask if it was okay for her to come over and ask a few more questions. Marie was free every other Friday, and luckily this was one of her days off.

It was perfect weather for a walk. A feeling of summer still lingered in the air, and Irene had left her jacket in the car. Marie was wearing a pink short-sleeved polo shirt with a thin white scarf. *She'll be able to wear high-necked sweaters in the winter*, Irene thought. As if that was any consolation.

Hanko was delighted to see Irene. They knew each other now, and he liked her. They set off, with Hanko making frequent stops to investigate interesting smells. Irene felt a pang of longing; she really did miss taking a dog for walks.

They came to a fork and chose the narrower path leading to a clump of birch trees that, with a little imagination, could be described as a copse. Thickets of hazel bushes grew at the base of the trees. A light wind was blowing through the tops of the birches, reinforcing the feeling of summer. There was hardly a cloud in the sky.

Hanko spent a long time investigating one particular patch, then he raised his big head and stared attentively at the nearest group of bushes. He pricked up his ears, concentrating hard.

"Has he seen something?" Irene asked.

"It looks that way. Or maybe he heard something."

They both stopped, and suddenly the crack of a gunshot split the air. Irene's heart did a somersault.

"Get down! Get down on the ground!" she yelled.

Marie tightened her grasp on Hanko's leash and dropped to her knees. As she was about to lie down, she looked at the dog.

"Hanko," she said quietly.

The dog was still staring at the bushes. Slowly he began to wag his tail. They heard another shot, but Hanko didn't move.

This time Irene paid more attention to the sound, and realized the shot hadn't come from a large-caliber firearm. She raised her head and yelled, "Hey! Who's shooting? We've got a dog here who's scared of gunfire!"

There was total silence. Irene got to her feet and looked in the direction from which the shots had come. After a moment she heard strange noises, as if someone was trying to suppress a fit of the giggles. Suddenly paroxysms of laughter exploded from the bushes.

"It's not Hanko who's scared. It's you guys!" howled a boyish falsetto.

"Oh, it's Jonathan," Marie said.

Hanko was wagging his tail as hard as he could, and he barked joyfully at the three boys who came crawling out of the bushes. They were holding toy guns that looked horribly real. The boy called Jonathan had a small rifle in one hand.

"You were terrified!" he shouted triumphantly.

Irene tried to hide her embarrassment at her extreme reaction by smiling. "Of course! We didn't know whether the shots came from a real gun or—"

Jonathan interrupted her. "This is a real gun!"

He aimed the rifle at her, and his two pals started waving their pistols around.

"I wonder what Katrin would say if I told her you were going around frightening people and animals," Marie said. "I think she might take away your gun." She wagged her finger at Jonathan, her expression half-joking, half-serious.

"Ha—in that case I'll tell my dad what you were doing yesterday!"

Once again the boy's face was suffused with triumph. Power. He obviously had a taste for it. *The signs are there from an early age in some people,* Irene thought. When she glanced at Marie, she was shocked. All the color had drained from her face, and she looked as if she was about to faint.

"I was just . . . joking," she mumbled.

Marie started tugging at Hanko's leash, keen to get away. The dog seemed surprised, but after a brief hesitation he trotted along obediently.

Irene followed a little more slowly. She turned and gazed back at the boys. Jonathan's two friends didn't seem quite sure what to do, but their leader answered their unspoken question by raising the rifle to his shoulder, taking careful aim at Marie, then firing off another shot.

As they walked through the clump of trees, Irene said, "Jonathan saw something going on between you and his mom yesterday. Something tells me Katrin is your girlfriend. The one who's married with kids. The one who saw someone in your garden."

Marie didn't reply; her shoulders were hunched, eyes fixed on a point straight ahead. She started walking faster, as if she was trying to get away from Irene. She had no chance. After a while Marie was puffing and panting. *She may go to the gym, but her lung capacity isn't up to much,* Irene thought with a certain amount of satisfaction. Her own pulse rate hadn't even increased.

Marie stopped so abruptly that Irene carried on for a short distance without her. Hanko had decided it was high time his mistress made use of one of the black plastic bags she had brought with her, and he crouched down at the edge of the path. Irene noticed that Marie's shoulders were shaking, and realized she was crying.

"We have to talk about this. And a number of other things. We haven't even touched on my reason for coming over here . . ."

Marie spun around and hissed, "You . . . bastard cop!"

Tears were pouring down her cheeks, and her face was contorted in anger. Irene was surprised Marie's aggression was directed at her. Then she understood: she had unmasked the secret girlfriend, and Marie was worried that the police would contact Katrin.

Irene sighed. "Calm down. I've been an investigator for many years, and I know how to put two and two together. But I'm not the only one. I'm guessing young Jonathan has done the same thing. Even if he doesn't understand the implications of whatever he saw yesterday, he knows it's something that gives him power. Power over Katrin, and you. Sooner or later he's going to tell his dad what he saw. Things have moved into a new phase for all of you. But that's got nothing to do with me. I just need to speak to Katrin about what she saw through the window that evening in February."

Marie was sobbing, trying to wipe away her tears, and fumbling with a plastic bag at the same time. Her hands were shaking and she couldn't get it open.

"Give it to me. I spent almost fifteen years picking up after my dog," Irene said.

She took the bag and slipped it over her hand. With a practiced gesture she scooped up what Hanko had produced. There was quite a lot of it—considerably more than Sammie had ever managed back in the day.

There was a black metal trash can with a lid not far away. Irene went over and dropped the bag inside. When she turned around, Marie hadn't moved.

"Come on, let's go home. Hanko has done what he came out to do," Irene said.

Without looking at Irene, Marie started walking. She turned off onto an even narrower path, and after a few yards they were back where they started, not far from Marie's house. She didn't say a word.

As soon as she had opened the door and let Hanko off the leash, she went into the kitchen. Irene closed the front door and followed her. Marie was standing by the sink pouring a tumbler of red wine from a bottle that was already open.

"I'm not offering you a drink. This is all I've got in the house and I need every last drop," she said grimly.

"No problem. I'm driving. And I'm working."

Irene watched with surprise as Marie took two huge gulps, her face expressionless as if it were water.

"I don't often drink, but sometimes . . ." Another gulp. Marie had stopped crying, and some of the tension in her shoulders had begun to ease.

"Maybe we should go and sit in the living room?" she said. Without waiting for a response she marched out of the kitchen and sank down in an armchair. It almost looked as if her legs had given way, as if they could no longer carry her.

"You're right. Jonathan isn't going to keep his mouth shut. Sooner or later . . ." She fell silent, her hand tightening around the glass of wine, but she didn't raise it to her lips. Slowly she looked up at Irene, who was still standing.

"I don't know if I'm going to be able to cope," she said quietly.

She started gulping the wine as if her future well-being depended on how quickly she could knock it back. *She's going to throw up if she carries on like this*, Irene thought. *I hope I'm gone by then.*

"Only you and Katrin can sort that out," she said. "I just need to speak to her about her observations that evening. Ask her to contact me as soon as possible, please. You already have my card; here's another one to give to her."

Marie glanced at the card Irene placed on the table but didn't pick it up.

"I actually came to talk to you about where we are with regard to the Package Killer," Irene went on. There was a glimmer of interest in Marie's eyes, but she didn't say anything.

"We've made a number of discoveries in Ingela Svensson's and Elisabeth Lindberg's apartments that suggest they might have been the victims of a stalker in the period before their deaths."

Marie gave a start. "A stalker? But nobody was stalking me before . . . before the attack," she said, unconsciously touching the scarf around her neck.

"Are you sure? The guy who was watching through the window? He could have been following you for a while without your knowing. We think this is a guy you wouldn't necessarily notice, but his behavior might have been a little odd. He might have turned up in different places. Said strange things. Or nothing at all."

"I meet thousands of people through my job, each one crazier than the last. No, that's not true—most of them are okay. But there are plenty of nut jobs out there," Marie said, making a face. She threw back her head and finished off the wine. She looked in surprise at the empty glass, and started to get to her feet.

"Sit down!" Irene said sharply.

Hanko immediately pricked up his ears. He got up and positioned himself between his mistress and the visitor. Did he need to intervene? Apparently not. With a final suspicious look at Irene, he sank back down.

"You can carry on drinking when I've gone, I don't care. But

I need you to keep a reasonably clear head. This could be a matter of life and death."

"What are you talking about?" Marie said, her voice less than steady. She couldn't look Irene in the eye. It was obvious the same thought had haunted her ever since the attack.

"You survived. The Package Killer may think you saw more than you did. I presume he's realized we may have made the connection between you and the two homicides. You have to help us catch him before he kills again," Irene said in a calmer tone of voice.

"I will. I'll do whatever I can to help you." Marie was slurring her words slightly. *She must have drunk the tumbler full of wine in less than five minutes,* Irene thought.

"We believe the killer is a strong man aged between twenty and forty. Average height, powerfully built."

Marie nodded. "That's exactly what I told the police in the first place." Suddenly she gave a start and looked Irene straight in the eye. "He stank!" she said.

Irene couldn't remember seeing anything about the perpetrator being smelly in the transcript of Marie's interview. Was it the wine that had made her remember this detail? It could be important.

"What do you mean?"

"It was disgusting—an acrid smell. Sweat and . . . kind of unwashed. Urine."

As she spoke her face took on a greenish tone. She leapt to her feet and rushed out of the room. She left the door open, and Irene could hear the vomit splashing into the toilet bowl. *I guess I didn't get away in time,* Irene thought resignedly. As a hardened homicide investigator she could cope with most unpleasant things, but she had a problem with vomit. Presumably because of the smell.

She heard Marie rinsing her mouth and spitting several times. When she came back, she was pale but composed.

"Sorry. I only have myself to blame," she murmured.

"Alcohol is never the best way of dealing with a crisis," Irene said. *God, I sound holier-than-thou!* she thought to herself.

"No, but today has been a bit much." Marie gave a wan smile as she delivered the understatement of the week.

"Was it so bad, whatever Jonathan saw?"

"Probably. Yes. It wasn't full sex, but it was a long, deep kiss . . . you know."

"It can't be explained away?"

"Not really," Marie said with a sigh.

Irene decided to leave it there and go back to the real reason for her visit. She was about to ask her next question when Marie said:

"I reacted so strongly because . . . because I think I might know who he was. Maybe."

"The Package Killer?"

"The man who attacked me. When you reminded me of the description I gave back in February . . . I suddenly remembered his smell. I'd forgotten about that. Or suppressed it."

She paused and slowly stood up. "I'm just going to fetch a glass of water."

She came back and took a few sips. "The smell . . . it made me remember him. I'm responsible for fruit and vegetables at the ICA Maxi store, and I coordinate staff resources. I sort out the shifts, bring in part-time staff when necessary, that kind of thing. So even though I do a lot of admin, I'm often out on the shop floor. There's a guy who kept coming in toward closing time. Occasionally he would pick up a basket and do a little shopping. I first noticed him when one of the assistants whispered to me that he really stank. She pointed to a well-built guy who was walking up and down the aisles. While we were looking at him he turned his head and stared back at us. We glanced away and kept chatting. I don't think he realized we were talking about him."

Hanko started snoring. Order had been restored, and he could relax.

"When was this?" Irene asked.

"In the middle of January. We were taking down the Christmas decorations, so it would have been after the thirteenth."

"Did you see him again?"

"Yes. It was the smell that got my attention . . . I was filling up the tomato display when I suddenly became aware of a stench. Like someone who had been living rough for months. When I turned around, the guy Sonja had pointed out was standing right behind me."

Irene felt her heart leap with excitement. Marie had been face-to-face with a man who fitted her own description of the perp!

"He asked me something about rolls . . . That's it! He asked me if it was possible to freeze sweet bread. Which was a weird question, because we have rolls in the freezer. But I'm used to odd questions from customers, so I said it was fine. He turned on his heel and left. Didn't say a word. Just walked out."

"When was this?" Irene asked again.

"About a week after I first saw him. And there was another time when he asked me a strange question."

Her voice gave way and her hands started shaking. She had to hold the glass with both hands to stop the water spilling over. Irene waited for her to calm down.

"It was at the beginning of February. I came out of the office to do something—I don't remember what it was. He suddenly popped up in front of me. Jumped out from behind a shelf. He must have been hiding . . . and there was that stench again . . . He asked me which dish soap I would recommend."

"Which dish soap would you recommend? Is that what he said?"

"That's exactly what he said. I was taken aback—maybe a

little scared, too. He gave me a bad feeling. Negative vibes, you know? This isn't something I've made up in retrospect—I definitely recall the way I felt."

"And you haven't seen him since that occasion at the beginning of February?" Irene asked, just to clarify things.

"No. I'm pretty sure about that."

Irene tried to sound calmer than she felt as she asked the critical question:

"What did he look like?"

Once again Marie's hand fluttered involuntarily up to her scarf before she replied:

"Just as you described him. Average height, powerfully built . . . or rather kind of stocky. Dark clothes, like work clothes. A baseball cap pulled well down over his forehead. Heavy nylon jacket. His clothes were very dirty."

"Any writing on the cap or the jacket?"

"Not that I remember . . . No, I don't think so."

"Age?"

"Between thirty and forty."

"What did his face look like?"

Marie closed her eyes and remained silent for a little while. When she opened them, Irene caught a glimpse of something that could be fear.

"I'm not sure . . . and we were only a couple of feet apart! But it was the cap . . . He had a round face. Rounded cheeks. Stubble. Discolored teeth. His eyes . . . were staring! He didn't blink. Unusually pale eyes. Grey or blue-grey. It was hard to see, because the cap was pulled down so far."

Irene nodded. "I need you to come down to the station with me right away. We'll go through some photographs, and I'll introduce you to a guy who produces facial composites using a special software package."

"Can I bring Hanko?" Marie asked, her voice trembling.

"I'll ask if it's okay," Irene promised.

She called the Unit and explained that she would be coming in with Marie Carlsson and her German shepherd to put together a facial composite of a man who could well be the Package Killer. Then she turned to Marie and said:

"We don't need to speak to Katrin just yet. And we can take Hanko with us."

A smile of relief flitted across Marie's face.

A ROUND, CHERUBIC face below a pulled-down cap, plump lips, blond eyebrows and something of a potato nose. It would have been a jolly face except for the eyes, which were unusually pale and expressionless. The thick neck and the cold eyes removed any hint of childishness from the features that possibly belonged to the Package Killer.

"He looks like a young Al Capone, but with fair hair," Irene said.

"He's not in our database," Hannu stated.

There was no reason to doubt him. If a picture of the blond version of a young Al Capone had been in the police records database, Hannu would have found it. This was a face you wouldn't forget.

"Where does he live?" Irene wondered aloud.

"Set the parameters between the victims' homes and the Frölunda torg shopping mall. It's likely he lives somewhere in that area, in the west part of the city," Hannu said.

Irene walked over to the map on the wall and did as he said, then she took a step back.

"All three victims live between three and four kilometers from the mall. Both Marie Carlsson and Ingela Svensson worked there. But Elisabeth Lindberg worked at Sahlgrenska Hospital," she said.

"But she did her shopping at the ICA store in the mall," Hannu pointed out.

Irene thought for a moment, then turned to Hannu. "Ingela

Svensson worked at the florist's in the mall. It's very likely that she often did her shopping in the ICA store before she went home to Såggatan. Marie Carlsson works in the ICA store and spoke to this guy on at least two occasions at the beginning of this year. We know that Elisabeth Lindberg shopped there in the hour before she was murdered. The killer could have been inside the store, or he could have been standing outside, checking out the women going in and out."

"Mmm. But then you'd think someone would have noticed him," Hannu said thoughtfully.

Irene and Hannu were alone in the room. Pictures of Ingela Svensson and Elisabeth Lindberg were up on the wall, next to close-ups of the strangulation marks on Marie Carlsson's throat and neck. She might have survived, but she would be physically and mentally scarred for life by her encounter with the killer.

THE FACIAL COMPOSITE was published in the media, with the caption: A WITNESS SAW THIS MAN IN THE VICINITY OF THE PLACE WHERE ONE OF THE PACKAGE KILLER'S VICTIMS WAS FOUND. It also said that the man was not suspected of homicide, but that he might have seen something important, and that the police would like to speak to him. The usual crowd of nut jobs and confused individuals got in touch. "He's my brother-in-law. He's bat-shit crazy! Sixty-two years old and fights like a madman whenever he gets drunk!" "The guy is my next-door neighbor. Those eyes . . . he's a killer! I've put two extra locks on the door!" And so on. The team spent the next few days following up every call, but most of them could be dismissed fairly quickly.

Eventually they were left with nine individuals who seemed interesting, all living in the western part of the city. The youngest was twenty-one, the oldest forty-two. Irene and Jonny took five of them, Sara and Hannu the other four.

The first one on Irene and Jonny's list was the forty-two-year-old, but on closer inspection they were able to rule him out straightaway. He was a carpenter, and had been working in Norway for the past year and had been there at the time of the attack on Marie Carlsson. He also had a wife and three kids who wanted to spend time with him when he came home at the weekends. The guy didn't have time to stalk anyone.

They were able to rule out the second man just as quickly: a twenty-six-year-old who was on an orthopedic ward encased in plaster following a car accident five weeks earlier. He could move his head and his left arm, but not much else.

The third person on the list was called Ants Hüppe. He was thirty-seven, and taught German and Swedish at a high school in Västra Frölunda. A female colleague had called in. According to her Hüppe was a weird loner who never hung out with the other members of the staff. "And he looks exactly like the picture in the papers!" she had said, delivering the knockout blow.

Irene managed to get ahold of Ants Hüppe on the phone during recess. He was utterly bewildered when he realized the police wanted to interview him.

"You can't come here—everyone will get the wrong idea! I'll come to you. I finish at twenty to four today—I'll be straight over," he said.

"That's fine," Irene said, and ended the call.

Hüppe didn't have an accent, but his dialect revealed that he came from Småland or Blekinge, and Irene assumed that at least one of his parents must have foreign antecedents, given his name.

As soon as she met Ants Hüppe in the waiting room on the ground floor, she had her doubts about his potential as the Package Killer. Admittedly he had round cherubic cheeks, pale eyes and full lips. What he lacked was the strength. Marie Carlsson had mentioned it specifically, and the injuries to the two homicide victims also bore witness to his physical power. This guy's handshake was as limp and damp as a Wet Wipe. There was something shapeless about him, and there was not a hint of muscle in his doughy body. He was sweating profusely, even though it was quite a cool day. As they traveled up to the fourth floor in the elevator, Irene was aware of a distinct smell of sweat, mixed with deodorant and some male fragrance. Marie had talked about the disgusting stench of her attacker; that didn't fit with Ants Hüppe. He was casually dressed in jeans, a black T-shirt and a black corduroy jacket. She could see in the mirror that he was somewhat shorter than her. His hands were surprisingly small and feminine. A wide gold ring glinted on the third finger of his left hand, deeply embedded in the flesh.

When Irene took his details it emerged that he was engaged but didn't live with his partner. He was in a rented apartment in a two-family house on Kungsladugårdsgatan. He had been there for five years, ever since he moved to Göteborg. Before that he had worked in Växjö.

"Why did you leave Växjö?" Irene asked.

"It's boring. I was born in a little village just outside the town. I wanted to see something new," he said with a shrug.

He couldn't quite meet Irene's gaze, and she instinctively felt he was hiding something. *Maybe I should take a closer look at you after all*, she thought.

"As I already explained, you're here because someone told us you bore a resemblance to the facial composite we published in the media. It's the picture of a man seen by a witness close to at least one of the locations where a homicide victim was found. So I hope you understand that I need to ask you a few questions," Irene said.

Hüppe merely nodded without speaking. He wiped the beads of sweat off his forehead.

"Can you tell me where you were on the evening of March second this year?"

"Absolutely!"

He reached into his jacket pocket and took out a small diary. He leafed through the pages. His face brightened and the hint of a smile played around his lips as he found what he was looking for.

"I landed at Landvetter at eleven-thirty that night. My brother lives in Florida. I'd been to visit him and his family."

So when Marie Carlsson was attacked, Ants Hüppe had been on a plane thirty thousand feet in the air somewhere over Denmark. He was able to supply Irene with his ticket number, the name of the airline and precise flight details. Something told Irene this was an alibi she wasn't going to be able to crack. Suddenly she was struck by a thought: something didn't fit.

"How come you were able to go to Florida in the middle of term?" she asked.

Hüppe's smug expression immediately disappeared, to be replaced by that evasive look. "I was due some leave. And it was only a week."

"Isn't it rather difficult for a specialist teacher to take time off in the middle of term?" Irene persisted.

There was something there, she could feel it. But what? She realized it almost certainly had nothing to do with the Package Killer, but she couldn't let it go. Ants Hüppe was sweating profusely once more. He dug a pack of tissues out of his pocket and managed with some difficulty to extract one. He wiped his brow and shoved the used tissue back in his pocket, clearly embarrassed. He took a deep breath; his eyes slid across Irene's face, then settled on a fixed point somewhere over her left shoulder.

"I . . . I was signed off sick. Burnt out. But I felt a bit better, so the doctor gave me permission to go over and see my brother. I've got a medical certificate," he said quietly.

It was that simple. Irene realized there was no point in taking up any more of his time. Before she went home she would just check his details so that she could eliminate him from their inquiries.

IT TOOK LESS than half an hour to confirm Ants Hüppe's alibi, which left just two names on the list she and Jonny were working through. She hadn't heard anything from Sara and Hannu, and she would have done if anything of interest had come up. Perhaps the fair-haired Al Capone was just a red her-ring. The smelly nut job had turned up by sheer coincidence at the ICA store a few weeks before the attack, and asked Marie Carlsson weird questions . . . Irene stopped herself. The man who had attacked Marie had also stunk. Her reaction had been very strong when she remembered the stench, and that wasn't only down to the red wine she had drunk. Irene had a feeling that the man with eyes like a cod probably had something to do with the case. All they had to do now was track him down and find the evidence to prove that her gut was right.

She logged out and shut down the computer. She was tired; it was time to go home. A hot meal and an early night seemed like the perfect plan for the evening. She suppressed a yawn and stood up just as Sara appeared in the doorway.

"I can't get ahold of Ann-Britt Söderström."

"Who?" Irene wasn't really interested.

"The woman who found Ingela Svensson's body. You were there, weren't you?"

It might have been her imagination, but Irene thought there was a faint air of reproach in Sara's tone of voice. A vague recollection of a stocky woman in her sixties popped into her head. Irene hadn't spoken to her personally, but she suddenly remembered that it was the woman's dog that had found the first victim in the churchyard. It felt like a long time ago, but it was just over a week.

"Oh, that Ann-Britt Söderström. Why are you trying to contact her?"

"Thylqvist told us to talk to the people who found the bodies again, just in case they've thought of something that didn't occur to them at the time. Hannu's spoken to the paperboy who found Elisabeth Lindberg—nothing new there. But as I said, I can't get ahold of Söderström."

Irene had completely forgotten Thylqvist's directive, but she had no intention of telling Sara that.

"I expect she's gone away," she said airily.

"No. I've just spoken to her daughter, who lives in Stockholm. She says her mother has heart problems, and doesn't really like going out. That's why the daughter gave her Egon for Christmas."

"Egon?"

"The dog. So that her mother would have to take him for walks. Apparently it wasn't working too well."

"So how long have you been trying to contact Söderström?" Irene asked with a sigh.

"Since yesterday afternoon."

A woman with heart problems had been unreachable for over twenty-four hours. According to her daughter, the woman didn't move around much, and never went out for long periods of time. There was only one thing to do.

"Okay, let's get over there, check things out," Irene said with an encouraging smile. The relieved expression on Sara's face told her that was exactly the response her young colleague had been hoping for.

ANN-BRITT SÖDERSTRÖM LIVED in a renovated governor's house with a view over Gröna vallen. It was no more than five hundred meters from the spot where she—or rather Egon—had found the first homicide victim, and Ann-Britt had driven there, if Irene remembered correctly. Her daughter was probably right; the dog walking wasn't working out quite the way she had hoped.

"Second floor, no elevator," Sara said as she read the list of residents' names next to the main door.

They pressed the button next to Ann-Britt's name, but there was no answer. After a while a young woman came out of the building. Irene and Sara showed their ID and asked her to let them in. She complied.

They could hear him from the ground floor. A faint

whimpering, almost like a sob. A few seconds' silence, then it came again.

"Egon is crying," Irene said.

"Crying? Can dogs cry?" Sara asked in surprise.

"Of course. All animals can cry. And I recognize that sound. That's one very unhappy dog."

"I'm not used to dogs . . . but it sounds desperately sad."

When they reached the second floor, it was obvious that the dog was sitting right behind the door. They rang the bell, and he started barking and scratching.

"He sounds hoarse," Irene said.

She pushed open the mail slot, which made Egon hurl himself at the door. Then he stopped and looked straight into her eyes through the gap. Scared and unhappy, Irene concluded. She was starting to get worried. She couldn't hear anything to suggest that Ann-Britt was on her way. In fact she couldn't hear anything at all, apart from the dog's frantic barking.

"I'll call the locksmith," Irene said, taking out her cell phone.

EGON LEAPT INTO Irene's arms, whimpering and shivering, when they opened the door. Instinctively he pressed himself against her. Nothing in the world was going to persuade him to get down on the floor.

"He's terrified," Irene said, unzipping her jacket.

She tucked the dog inside, and held him close, with only his head sticking out. The long-haired dachshund was very small and didn't weigh much. Irene could feel his body shaking, his little heart pounding. *Poor baby*, she thought. *What's made you so scared?*

The apartment was furnished in a style well-suited to its era, the 1920s. Irene glanced into the bright kitchen with its yellow cupboard doors, and saw an old table with four chairs. They could have been there since the place was built. Beneath the table were a large puddle and a little pile of dog crap. Poor Egon had had to do his business indoors. Irene also noticed two empty dog bowls in the corner.

"Irene," Sara called quietly.

Irene went through the neat little living room and over to the doorway where Sara was standing. Irene looked over her shoulder into a bedroom. Ann-Britt Söderström was lying on the bed. It was obvious that she was dead.

"The door was closed," Sara said.

Good, that meant Egon hadn't been able to get in. Over the years Irene had been in a number of places where one or more dogs had had access to the dead bodies. It was never a pretty sight.

IRENE AND SARA stayed until reinforcements arrived. There was no sign of external violence; all the indications were that Ann-Britt had died in her sleep. Irene found the dog leash hanging on a hook in the hallway and took Egon for a short walk while Sara called the local police in the Stockholm suburb where Ann-Britt's daughter lived. She explained the situation, and her colleagues promised to deliver the sad news in person. They also promised to pass on contact details for Irene and Sara.

"She's bound to wonder what's happened to Egon. Ask them to let her know I'm taking him home tonight, and I'll try to find somewhere for him tomorrow," Irene said before she went out.

The dog still refused to leave the safety of her arms, so she had to carry him down the stairs. Once they reached the inner courtyard he happily jumped down onto the cobblestones and ran straight over to a rug-beating rack in the middle. He cocked his leg and stood there for a long time. It was obvious he had done it before; no doubt Ann-Britt had sneaked down here in the evenings instead of taking him for a walk.

"You poor little soul," Irene said quietly.

Back in the apartment she gathered up Egon's bowls. She found a bag of dry food in the pantry, and his basket was in the hallway; that might come in handy. She couldn't see any toys. Strange—he was only a puppy. She put the bowls and food in the basket and tucked it under her arm, then set off down the stairs once more, with Egon trotting happily along beside her on the leash. Sara stayed behind to report to the CSIs.

"SO WE'RE DOG owners again," Krister said with a contented smile.

He was sitting with Egon on his lap, scratching him behind the ear. The dog belched discreetly. He had gobbled up his dry food, mixed with a little liver pâté and the remains of the previous day's stew.

"Not owners. Foster parents," Irene corrected him.

"Pity. He's a sweet little guy. But he needs a bath," Krister said.

Egon knew they were talking about him and wagged his tail with enthusiasm. Lovingly he licked Krister's chin. Irene got up to sort out his basket. She put it in the corner of their bedroom, where Sammie used to lie on a little soft rug. He had never been interested in a basket; he had always preferred his master and mistress's bed. In spite of the fact that they had agreed that he would never be allowed on the bed, that was where he had spent virtually every night of his fifteen years. Irene hadn't thought she would miss him rooting around at the foot of the bed, but she did. She even missed his snoring.

Egon obediently clambered into his basket when Krister and Irene got into bed, but just a few minutes after Irene had switched off the light, she heard the patter of little claws on the floor. The impact was hardly noticeable as Egon landed at the foot of the bed. He turned around a few times, then settled down with a contented sigh. Irene could feel the warmth of his small body through the covers. She smiled into the darkness and fell asleep straightaway.

"Whose dog is that?"

Superintendent Thylqvist was standing in the corridor, looking at Egon with distaste. He was sitting on the floor, looking up at her expectantly as his tail swished to and fro across the floor. In his mouth was a little ball Irene had found—one of Sammie's old toys. It was great fun when someone threw the ball down the corridor for him to run after, but he was beginning to realize that the woman with the powerful smell and the harsh voice wasn't about to join in with the game. On the contrary, she seemed cross. Egon was confused. He dropped the ball and sneezed a couple of times before rushing into Irene's room. She was on her way out and nearly tripped over him.

"Oh, there you are," she said, picking him up.

She had heard Thylqvist's question, and went up to her boss.

"This is Egon. His owner was found dead on Friday evening: Ann-Britt Söderström. She's the person who stumbled across Ingela Svensson's body. In fact it was Egon who made the discovery," she said.

Irene smiled at Thylqvist and held out the dog so that she could stroke him. Irene was quietly congratulating herself on having spent Saturday giving him a bath and clipping his claws. He hadn't been too keen but had gone along with it.

Now he smelled good, and his russet coat was shining. Neither she nor Krister had been working over the weekend, and had taken Egon for several long walks. Irene had even taken Monday off and had urged Krister to do the same. It felt good to have a dog in the house again.

Thylqvist reached out and tentatively stroked the puppy's head. Irene felt him press closer against her body, but thank God he didn't start growling. He did, however, sneeze loudly once more. He obviously couldn't cope with Thylqvist's perfume.

"Sweet. But why have you brought him here?"

"It was late in the evening when Sara and I found Ann-Britt Söderström, so I took him home for the night. I couldn't find anywhere for him to go over the weekend, so he stayed with me. I'll contact Ann-Britt's daughter today to see what she wants me to do with Egon. The plan was for him to spend the day in my office, but he sneaked out with the ball, and . . . he's been having a lot of fun in the corridor."

"He goes like a rocket when you throw the ball. Maybe he's going to be a racing dog? Are you going to be a racing dog and earn lots of money for Uncle Jonny?"

To Irene's astonishment, Jonny had fallen head over heels for Egon. He came up to the dog babbling baby talk, seemingly oblivious to his colleagues standing nearby. He took Egon out of Irene's arms and put him down on the floor, then he picked up the ball and threw it down the corridor. Egon raced after his new toy, claws scrabbling on the floor.

"Would you look at that!" Jonny said with a grin.

"This is not doggy day care. Keep him in your room," Thylqvist said, turning on her heel and marching to her office.

At least she didn't tell me to get rid of him right away, Irene thought. She called Egon, and without any fuss he settled down in his basket, with the ball beside him. He'd probably had more stimulation in the last hour than he'd had in weeks.

He looked utterly contented as he closed his eyes. Irene paused for a second to listen to his steady breathing before she left the room.

HANNU AND SARA had one name left on their list of the men who could be Cod Eyes, as they had started to call the man in the facial composite. They hadn't managed to track him down, but that was their priority today. Irene and Jonny had two left, and were planning to take one each.

The preliminary report from the pathologist indicated that there was no reason to suspect that Ann-Britt Söderström had died of anything but natural causes. The autopsy would take place in a few days.

Sara gave Irene the contact details for Ann-Britt's daughter in Stockholm, Anna Hallin. A faint voice answered after the phone had rung several times.

"My name is Detective Inspector Irene Huss from Göteborg. First of all, my condolences on the loss of your mother. DI Sara Persson and I were the ones who found her."

"Thank you . . . thank you. It wasn't entirely unexpected. Mom had been having problems with her heart for a few years, but I thought . . . I thought she'd be okay for a while longer," Anna Hallin said, clearly on the verge of tears.

"All the indications are that she passed away in her sleep. She was in bed, and she looked very peaceful when we found her."

"It's good to know that . . . but she died alone. My father passed away several years ago, and I'm an only child."

Irene knew that already, but made sympathetic noises before asking:

"We have a little problem: Egon. What would you like us to do with him?"

"Oh, I'd forgotten about him! Egon . . . I don't know . . ."

"He spent the last few days with me. My husband and I are

used to dogs, so it was no problem. Can you come down to Göteborg to collect him?"

Anna Hallin took a deep breath. "Oh no, that's out of the question! My daughter is extremely allergic; we can't have any pets. We didn't know that when we bought Egon. My son really wanted a dog, but fortunately we found out about his little sister's allergy just before we went to pick up Egon. That's why I gave him to Mom. I thought he'd be company for her, and give her a reason to go out every day . . . but I'm not sure it was working out too well recently."

You're right there, Irene thought, but instead she asked again, "So what do we do?"

"I have no idea," Anna said helplessly after a brief silence.

"Would you like me to keep him for the time being? Until you come up with something?"

Irene was surprised to hear the words come out of her mouth; that wasn't what she had intended to say at all. She should have informed Anna Hallin that Egon would be taken to a short-term care facility for three weeks, then they would decide what was to be done with him. If no one wanted him, in the worst-case scenario he would be put down. That was the normal routine, but Irene didn't want to move him to a new environment again. He had spent at least twenty-four hours in the apartment with his dead owner. He had been crying by the door, frightened and alone, without food or water. Both Irene and Krister liked him, and wanted to give him the warmth and security he so badly needed. Decision made. Fortunately Anna was happy to go along with Irene's suggestion. They agreed to speak in a couple of weeks, when Anna was feeling a little better and had had time to think things over.

Niklas Johansson's appearance fit pretty well with the facial composite. He was thirty-one years old and "seeking work." He had a police record because he had stabbed a man during a fight four years prior, causing serious injuries. The victim had hovered between life and death for a long time. His condition had been stabilized after several months, and the doctors had stated that he would survive, but with long-term disabilities. Niklas Johansson had been convicted of attempted manslaughter, and had been sentenced to three and a half years in jail. The relatively lenient sentence was handed down because witnesses had testified that both parties had been extremely drunk, but it was Niklas who had been holding the knife. His opponent had grabbed a bottle to use as a weapon, but had dropped it during the fracas after smashing Johansson across the face and breaking his nose. His mug shot therefore showed him with the fractured nose in plaster, but the pale eyes gazed expressionlessly into the camera, and it was possible to see the rounded cheeks and the full lips.

"The picture is four years old, and he's done jail time since then. We don't know what he looks like today," Jonny said.

"Then let's find out," Irene suggested.

She hid a smile as he got up with a groan. Jonny wasn't too keen on good old-fashioned foot slog.

• • •

Niklas Johansson lived on Smyckegatan in Tyn-
nered. Before they left the station Irene checked the address;
over the past few months there had been several complaints
from neighbors about disturbances in the apartment.

Jonny rang the bell. From the other side of the door came
the deafening sound of hard rock.

"There's no chance of him hearing the bell," Jonny said,
pushing down the handle. A searing guitar riff hit them like a
tidal wave.

A man in his thirties with a haggard appearance came into
the hallway. He had changed a great deal since the mug shot
was taken four years ago, but Irene recognized those pale eyes.
He blinked at the two cops in the doorway and yelled:

"Get the hell out of here! Or shall I help you on your way?
Is that what you want?"

As he was speaking he came toward them, fists clenched.
Jonny showed his police ID.

"Calm down. Police. We'd like a word."

The man was standing right next to them now. He was
shorter than Jonny, but was staring him straight in the eye.
"Fuck off!" he shouted.

At such close quarters Irene could smell not only booze
but also his unwashed body. His clothes were dirty and stank
of piss and something else. The pale eyes were terrifyingly
empty and expressionless. So far he was a good match for
Marie Carlsson's description of Cod Eyes, but the body didn't
fit at all. Niklas was skinny, little more than skin and bone.
Only loose pouches remained of those cherubic cheeks. His
movements were jerky and uncoordinated. Both Irene and
Jonny had seen this many times before: Johansson was under
the influence of narcotics.

Jonny gave Niklas a gentle push. The thin body wobbled,
and he staggered back a few paces. He tripped over a sneaker and
fell flat on his back.

"Oops-a-daisy. There you go, we have to come in now—make sure you haven't hurt yourself," Jonny said in a deceptively friendly tone.

"You're . . . you're trespassing," Niklas gasped without any real conviction.

"So report us."

Jonny went over and helped Niklas to his feet. All the fight had gone out of him; he was as limp as a rag doll, and he allowed himself to be led into the living room.

Irene closed the front door and followed them. Quickly she took in all the details: the dirt, the stench, the mess, the few shabby pieces of furniture, the cigarette smoke, the young man lying on his back on the floor. At first she thought he looked as if he was dead, but on closer inspection she could see that his chest was moving up and down. *Drugged up to the eyeballs*, she concluded. He was wearing nothing more than a pair of scruffy jeans. She picked up a grubby blanket from the sagging sofa and placed it over him.

"Don't you fucking worry, I will fucking report you . . ."

Niklas was trying to work himself up into a frenzy again, but Jonny interrupted him.

"I don't think so. You are a person of interest in a homicide investigation. Refusing to answer questions under the circumstances would be regarded as suspicious behavior, which means you would have to come down to the station. You would be questioned, over and over again. Until you talk. That can take quite a while, and you would be held in a very, very, *very* small cell. Tiny, in fact. For a very, very, *very* long time. But of course you know all this already," Jonny said with a false smile.

Any courage that Niklas had managed to summon up disappeared in a second. His slack face became even paler, if that were possible.

"What homicide investigation? I don't know anything about any fucking homicide," he croaked.

"We'll see," Jonny said curtly.

He paused for effect, his eyes boring into Niklas.

"How often do you visit the mall at Frölunda torg?"

"Frölunda torg . . . is that where the homicide . . ."

"I'm asking the questions!" Jonny snapped.

He was outstanding when it came to playing the bad cop. So far Irene couldn't see any reason to interrupt; her job was to gather impressions and try to spot any clues. She could see little plastic bags and scraps of aluminum foil all over the floor. Some of the bags were on top of the box that served as a coffee table and appeared to contain different-colored pills. In one corner of the room there was a small fortune in empty bottles that hadn't been returned. There were greasy, smelly pizza delivery boxes everywhere. The sink was overflowing with dirty dishes and the remains of unidentifiable substances. The man on the floor hadn't moved.

"How often do you visit the mall at Frölunda torg?" Jonny repeated.

"Once a week . . . maybe."

"How about several times a week?"

Jonny's tone of voice was almost paternal now. This made Niklas nervous: his eyes were darting all over the place.

"Maybe."

"Do you sometimes shop at the ICA Maxi store?"

"No—why the hell would I do that?"

The surprise in Niklas's voice sounded genuine.

"We all shop for food and other stuff. How often do you go to the ICA Maxi store?"

"Never," Niklas said firmly.

"But surely you . . ."

"I don't cook."

"But surely you must buy . . ."

"I buy fast food. Hot dogs, burgers, pizza."

● ● ●

"IT'S NOT HIM," Irene said as they were walking back to the car.

"I agree. Although just to tidy things up, tell me if there's anything in particular that makes you think he's not our perp," Jonny said.

"He's a complete wreck thanks to the drugs. He's weak and emaciated. Doesn't fit the description. Even if a junkie can be as strong as a bear when he's taken something, I don't think Niklas would be able to overcome Marie or the other two women. Both Marie and Elisabeth were used to working out. And Niklas's main interest in life isn't stalking women. The only thing that matters to him is making sure of his next fix. He doesn't care what it is, as long as it does the job. Which is probably when he heads for Frölunda torg."

"You're right. Shit!"

The last word slipped out as they reached the unmarked police car. Someone had smashed the rear side window.

"Nice of them to go for that one so we don't get broken glass in our asses on the way back," Jonny said through gritted teeth.

WHEN THEY PUSHED open the door of the unit they both stopped in their tracks. They could hear Egon yapping with delight, and a voice saying:

"There's a good dog! Fetch your ball—go on, fetch it! Good boy!"

Irene and Jonny exchanged a look of mutual understanding. They tiptoed along the corridor and peered around the corner. They had heard correctly, and they had drawn the right conclusion.

"I see the boss of doggy day care is exercising her little charge," Jonny said.

Efva Thylqvist spun around, caught in the act. Egon raced past her with the blue ball in his mouth.

"He was whimpering, so I thought maybe he needed to go

out . . . but when I opened the door he ran past me. He took the ball with him," she said apologetically. Then she straightened up and added, "This really isn't a suitable environment for a dog. And as I said, this is not doggy day care."

She gave Jonny a poisonous glance. *Maybe referring to her as "the boss of doggy day care" wasn't all that smart,* Irene thought.

"I'll take him for a walk," she said, heading for her office to fetch his leash. She had trouble hiding a smile as she passed Thylqvist. It was the first time in two years that Irene had seen any indication that the superintendent cared about anyone else's feelings. Okay, so it was only a dog, but it had to be regarded as a major step forward.

THE LAST PERSON on Jonny and Irene's list was Daniel Börjesson, a single thirty-three-year-old park operative living on Basungatan.

They had been given his name over the phone by a young woman who wanted to remain anonymous. From past experience the police knew this could be a question of revenge on the part of an ex-girlfriend or a wannabe girlfriend. According to the colleague who had taken the call, she had given Daniel Börjesson's name and address in a clear, steady voice. Then she had paused for a little while before going on, her voice shaky now: "He won't . . . he won't be able to find out who . . . you're not going to trace my number, are you?" When the officer had reassured her, she said: "He's just so strange. It's his eyes. He never says anything weird, it's not that—but there's something . . . wrong." Then she had ended the call.

Just a few hours later the owner of a convenience store in the area where Daniel Börjesson lived had called; he had also been struck by Daniel's resemblance to the picture in the paper.

"Two calls about the same person. Interesting," Jonny said.

"Yes—or he just happens to look like the facial composite," Irene replied.

THEY STARTED BY talking to the store owner the following morning. It was pretty small—more of a well-stocked kiosk, really. It also had a terminal for placing bets on harness racing, and the line of customers was long. The girl at the register was working at full speed.

Jonny nodded to the cashier and said to Irene, "Everyone dreams of easy money, but the only winners are the state and the betting companies."

The owner introduced himself as Theo Papadopoulos. He was a short, stout man in his sixties who spoke almost perfect Swedish with a Göteborg accent, from which Irene concluded that he must have been born in the city. This turned out to be incorrect.

"I fled to Sweden during the junta in the 1970s, and I've lived in Göteborg ever since. I fell in love and got married. The girl on the till is our youngest daughter. We have four children, but Melina is the only one who works here, along with my wife and me. We also have two general staff, young guys who work evenings and weekends. I don't want Melina or my wife to do that," Theo explained.

"Things seem to be going well," Jonny said, nodding in the direction of the line.

"We get by," Theo said with a smile.

Looking at Melina, Irene could see why the line consisted mainly of men. Her long, honey-blonde hair flowed down her back. She was beautiful, and every customer received a beaming smile as they paid.

On a TV screen above Melina's head a commentator was starting to yell hysterically. Apparently it was a photo finish, so it wasn't clear which horse had won. Irene decided it was time to get down to business.

"We'd like to talk to you about the call you made with regard to the picture in the papers," she said.

Papadopoulos immediately became serious, and rubbed his hand several times over his balding head. He showed them into a room behind the counter, with four chairs around a worn Formica table.

"I've owned this place for thirty years, and Daniel has lived there all that time," he began, pointing to the apartment block next door.

"Thirty years . . . so he must have been three," Irene said after a quick calculation.

"I guess so. He lived with Signe, his grandmother. She was a regular customer right from the start. She liked a chat, and she often brought the boy with her. My eldest son and Daniel are about the same age, but Alexander never wanted to play with him. They tried it a few times, but it didn't work. Alex thought the kid was strange."

The anonymous young woman had used exactly the same word in her phone call. Strange.

"Strange in what way?" Irene asked.

"It was as if . . . as if he wasn't quite there. He didn't say much, and he seemed very slow. Sometimes he said weird things, but mostly he kept quiet."

"So you live in the area?" Irene gestured vaguely in the direction of the nearby apartment blocks.

"Not far away—in Järnbrott. Rundradiogatan. We've been there ever since we got married."

"So you've seen quite a lot of Daniel over the years. What else can you tell us?" Irene said encouragingly.

Theo got to his feet. "Could you excuse me for a moment while I go and help Melina? I won't be long—help yourselves to coffee," he said, pointing to a pot on the stove with a stack of paper cups beside it. Irene poured two cups, dropped two sugar cubes in one and passed it to Jonny. On the table there was a large tin of cookies. Without hesitation Jonny took off the lid and helped himself. Irene resisted for two reasons. Firstly she thought it was impolite to take one without asking, and secondly her jeans had started to feel a little tight around the waistband lately. She couldn't step up her exercise regimen, she was already doing all she could, so her only option was to cut down on the sugary treats.

Theo came back and poured himself a coffee before sitting down.

"Daniel . . . He lived with his maternal grandparents. As I understood it, both his mother and father were dead. Which is unusual—for both of them to die at such a young age, I mean."

His expression was pensive as he took a cookie and broke it into smaller pieces. Irene gave a start; her former chief, Superintendent Sven Andersson, used to do exactly the same thing. Efva Thylqvist didn't eat cookies, of course. The thought of Thylqvist made Irene take a cookie out of sheer defiance.

"Daniel has always been . . . odd. I don't think he has many friends today either. Not that I've noticed, anyway. And he's never had much to say for himself, but he was always there for his grandmother. His grandfather passed away . . . It must be twenty years ago now, but Daniel stayed with his grandmother until her death."

"And he still lives in her apartment?"

"Yes—it's a rental property, but he was able to take over the contract. I think it was good for him. He was terribly upset when she died. He looked pretty rough for a while, but he's back on his feet now. Back to normal. Well, as normal as Daniel can be."

"Do you know if he takes drugs or drinks alcohol?" Irene asked.

"I've never seen him under the influence of anything. I don't think he drinks or smokes. That's certainly the way he was raised. Signe was a churchgoer, and she used to take the boy with her. She was kind to him, but I've got the feeling she was pretty strict, too, kept him in line. Maybe that's why he doesn't take drugs. There's a lot of that around here."

"Have you ever seen or heard of any violent behavior from Daniel?" Jonny asked.

"No, never. Although of course I don't know him very well. I don't think anyone does."

"And you think he looks like the picture in the paper?" Jonny went on.

"Absolutely. It was Melina who saw it, and right away she said: 'Look, it's Daniel!'"

"Have you noticed whether he smells?" Irene asked.

Theo raised an eyebrow but said nothing. He thought for a moment before he answered.

"When he was little he used to smell of . . . piss now and again. He wet himself when he started school. The other kids gave him a hard time, but he didn't seem to care."

"I was thinking more of now, as an adult," Irene clarified.

"He often comes in here in his work clothes, and they don't smell too good. Melina has said several times that even if they are work clothes, surely he could wash them occasionally. But I can't say whether he smells worse than anyone else. I'm a heavy smoker, and my wife says I've destroyed my sense of smell." He grinned, showing them an uneven row of nicotine-stained teeth.

Irene and Jonny stood up and thanked him for the coffee and his help. They couldn't help feeling a certain amount of expectation as they headed for Daniel Börjesson's apartment block. Several things that Theo had said seemed to fit with the profile of the Package Killer.

DANIEL LIVED ON the fourth floor. The name plate on the door said s. BÖRJESSON, so he obviously hadn't bothered to change it. It was just after five when they slipped in through the main door behind a female resident. Irene and Jonny wanted to take a look at both Daniel and the apartment, so it was important that they arrive unannounced.

Jonny had to ring the bell twice before they heard footsteps approaching. The door opened and Irene found herself looking straight into those cod eyes, which were so familiar by now. She should have been prepared for the total lack of expression or emotion, but she still reacted with an intuitive feeling of unease.

Jonny seemed completely unmoved, and merely said: "Daniel Börjesson?"

The man in the doorway was powerfully built and stocky, but almost as tall as Irene. His shaven head appeared to be sitting directly on his shoulders, with no neck in between. The large hand resting on the door handle had short, strong fingers with dirty, flaking nails. His grey T-shirt strained across his broad chest. The short sleeves exposed impressive biceps and meaty forearms. His jeans were baggy and grubby, as were the scruffy socks that had presumably been white in a former life. Irene took a deep breath. Daniel exuded a noticeable smell of sweat, but it wasn't suffocating. There was something else hovering around him that she vaguely recognized, but couldn't quite place. Some kind of soap? Shower gel? No, something else. But what?

When the man didn't reply, Jonny repeated his question. This time it elicited a faint nod of the head. Jonny introduced himself and Irene with full names and titles, then said firmly that they needed to speak to Daniel on a police matter. He stared at them blankly and didn't move. Eventually Jonny pushed him to one side and walked in, with Irene right behind him. She didn't take her eyes off Daniel Börjesson. Everything about him was giving her bad vibes. She couldn't pin it down. Maybe it was her gut instinct as a cop.

The hallway was cramped, and led into a dark passageway.

The walls were covered in grey-ish brown well-worn textured wallpaper, and there was a dirty blue and white rug on the linoleum floor.

"Could we sit down somewhere? We'd like to ask you a few questions," Jonny said.

Börjesson shrugged and set off along the passageway. As they passed the half-open door of the bathroom, Irene picked up that same smell again. Soap? Close, but not quite.

The living room lay at the end of the passage. On the way Irene saw an untidy kitchen and a bedroom that appeared to be in darkness; she had a fleeting impression of closed blinds and an unmade bed. There was a closed door opposite, presumably another bedroom or a study. The whole apartment smelled dirty, and the floor felt gritty beneath her feet. She couldn't see any signs of drug use, and there was no trace of cigarette smoke, just a general stuffiness and a lack of fresh air.

The living room was sparsely furnished. There should have been plenty of light flooding in through the big window leading out onto the balcony, but the effect was somewhat spoiled by the thick layer of dirt on the outside. The moss-green patterned wallpaper absorbed any light that did manage to find its way in. The armchairs and sofa were upholstered in a brown woolen fabric, and the same shade of brown was echoed in the threadbare rug. The bookcase contained a few copies of abridged novels from *Reader's Digest*, plus some attractive leather-bound volumes and several Bibles and hymnbooks. In the middle was a space for the TV. Daniel had an old model, and no video player. Irene couldn't see a computer or CD player either. Daniel obviously wasn't into computers or electronic gadgetry, unless of course they were behind the closed door. She planned to try to take a look in that room before they left.

Irene was particularly surprised that there were no pictures on the walls. She could see paler rectangles here and there where pictures had obviously been; she could even see the marks left by the hooks.

Jonny and Irene went over to the sofa and sat down. Daniel remained standing until Jonny told him to sit. He plodded over to the armchair and flopped down. The expression in those empty eyes hadn't changed, and he still hadn't said a word.

"The thing is, Daniel, a witness saw a man near the scene of a crime. We're talking about the so-called Package Killer. I'm sure you've seen the facial composite in the papers; that was based on the description provided by the witness. Two different people have contacted us to say that they think you look like the picture we put out, so of course we wanted to come and see you, and to ask if you were anywhere near the scene of the crime. You might have seen something that could help us in our inquiries. Needless to say we're very interested in any witnesses we can find," Jonny concluded.

Daniel stared at him for a long time without blinking.

"Where?" he asked eventually.

"What?" Jonny said.

"Where?" Daniel repeated.

Jonny was lost, but Irene realized what Daniel meant.

"In the western churchyard," she said.

Without looking at her Daniel said tonelessly, "When?"

There was no time to think; Irene had to improvise.

"We're not at liberty to say at the moment."

"Who?"

Jonny's expression was grim as he contemplated the weird guy who was staring at him with those colorless eyes. "We're asking the questions," he said in an attempt to reclaim the initiative.

"I have a right to know."

Daniel's voice sounded hoarse and scratchy, as if he had a cold. Or as if he wasn't in the habit of using it. He spoke slowly and without intonation. Perhaps he had hearing difficulties.

That would explain his reluctance to talk. Then again, he had definitely heard their questions. Irene couldn't figure him out.

"We never reveal the identity of our witnesses. Their anonymity is guaranteed," she said.

"In that case I can't answer."

Daniel was still staring at Jonny. He was responding to what Irene said, but he refused to look at her. He really was strange, just as Theo Papadopoulos had said.

"Why not?" Jonny demanded.

"I must know those who slander me," Daniel replied implacably.

That's an odd way of putting it, Irene thought. *Old-fashioned.* She became aware of a strong odor of sweaty feet.

Daniel was sitting with his legs stretched out under the cracked glass coffee table, and Irene could see his dirty toes through the gaping holes in his socks. The nails were long and filthy. *He's dirty and unwashed,* Irene thought, *but I wouldn't describe it as an overwhelming stench.*

"Daniel, if you don't answer our questions, we will have to ask you to accompany us to the station," Jonny said. "Although I'm sure that won't be necessary."

Jonny had once again adopted the paternal tone of voice that he occasionally used. Most of the time it worked, but Daniel seemed to be immune.

"I'm just going to the bathroom to blow my nose," Irene said, getting to her feet.

She had left the room before Daniel had time to protest. She pushed down the handle of the closed door, and it swung open to reveal a bedroom. A narrow single bed was covered in a white crocheted bedspread with a matching pillow. The white curtains were also crocheted. They had gone slightly yellow from the sunlight, but looked as if they were starched. On the floor was a green and white rug. A small dressing table painted green and a plain wooden chair completed the furnishings. There were no pictures in this room either—just a big black crucifix above the headboard.

The room was clinically clean. Irene was aware of the same smell that hovered around Daniel, and she suddenly realized what it was: Yes-brand liquid soap. She had used it herself for many years. Why did Daniel smell of dish soap? And why was this room pervaded by the same aroma?

She quickly stepped back into the hallway and closed the door.

"Sorry, my mistake," she called in the direction of the living room.

The first thing she saw when she switched on the bathroom light was a big bottle of Yes on the side of the bath. There had been traces of some kind of soap on both Ingela Svensson's and Elisabeth Lindberg's bodies. Could it be Yes? There was every reason to bring Daniel in for questioning.

When she got back to the living room, Jonny was on his feet.

"We'll be in touch. Perhaps you'd like to think about whether you've been in either of the churchyards I mentioned," he said to Daniel, who stared back blankly.

"I have."

Jonny stiffened. "Which one?"

"Both."

Daniel's calm demeanor was extraordinary. His expression hadn't change a bit.

"When?"

Irene could hear the tension in Jonny's voice. He had picked up the scent, and he had no intention of letting go.

Daniel shrugged. "Now and again."

"Now and again? What the hell . . ."

Irene jumped in before Jonny lost his temper. "Do you visit different churchyards?"

"Yes."

"And why is that?"

"Work."

"So you've worked in different churchyards?"

"Yes. They call. When they need me."

He was described as a "park operative," so presumably the church administrators brought him in from time to time. Irene and Jonny informed their colleagues that they would be bringing in a person of interest for questioning that evening. Hannu and Jonny would conduct the interview, thank goodness. Irene was exhausted.

By the time Irene and Egon got home, there was a light drizzle in the air, and it was starting to feel chilly. Krister had promised homemade tomato soup and cheesecake for dinner. Just the thought of the soup made her feel warm inside. Before she had time to put Egon on the leash, he leapt out of the car and trotted purposefully up the path. Did he already regard their house as his new home? Irene smiled in the darkness. Egon was waiting at the door, barking to make his point. Through the window Irene could see Krister stirring a steaming pan. When he heard the dog, he immediately came to the door. He bent down, and Egon leapt joyfully into his open arms. Irene joined them, and her husband's welcoming kiss was mixed with sloppy doggy kisses. It wasn't exactly hygienic, but when she saw the contented looks on Krister's and Egon's faces, she couldn't help laughing.

Krister put the dog on the floor, and he scampered off to his food bowl in the kitchen. He quickly demolished the contents, had a big drink of water from his other bowl, then trotted off up the stairs. They could hear him belching on his way up, then there was silence.

"Guess who's sleeping on our bed?" Irene said.

"Shall we chase him off?" Krister asked with a smile.

"Oh, let's eat first."

She inhaled the wonderful aroma of tomatoes, garlic and fresh basil. She could see the cheesecake browning nicely in the oven.

The soup was every bit as delicious as she had imagined it would be. The warmth and the spices spread through her body. When Krister served the cheesecake with freshly made black-berry compote, life seemed almost perfect. Irene reached out across the table and Krister took her hand.

At that moment the kitchen window exploded in a shower of broken glass, the fragments raining down on Irene and Krister. One of the empty cast-iron flower urns landed on the table with a dull thud, before rolling onto the floor. Irene had left the attractive urns on the steps even though the asters had been uprooted since she had been planning to plant them with a variety of heathers later in the season.

Her first thought was to close the kitchen door so that Egon couldn't come in and get splinters of glass in his paws. Then she looked at Krister, who was bleeding from several scratches on his face. Cautiously she touched her own face; it hurt. The palm of her hand was spotted with blood. The sight of the blood enabled her to overcome the paralysis in her brain, and she quickly looked out of the broken window. There was no one in sight, but she heard the hinges of the gate squeak. Was there any point in giving chase? Then she noticed the back of Krister's hand. A large shard of glass was sticking up like the blade of a knife. It was the hand he had placed over hers.

"Oh my God! Don't touch the glass, honey! I'll call . . . where's my cell phone?"

She rushed into the hallway and scrambled through her pockets with shaking hands. She couldn't find her cell, so she grabbed the house phone on the wall and dialed emergency services. She forced herself to speak calmly and clearly as she gave her name and title. The operator promised to send a patrol car right away. As she was speaking, Irene caught a glimpse of herself in the mirror. She flinched when she saw her face, streaked with blood, but at least her eyes were unaffected. Most of the damage was to the right side of her face, the side that had been toward the window. Would she need any stitches? She heard the sound of little paws padding down the stairs.

"Go back to bed, there's a good boy."

The dog stopped and whimpered, then obediently turned and went back upstairs. She followed him and closed the bedroom door. She called to Krister and told him to come up, too, then she went into the bathroom to take a closer look at her injuries. In the bright light she could see two places where there were fragments of glass in the wound; she picked at them carefully with her nails and managed to remove them. None of the cuts seemed to be particularly deep. She ran a cotton wool pad under the cold tap and dabbed away the blood. She rummaged in the cabinet and managed to find a box of assorted bandages, but unfortunately there were none of the small ones left. All she could do was to stick a great big bandage over her cheekbone. Krister came in, and managed a faint smile at the sight of her, but he didn't say anything. Irene gently washed the blood off his face. A cut on his temple wouldn't stop bleeding, even though it didn't look particularly deep. To be on the safe side she rolled a piece of toilet tissue into a hard ball, pressed it against the cut and fixed it in place with a Band-Aid. She wasn't worried about any of his other injuries, apart from his hand. The piece of glass had penetrated a long way, and they didn't dare touch it.

"It hurts," Krister said with a grimace.

"We need to get you to the ER," Irene said.

They heard the sound of approaching sirens. Irene went back downstairs and into the kitchen; she could see the patrol car pulling up at their gate, with a second car close behind. The relief was much more overwhelming than she had expected, and to her surprise she found herself on the verge of tears. She tried to pull herself together as she went to open the door.

"Wow—I'm honored," she said, forcing a smile.

"I had to come out when I heard it was you," Detective Inspector Lars Holmberg said.

All at once Irene felt completely safe. She explained what had happened, and she also ran through the previous incidents in the garden, the theft of Krister's wallet, and the other problems the family had had recently. Meanwhile the second patrol car drove Krister to the ER at Sahlgrenska Hospital. Irene made sure he took his cell phone so that they could keep in touch.

Holmberg's expression had grown more and more concerned during Irene's account. When she had finished he said:

"You can't stay here tonight. Two of our guys will stay until the glazier arrives; we've already got two cars patrolling the area looking for suspicious persons. We'll drive you to a hotel, and Krister can join you. Go and pack what you need."

Irene's first instinct was to protest, but then she realized there was no point. It wasn't an offer; it was an order. Her colleagues needed to be able to work in peace. She was well aware that it was regarded as extremely serious when a police officer or anyone else working within the justice system was attacked in their own home. She had no choice but to pack what they needed for the night and the next day.

She got out a small suitcase and went up to the bedroom. In vain she tried to think of what ordinary people took with them for an overnight stay. She realized she was in shock and tried to gather her thoughts. Her brain remained empty. What clothes would they need tomorrow? *Breathe, Irene, breathe*, she told herself at regular intervals. It helped a little, but her hands were still shaking, and her heart gave an extra beat now and again. Her throat felt thick with unshed tears. This couldn't be happening to her. In her own home! Someone out there in the darkness was watching them, wanting to do them harm. It was like a bad dream, but the worst thing was that she knew she wasn't going to wake up from this dream. Before she had finished packing, Lars Holmberg appeared with something in his hand.

"This was in the urn," he said gravely.

He was wearing latex gloves and holding the very edge of a piece of paper, which on closer inspection looked more like a torn-off scrap from a cardboard box; it was stiff and pale brown. Holmberg turned it so that Irene could read the scrawled words:

> *You think you're going to get away with it but you are going to suffer, too! You are going to die! My vengance is coming!*

Irene read the message several times. This wasn't possible. Her life and her family's lives were being threatened.

"Katarina!" she said, looking at Holmberg.

"Who?"

"My daughter. My other daughter, Jenny, lives in Amsterdam—she's the one whose cell phone was blocked after Krister's wallet was stolen—but nothing has happened to Katarina yet. We need to contact her, tell her what's happened. She thinks we're just having a run of bad luck. She doesn't realize . . ."

Irene knew she was rambling, but right now she couldn't help it. Anxiety about her daughter took over, and she went over to the phone on the bedside table. She called Katarina; it took a while before her daughter picked up, mumbling her name and sounding half-asleep. As gently as possible Irene explained what had happened. Katarina was wide awake in a second, wanting to know all about her parents' injuries, but Irene reassured her as best she could before telling her about the note in the urn.

"Obviously I'm worried about you. You're the only member of the family who hasn't been affected so far. I want you to be extra careful. Don't take any risks. Don't go out on your own after dark. That kind of stuff."

Irene could hear how ridiculous she sounded. Katarina trained in capoeira two or three evenings a week. She usually cycled to and from training with Felipe, but not always. Plus she had lots of friends she met up with in the evenings and at weekends. Irene just had to accept that Katarina's entire social life took place after dark.

There was a pause before Katarina answered. To Irene's surprise, there was a palpable tension in her daughter's voice.

"Actually . . . I think something has happened to me. I've got huge Band-Aids on both knees and on the palms of my hands. They're badly grazed."

Irene tightened her grip on the receiver. "How come?"

"The brakes on my bike didn't work—neither the handbrake nor the foot brake. I was late, and I was racing down the hill from Redbergsplatsen. A car pulled in toward the sidewalk. I tried to brake, but nothing happened, so I had to hurl myself to the sidewalk. I went one way, the bike went the other. My new jeans are ruined—so annoying!"

"But you . . . you were just grazed?" Irene asked anxiously.

"Yes. Fortunately Felipe was home, so I called him, and he came out to help me. But the bike is toast. He said someone must have sabotaged the brakes. They'd been bent outward, so they didn't make contact with the wheel rims when I tried to slow down. I didn't notice until it was too late!"

The lump in Irene's throat grew bigger, but she swallowed several times to force it down. Eventually she managed to speak. "When did this happen?"

"This morning. I had to miss a couple of lectures, but I managed to go in this afternoon."

"Katarina, tell Felipe not to touch the bike. The police will pick it up tomorrow. We need to examine it to find out if it is sabotage, or if there's some other explanation for the damage to the brakes," Irene said, her eyes fixed on Lars Holmberg.

She ended the call and quickly explained the situation. Before Holmberg went back downstairs he promised to contact Katarina and to make sure the bike was collected.

Irene sat down on the bed. Concentrating on her breathing was no longer helping. Her entire body was shaking, and her heart was racing. Only when Egon crept onto her knee and settled down did she begin to feel calmer. She sat there for a long time, stroking his soft, silky fur.

She could deal with being exposed to danger herself. Sometimes that went with the job. But she had no intention of passively accepting the threat to her nearest and dearest. An idea began to form within her. She wasn't about to run away and hide. She was going to become the hunter.

"Watch out, you bastard," she said quietly.

THEY HAD BEEN given a very pleasant double room at the Heden Hotel. Krister arrived just after midnight; to his relief the doctor had said there was no serious damage to the sinew and the wound should heal within a week. He had needed sutures to stitch some large blood vessels, and a specialist hand surgeon had been called in to carry out the procedure. The surgeon had given Krister a shot to prevent cramps, and antibiotics since the cut was so deep. The worst thing for Krister was that he was going to have to take some time off work, which he insisted was impossible. However, the doctor refused to be swayed, and signed him off sick with strict orders to do nothing for at least a week. Muttering darkly to himself, Krister had been forced to agree.

When Irene told him about Katarina, Krister was distraught. His first reaction was that they should go and pick up both Katarina and Felipe and bring them to the hotel, but he soon realized that wasn't necessary. Their daughter and her partner were both adults who had spent eight months living in Brazil, almost as far away from Mommy and Daddy as it was possible to be, and they had coped perfectly well. They were aware of the danger, and they could take care of themselves.

Irene had forgotten their toothbrushes and toothpaste, but they were able to buy what they needed at the reception desk. After showering they slid between the clean, fresh sheets, but neither of them could sleep. Egon had no such problems, and sighed contentedly at the foot of the bed. Irene and Krister quietly talked over the evening's events. Who wanted to hurt them? Why? And how serious was the death threat? It was frustrating to conclude that they didn't know the answers to any of their questions. Krister fell asleep in the small hours while Irene lay there listening to his snores, accompanied by Egon's gentle snuffles. She didn't sleep a wink that night.

IN THE MORNING Irene managed a cheese roll and several cups of coffee in the hotel's breakfast room. Krister had ordered room service so Egon wouldn't be left alone, then he would go home to Fiskebäck to take care of all the practicalities, such as contacting the insurance company to report the damage to the house, and the injuries he and Irene had sustained. Irene would be home in a few hours; she wasn't planning on staying at work for very long.

She walked the short distance to police HQ. The air was chilly and damp, but the sky seemed to be clearing in the west. Heden's football pitches were deserted, although on the field closest to Södra vägen, several brightly painted trucks were being unloaded. Apparently the circus had come to town. *Life goes on as usual for most people, but not for the Huss family*, Irene thought gloomily. *Our sense of security has been shaken to its foundations.*

WHOEVER HAD THROWN the urn through Irene's kitchen window, it couldn't have been Daniel Börjesson. He had spent the evening at the station being interviewed.

"That guy is seriously weird," Jonny stated.

"Do you want me to have a go?" Irene asked.

"Good luck," Jonny snorted, slurping his sweetened coffee.

Superintendent Thylqvist entered the room. "Good morning! Has our suspect confessed yet?" was her first question.

Lack of sleep meant Irene wasn't in the best of moods, and she thought Thylqvist was being ridiculous. As if they could pressure someone like Börjesson into a confession! She pulled herself together and realized that maybe coming into work hadn't been such a good idea. However, she had a strong feeling that the investigation into both homicides had entered an important phase, and she wanted to be there.

"Daniel Börjesson was interviewed for three hours late yesterday evening," Jonny began. "He barely answers our questions, and when he does say anything, it's fucking crap. He's a nut job, but we can't eliminate him from our inquiries." He stared morosely into his empty cup, as if the resolution to the case might be written in the coffee dregs. But there were only a few soggy cookie crumbs, which didn't provide much in the way of clues.

"Why not?" Thylqvist wanted to know.

Jonny took a moment before he responded. "He sits there saying nothing and . . . just glaring. But I get the feeling he knows exactly what he's doing, and exactly what we're after. He's a slippery bastard."

"Has he admitted to anything?"

"Depends what you mean. He admits that he sometimes shops at ICA Maxi in the Frölunda torg mall. He thinks he might have been in the flower store once or twice. And it's possible that he might have seen Marie Carlsson at ICA and Ingela Svensson in the florist's. And of course he's been to the ER at Sahlgrenska Hospital; it's not impossible that he met Elisabeth Lindberg there. Apparently he was at the ER several times with his grandmother when the old lady was dying. But he doesn't remember any of the women specifically, and can't say he's spoken to any of them. And yes, of course he's been to both churchyards—many times, in fact. He works there sometimes. God help us!"

Jonny looked every bit as frustrated as he sounded. Thylqvist didn't seem to notice.

"So he won't admit to having made contact with any of the women?"

"No. He just keeps quiet, or flatly denies it. I can't find anything that we can hold him on."

"Have you asked him what he was doing on the evenings when Ingela Svensson and Elisabeth Lindberg were killed?"

"Of course. He just says he can't remember exactly; he was probably home watching TV."

The look on Jonny's face said it all.

"Can we get a warrant to search his apartment?" Irene asked.

"I'll speak to the prosecutor. Obviously a search would be helpful, but what we have at the moment isn't sufficient grounds—even with the dish soap in Börjesson's apartment. Yes is a common brand," Thylqvist said.

"Let Marie Carlsson take a look at him," Hannu suggested.

In a lineup, Marie would have the opportunity to state whether or not it was Daniel Börjesson who had been in the ICA Maxi store at the beginning of the year. Irene thought for a moment.

"That's not enough for an arrest. It would just prove that he asked Marie some weird questions. That's not against the law.

And he's never denied being in the store. We need solid evidence. DNA, fingerprints, strands of hair . . . and I didn't see any sign of a cat in his apartment. I looked specially," she said.

"In that case, carry on questioning him," Thylqvist said, getting to her feet. "Report back to me this afternoon." With that she swept out of the room.

There was a brief silence, then Jonny said, "I need another coffee before I start the next round with Mr. Looney Tunes."

"It's probably best if you all get yourselves a coffee. I've got something to tell you," Irene said.

She went through the dramatic events of the previous evening, and informed them that she would be going home after lunch to take care of her damaged house and her injured husband.

"And what about you?" Sara said quietly. "How are you feeling?"

It was the first time she'd spoken all morning. What was Irene supposed to say? She tried a reassuring smile, but she knew exactly how strained it must look. Sara didn't look too convinced either.

"That explains the marks on your face. I wondered if you'd cut yourself shaving again," Jonny said with a grin.

Irene stuck out her tongue at him, the others laughed, and the atmosphere in the room lightened somewhat.

"I'd really like to speak to Daniel Börjesson. I had a good look around his apartment, and I'd be interested to hear his explanations for certain things. And they'd better be convincing," Irene said.

She was doing her best to sound feistier than she was feeling. She would go straight home after the interview with Börjesson, she promised herself.

DANIEL BÖRJESSON LOOKED exactly the same as he had done the previous evening. Yesterday's questioning didn't seem to have affected him at all. He was wearing the same clothes, and his face was just as expressionless. He was surrounded by a miasma of stale sweat, and Irene thought she could also detect a faint whiff of dish soap.

Before Jonny and Irene could begin the interview, Thylqvist came into the room. She looked very smart in her impeccable uniform, which sat perfectly over her hips and shoulders. She always wore it for official events; presumably she had put it on in readiness for the afternoon's press conference. Daniel gazed at her, then looked away. He knew who would be conducting the interview and focused on Irene. The superintendent stared at him for a moment before turning to Jonny, who had positioned himself by the wall, just out of Börjesson's line of sight. He wanted to make it clear that Irene was running the show.

"I think you've got the keys to one of the cars," Thylqvist said, holding out her hand.

Jonny patted his pockets and handed over the keys with a mumbled apology. Thylqvist smiled sweetly, turned on her heel and left the room.

Irene decided to start by playing the good cop.

"Hi Daniel—we meet again! We just need to clear up one or two things; it shouldn't take long."

She gave him an encouraging smile, but that blank face made her heart sink. She didn't feel comfortable with him, probably because she couldn't interpret his reactions—for the simple reason that he didn't show any.

"I know you're a park operative, but I'm wondering where you're working at the moment," she began.

For a long time he stared her straight in the eye without blinking. *I'm not going to look away*, Irene thought. Just as she was beginning to feel she couldn't hold out any longer, he shifted his focus to a point on the wall behind her head.

"On benefits," he replied.

His voice sounded just as scratchy as it had the previous

day, and once again it struck Irene that he wasn't accustomed to using it.

"How long have you been on benefits?"

He remained silent for some time, his gaze fixed on the wall. Irene was convinced he wasn't going to answer, when suddenly he mumbled.

"January."

It seemed a little odd for a park operative to be out of work during the spring and summer. What was that all about?

"So you didn't have any work through the spring and summer?" she said, keeping her tone casual.

"No."

"How come?"

He merely shrugged; he clearly had no intention of explaining. Irene made a mental note to ask Hannu to check on the reasons behind such a long period of unemployment.

"So you haven't worked since January . . . Was that when your grandmother died?"

For the first time, Irene saw something that could be described as a reaction. He glanced at her, then down at the table. His hands twitched, and something flickered across his face. The expression was too vague for Irene to be able to interpret it; when he gave a brief nod, the mask was back in place.

"What date did she pass away?"

"January seventh."

He answered without hesitation, and raised his head to look her in the eye again. Irene pretended she hadn't noticed.

"When was the funeral?"

"Thirty-first."

"January thirty-first?"

He nodded.

"Did you buy the funeral flowers from the florist's in the Frölunda torg mall?"

Not a blink, not a movement, but intuitively Irene felt him stiffen. After a while he gave a brief nod.

"How often do you shop there?" she went on.

He shook his head.

"Yesterday you admitted you'd shopped there."

"Funeral," he stated implacably.

"So you've never been in there at any other time, either before or since?"

A firm shake of the head.

"Do you remember when you ordered the flowers?"

He was about to shake his head yet again, but stopped himself.

"Eight or nine days after she died," he muttered.

Around January sixteenth. According to Marie Carlsson, she had noticed the smelly customer some time after the thirteenth, when she and her colleague were taking down the Christmas decorations in the ICA Maxi store. They had produced the facial composite with her help, and now two callers had suggested that Daniel Börjesson was that man. Daniel had just supplied them with an approximate date when he might have met Ingela Svensson. The florist's was bound to have the order form for the funeral flowers, and would be able to confirm exactly when Daniel had been in there. They would also know whether Ingela Svensson had been working that day. She probably had, but of course all that proved was that she might have taken the order. They weren't going to get any further with Ingela, so Irene decided to see how he reacted to questions relating to Marie Carlsson.

"I believe you often shop in the ICA Maxi store in Frölunda torg."

"Sometimes," he corrected her.

"Okay, sometimes. How often?"

He shrugged but didn't speak.

"Once a week? Twice?" Irene pushed him.

Another shrug. The mall was within walking distance from Daniel's apartment, so it was hardly surprising if he shopped there. It was going to be difficult to trip him up where Marie Carlsson was concerned, too, so Irene quickly decided to try a different tack.

"I saw a big bottle of Yes in your bathroom yesterday, and you actually smelled of Yes, too. Do you use a lot of that particular soap?"

She could see that the question was totally unexpected. Once again that fleeting and almost imperceptible change flickered across his face. *He knows it's a sensitive point*, Irene thought.

"I favor Yes," he said.

"Favor" was an odd, old-fashioned word for a man in his thirties. "Use" would have sounded more natural. But there were a lot of contradictions about Daniel Börjesson. Irene decided to press on.

"For most things? As a soap? As a shower gel?"

He nodded, then turned his head and fixed his cod eyes on Jonny. Maybe he was beginning to realize that the bad cop hadn't been quite as dangerous as the woman sitting opposite him.

"You haven't developed any skin problems from using it in the shower?" Irene continued in a neutral tone, as if there was nothing remotely strange about the idea of washing in dish soap.

"Functional."

Functional. Weird answer.

"So you use Yes for all your cleaning?"

A shrug that could have meant yes or no.

"Did someone recommend it to you?"

A shake of the head.

"No one told you that Yes was the best dish soap?"

"Commercials." Yet another shrug.

Irene realized he wasn't about to walk into her trap. His body language really was contradictory.

"So no one told you to use Yes because it's the best product on the market?" she tried again.

This time the shrug was no more than a twitch. She made an effort to suppress a deep sigh. *Get a grip*, she told herself.

"Do you ever ask anyone who works at the ICA store for advice?"

"Sometimes," he said immediately.

"Do you find it difficult to shop for food and cleaning products?"

"My grandmother did all the shopping."

"In that case I can understand that it must have been hard to get used to dealing with all the everyday stuff after her death," Irene said sympathetically.

The faintest of nods in response. Once more Irene had the feeling that he was more switched on than he was showing.

"Do you remember who you asked for advice in the store?"

Shrug.

"Does the name Marie mean anything to you?"

"Mother."

"Mother?"

"Mother," Daniel repeated with an emphatic nod.

"Your mother's name was Marie?"

"Yes."

"And your father?"

"Per."

"So your mother was Marie Börjesson. What was your father's surname?"

Daniel frowned; for the first time it looked as if he was actually making an effort to think.

"Don't know," he said eventually.

Strange, but they could soon find out.

"When did your parents die?"

"When I was a baby," he said tonelessly.

"So you don't remember them?"

He shook his head.

"I believe they died in an accident?"

"My father. A motorcycle accident. My mother died of a burst gastric ulcer," he replied in a monotone.

So both parents had died suddenly and dramatically. At an unusually young age. Another point that needed checking out.

"I understand your grandmother was ill for some years before she died. What did she suffer from?"

"Heart."

"How many times did you visit the ER at Sahlgrenska Hospital with her?"

Börjesson stared at Irene with his pale eyes until her flesh began to crawl. Something was stirring in the depths of those eyes. She couldn't interpret it, and she wasn't sure she wanted to know what it meant.

"Three times," he said eventually.

"Do you remember when?"

He remained silent for a long time, scrutinizing her in detail. Irene realized sweat was trickling down her back and from her armpits. In spite of the fact that she was leading the interview, he was making her nervous. Ridiculous—he's just another suspect, she tried to tell herself, but without success. Discreetly she wiped her damp palms on her jeans under the cover of the desk, but she could see that he had noticed. *I must be incredibly tired to let him affect me like this*, she thought.

"November. Heart attack. Then she was well. We went back again in an ambulance on Christmas Day. Then she was well. Pain in her chest on January seventh. They said she was dead."

"They?"

"The hospital."

That was the longest speech he had made during the entire

interview. His rasping voice was completely without intonation, as if he were deaf. And the way he expressed himself was odd: twice he had said "then she was well," which sounded childish. And he used words like "functional" and "favor." Irene couldn't get a handle on him at all.

"Did you go with her in the ambulance?"

A faint nod.

"Do you miss her?"

Once again that strange shrug that could mean anything at all.

Suddenly Irene was overcome with exhaustion. She couldn't think of one more sensible question to ask. She had established that Börjesson had been in contact with the florist in the middle of January, he had admitted that he shopped at the ICA Maxi store, and that he sometimes approached the staff for advice. This suggested that he could be the man who had asked Marie Carlsson strange questions on two occasions. He had also stated that he had visited the ER where Elisabeth Lindberg had worked. He used Yes for all types of cleaning, because it was "functional." That would have to do. To tell the truth, she hadn't added a great deal to the information her colleagues had gotten out of him the previous evening. She turned to Jonny.

"Is there anything you'd like to ask Daniel?"

Jonny got up and came over to the desk. He gazed at Börjesson for a long time before he spoke:

"You hold a driver's license, but you don't have a car—is that correct?"

Nod.

"But you used to have a car?"

Another nod.

"According to our records, you unregistered the vehicle almost two years ago. What happened to it?"

Daniel looked as if he hadn't heard the question. He fixed

his eyes on a point above Jonny's head; just as Jonny was about to try again, he spoke.

"Sold it."

"So you sold the car. Who to?"

Shrug.

"Why is there no information about the person who bought the car? It simply shows up as being unregistered."

Daniel slowly turned his head and looked at the mirror on the wall.

"The engine was shot. The car was worthless. It went for scrap," he informed his reflection.

"Who bought it?"

A shake of the head at the mirror was the only response.

"What make was it?"

He must have known that if he'd tracked down the records, but Irene realized Jonny was after something.

"Express," Daniel rasped after the obligatory pause.

"Exactly. A 1990 Renault Express. A handy little hatchback. Perfect for someone who travels around doing a variety of jobs. They stopped making it at the end of the nineties, and replaced it with the Kangoo. Why didn't you buy a new car, something along the same lines?"

So that was what Jonny was after. A car. The killer must have had a vehicle in order to transport the bodies to the location where he wrapped them in plastic, and then to the churchyards where they were found.

"Too expensive."

"But that meant you had to stop working for yourself, because you couldn't carry your tools around. Why didn't you buy a new car?"

Daniel's expression didn't change. He didn't even appear to have heard the question.

"How do you get to work?"

"I don't take any jobs that are far away."

"Okay—so how do you get to the jobs you do take?"

"Moped. Tram. Bus."

Jonny had come up with a really interesting question: Why didn't Daniel have a car? Was it important? Maybe the explanation really was as straightforward as he claimed—he couldn't afford it. Irene was too tired to work out whether it was significant or not. She couldn't do this anymore. It was high time she went home.

JUST AS SHE was putting on her coat, Sara came into her office waving a bundle of papers.

"I told you I had experience with stalking. Here's a case I was involved in last year, when we were called to the scene of a homicide. Do you remember the Emma murder?"

Irene searched her memory. Her weary brain felt as if it was stuffed with cotton wool, but eventually she realized what Sara was talking about.

"The bride-to-be who was murdered by her ex the day before the wedding," she said.

"Exactly. He stabbed her to death as she left her apartment block to go to the beauty salon. It eventually emerged that he'd been stalking her ever since they split up—three years. Both in real life and online, according to Emma's fiancé. The Americans call it cyberstalking. It's absolutely snowballing. We found the killer's blog, and the contents were terrifying. If you didn't know the truth, you'd think he was the one that was being stalked! He was sent to a secure psychiatric unit, but of course anyone who reads his blog won't necessarily know that. Stalker blogs are becoming more and more common, and whatever they choose to write stays online forever, purporting to be the truth. Nothing we can do about it." Sara held out the papers.

"What's this?" Irene asked.

"Your stalker's blog."

Irene simply stared at her colleague. "My stalker?"

"Yes. I looked you up on the Internet, and there it was. You're being cyberstalked."

The papers in Irene's hand suddenly felt red hot, and her first impulse was to drop them on the floor. Then her professional side took over. A faint glimmer of hope began to glow inside her. At last, a clue to whoever was hassling her family. She glanced at the first page. It was an extract from a blog with the heading: PERSECUTED BY THE COPS! The subheading read: OUR KIDS ARE IN DANGER! THE COPS ARE HARASSING THEM TO DEATH!

Irene sank down on her chair and started reading. The blogger called herself Angie, which meant nothing to Irene. However, the photograph next to the heading was a different matter. An attractive face with high cheekbones, almond-shaped brown eyes, and shiny dark hair cut into a flattering bob. The glossy lips were full of promise as she smiled into the camera. A face that had been the downfall of many a man.

"Angelika Malmborg-Eriksson!" she exclaimed.

"You know who she is?" Sara was clearly surprised.

"I certainly do. But it's an old story."

The flattering picture of Angelika Malmborg-Eriksson was at least twenty-five years old. They had met six years earlier, and Angelika had looked significantly younger than she was, with her neat, toned body. *She must be fifty by now,* Irene thought.

"Feel like telling me about her?" Sara asked.

"Sure. Of course."

Irene really wanted to read through the blog, but at the same time she was reluctant to do so. She had an idea of what she was going to find, and she didn't want to be confronted by it. Perhaps it was just as well to postpone that moment, and tell Sara the story of Angelika and her unfortunate children. Irene summed up the details of the case. She could almost smell the acrid smoke in her nostrils from the fire that had left

Angelika's husband dead. She and her colleague in the patrol car had been there at the cottage and seen the whole thing.

"At an early stage in the investigation, suspicion fell on Angelika's daughter, Sophie. It was thought that she could have started the fire before she left for her ballet class. She'd never gotten along with her stepfather."

"There was no chance that she could have been involved?" Sara asked.

"No chance whatsoever. She was teaching a class when the fire broke out." Irene paused, thinking back on the case that had long haunted her. "In January 1990," she continued, "I moved to the Violent Crimes Unit, and that was the first case I worked on. Needless to say, I failed completely. Sophie simply sat there as stiff as a poker, refusing to respond to any questions. It was only fifteen years later that we finally found out the truth."

"So you never found out the truth from Sophie?"

"No. She was referred to the child psych team, and the case was put on ice. Fifteen years later, the body of a young woman was found after a fire in an old storage shed out in the Högsbo industrial zone. It was Sophie."

Irene stopped, picturing a little heart-shaped face with unfathomable brown eyes gazing into hers. She had been eleven years old. Poor little Sophie. *If only I had understood back then,* Irene thought.

"Sophie was suspected of starting the fire in which Magnus Eriksson died, when in fact her brother did it."

"Her brother set fire to the cottage?" Sara exclaimed.

"Yes, Frej. Angelika told the truth in the end."

The room fell silent. Heavy raindrops started hammering on the windowpane. *Why does it have to start raining just when I'm about to go home?* Irene thought.

"What happened to him?" Sara asked.

"He was charged with manslaughter and causing death by

arson, but before the trial he broke down and was taken into psychiatric care. My daughter's partner Felipe is an old friend of Frej's, and tried to keep in touch with him, but that hasn't worked out too well over the past few years. And back in the spring, Frej took his own life. I don't actually know how he died."

"He hanged himself five months ago. And according to Angelika's blog, that's on you."

Irene looked down at the bundle of papers. So Angelika had written about her son's suicide. Both her children were now dead, and she believed everything was Irene's fault. For a second the room spun around her. *I'm not going to read it until tomorrow*, she decided.

KRISTER CAME TO pick her up. It was one fifteen, and she hadn't had any lunch. Krister said he would fix that when they got home, and he promised her a delicious spinach omelet with fresh chanterelles sautéed in butter. He had found the mushrooms during his morning walk with Egon. He also told her they had something to celebrate, although he refused to say what until they got home. Irene found it very hard to imagine there was much cause for celebration. She had failed professionally: she hadn't found anything that would enable them to hold or arrest Daniel Börjesson. In the worst-case scenario, they had just released a dangerous killer. Her family was being persecuted by a crazy woman, they had been physically attacked in their own home and now she had been hung out to dry on the Internet with no opportunity to defend herself. She told Krister who was behind the recent incidents, and about Angelika's blog.

Even the weather seemed to match her state of mind. It was pouring, and the wind was shaking the car. Yellow leaves stuck to the windshield, and the wipers had to work hard to push them aside.

"Looks as if the first storm of the fall is here," Krister said. "Although it's supposed to ease off tonight, according to the forecast."

He seemed remarkably positive. Was he just putting on a show in order to cheer her up? Hardly—he really was in a good mood. Everything would become clear when they got home.

Egon came racing down the stairs as soon as they opened the door. He was delighted to see them, and showered them with enthusiastic displays of affection. A warm glow spread through Irene's chest. It was wonderful to be welcomed by a happy dog. She had missed that more than she had been prepared to admit.

"Sit down, honey, and I'll fix us some lunch."

Krister had already set the table. The kitchen was spotless. He quickly wilted some spinach, diced an onion and whisked the eggs. His injured hand didn't seem to be holding him back. He sautéed the chanterelles in a small frying pan and seasoned them with a little thyme. The kitchen was filled with a delicious combination of aromas, and for the first time since the previous evening, Irene actually felt hungry.

"I can offer you a beer with lunch, but we only have low-alcohol," Krister said after checking the refrigerator.

"Fine by me—I think even that will knock me out," Irene said with a laugh.

She put together a simple tomato salad with a vinaigrette just to make herself feel useful. Having something to do prevented her from falling asleep with her head on the kitchen table.

"How's your hand?" she asked.

"Better, but I realize it's a good idea to take things easy for a few days."

Krister didn't sound at all upset at the prospect of this enforced leisure. The incident clearly hadn't affected his mood adversely. Irene decided to put it out of her mind. Right now the important thing was saving a life. Her own. She felt as if she was on the point of starving to death. She tried to exercise some control, but the food disappeared in no time. It was delicious. When they had finished Krister made coffee and produced a box of dark chocolates. Then he cleared his throat.

"I have something to tell you. Our family is about to increase."

His tone was ceremonial, as if he were making an important announcement. Irene didn't get it. Was one of their daughters . . .

"I've spoken to Anna Hallin," he went on.

"Who?"

The name sounded familiar, but she couldn't place it.

"Anna Hallin. The daughter of the woman who owned Egon," Krister explained patiently.

The penny dropped, and Irene nodded.

"She called this morning, wondering if we might be able to keep Egon. I said yes, provisionally. What do you think?"

At first Irene didn't know what to say. As if he realized they were talking about him, Egon scampered into the kitchen with the blue ball in his mouth and went straight up to Irene. He dropped it at her feet and looked up at her, his bright little eyes full of expectation. His tail was wagging furiously, and he couldn't keep still. Irene had to laugh. She picked up the ball and bounced it across the kitchen floor and into the hallway. Egon set off after his favorite toy, yapping ecstatically and sending the hall rug skidding into the living room.

"Of course we'll keep him. I think we're ready for another dog now. How much does she want for him?" she asked.

"She said we could have him for free, but I said that if he's going to be ours, then we want to pay. No less than a thousand kronor, I told her. It's only fair."

"Absolutely, I couldn't agree more. I want to feel as if he's really ours. Although we do have a problem."

"We do?"

"My boss doesn't like me taking Egon into work. 'This is not doggy day care,' according to her."

Irene adopted a particularly snooty tone as she imitated Superintendent Thylqvist. Perhaps that wasn't entirely fair—after all, police HQ was definitely not doggy day care—but it made her feel better.

"It's fine—I'll take him to work with me," Krister said.

Had he completely lost it? A dog in a restaurant kitchen? No chance. Environmental Health would be there in seconds, and they would close the place down. Irene was about to share these vital insights with him, but he got there first.

"I'm changing jobs," he said with a grin.

This was all too much. Irene suddenly felt just as exhausted as she had before lunch.

"You're . . . what?" was the best she could manage.

"It's not as dramatic as it sounds. I'm taking over the admin at the restaurant. As you know, the so-called restaurant king who's owned the place for the past few years has run into some problems with the tax authorities. Yesterday it all came crashing down. He's selling his entire empire, and guess who's buying Glady's and Sjökrogen? Janne Månsson!"

Krister was positively glowing. Irene was finding it difficult to take everything in, but she definitely recognized that name.

"Janne? Your old friend from The Ritz? He's buying Glady's?"

"Yes. He's selling his bar in Stockholm and moving back to Göteborg. He wants me to take care of all the admin—staff, purchasing, marketing, menu planning . . . everything except the finances. He's farming that out to a professional accountant. I'll be cooking one weekend a month, but I can choose when that is so it fits in with your shifts. I'll be working seventy-five percent of the week. When I'm in the kitchen you'll be at home with Egon, and when I'm in the office, he can come with me. It's next door to the restaurant, with a separate entrance from the loading bay. I'll be on my own in there, so no one will be disturbed by Egon."

It sounded like the perfect arrangement. Apart from one detail.

"Sometimes I have to work late. Pretty often, in fact," Irene said wearily.

"I know that, but it's not a problem. I'll be working office hours, and Egon will be fine on his own for a couple of hours in the evening if the worst comes to the worst. And I've made my mind up about the house, too. I think we should sell this place and move to Guldheden. That means both of us will be closer to work. I've actually spoken to a realtor today. Someone is coming over this afternoon to do a valuation. Apparently they have a long list of people who are keen to buy in this area."

Irene was at a loss for words. Krister had certainly been busy sorting things out. Which was just as well since she wasn't even sure she could get up the stairs to the bedroom.

"Darling, that all sounds fantastic, but I really do have to get some sleep. When I wake up I'm sure I'll be a much nicer wife who can actually appreciate what's going on."

She got to her feet and staggered upstairs. Summoning up the last of her strength, she removed her clothes. She was asleep before her head touched the pillow.

IRENE WAS AWOKEN by the sound of the alarm clock. She had set it for six o'clock, just to be on the safe side. She didn't want to sleep for too long, otherwise she would be facing another disturbed night. She could hear voices from downstairs. It took a while before the fog in her brain cleared, and she realized Krister must be talking to the realtor.

No doubt they would want to come upstairs, but Irene still allowed herself a long shower. The needles of hot water got her circulation going, and she finished off with an ice-cold blast. She pulled on her jeans and a sweater and went down. Egon shot out of the kitchen. Irene could hear a woman's voice talking to Krister. Suddenly she wasn't sure if it was the realtor; she had even more doubts when she walked in and saw the owner of the voice.

She was tall and slim, wearing stilettos and a beige suit, the short skirt exposing her long legs. Her blonde hair hung down her back, all the way to her waist. *She looks like one of the lawyers on* Ally McBeal, Irene thought. The woman turned around, smiling warmly.

"This is Madeleine Siegfrid from Siegfrids' Real Estate," Krister said.

"Hi," Madeleine said, extending a well-manicured hand. Her grip was firm and dry. *This lady knows what she's doing,* Irene thought.

"Okay, let's take a look upstairs," Krister suggested.

Irene glanced out of the newly repaired window and saw that it was no longer raining, although the dampness still hung in the air. Dusk was falling, the sky darkening.

The food bowls by the wall were empty. Egon was probably ready for a walk.

"I'll take Egon out," she said. She pulled on her jacket and put him on the leash, remembering to slip a couple of black plastic bags in her pocket at the last minute.

The air felt fresh and clear. Irene took several deep breaths. She had always loved the fall, and it was definitely on its way. She could happily live without the endless rain, but there was nothing like a crisp autumn day. The change of season made some people feel melancholy, but she was filled with a warm sensation of calm and happiness. It was nice to let go of all the stresses and obligations of the summer, take the time to breathe out and build yourself up before the long winter. The fall gave her strength.

She was so pleased that Krister had gotten a handle on the issue of where they were going to live. She remembered that evening in her mother's empty apartment, the powerful sense of Gerd's presence. Admittedly she would have mixed feelings when it came to leaving the house where they had spent almost twenty years, and she would certainly miss being so close to the sea. But there is a time for everything. The twins were grown up now, and hadn't lived at home for years. She and Krister were going to become city folk, and Egon would be a city pooch.

The twilight was gathering fast, blue-black clouds racing in from the sea. The wind was picking up, promising more rain. Irene decided they would take a quick walk around the local streets before returning home.

The path behind their house led down a small hill, which boasted a few trees and dense undergrowth. That would have to do as far as nature was concerned this evening, particularly as Egon and Krister had been out in the forest in the morning picking mushrooms. Irene glanced down at the little dog, who was happily trotting along investigating interesting smells. The leash gave him a range of five meters, and he was making full use of it. His silky fur was soon wet as he rooted around under the rain-sodden bushes. What kind of care did his coat need? Would he need to be clipped, or was a strip-comb more suitable? She would have to check it out. She looked down lovingly at her new dog, and immediately noticed the change in his body language. He stiffened, his gaze fixed on something deep in the dark undergrowth. Irene quickly turned and realized she could see straight in through the window of her own living room, where Krister and Madeleine Siegfrid were standing chatting. The neighbors had neatly clipped hedges, but the Huss family had never bothered to plant a hedge. Their property was separated from the path by a low fence.

The crack of a snapping twig made her quickly turn back, focusing on the undergrowth once more. She heard a sound like fabric rubbing on fabric—or was it just the dry leaves rustling in the wind? It was impossible to see—could it be a deer? Hardly—it would have run away as soon as it picked up the scent of the dog. There was silence now. Whoever was in there was standing perfectly still, watching her.

Egon started to whimper, tugging at the leash. He was scared, and wanted to get away. Alone and unarmed, Irene had no desire to push her way through the bushes to see who was hiding there. Could Angelika have come back to smash another window? Or was she planning a physical attack on Irene and Krister? Suddenly Irene wished she had read the printout of Angelika's blog. It's always best to know as much as possible about an opponent, so you are aware of what you're dealing with. Should she stay here and request a patrol car? No—what if it was just her imagination (and Egon's) playing tricks? Besides, it could take a while before a car turned up. The best thing would be to get away as quickly as possible.

Egon made a beeline for home, taking full advantage of his extending leash. Irene could feel eyes burning into the back of her neck, but she forced herself not to look around. Instead she concentrated on listening as hard as she could in case someone tried to creep up on her from behind.

Outside the front door she stopped and called the Unit. As she expected it was Hannu who answered. When she asked if they had picked up Angelika, he was very apologetic.

"The latest address we have for her is Distansgatan in Högsbo. We've tried there, but no luck so far."

"That means she's moved back to her old apartment, or at least to the same street. I guess her money ran out, and her relationship with that older guy came to an end."

"Probably. She's no longer working as a dance teacher either. We checked with the dance school. She gave it up five years ago."

Things had obviously gone downhill for Angelika if she was back on Distansgatan. Irene had been there a few times during the investigation into Sophie's death. Presumably the rich fiancé was out of the picture; he was hardly likely to be living in a two-room apartment. As far as Irene recalled, he had had big plans for the house in Änggården that Angelika had inherited from her daughter.

And now Angelika had disappeared—or at least she was keeping a low profile as far as the police were concerned.

"Have you got her apartment under surveillance?" Irene asked. She could hear her voice trembling.

"We have," Hannu replied.

Irene's heart was heavy as she opened the door of her safe, secure home. Or rather what had been her safe, secure home until yesterday.

• • •

"IT MIGHT HAVE been my imagination, but I'm getting kind of paranoid! I feel like someone was actually standing behind the bushes looking into our house . . . We're not safe in our own home!"

Irene had managed to hold onto her self-control until the realtor left, but as soon as the door closed behind her, everything had come pouring out. Krister had listened in silence as she told him about her reaction, and Egon's, to the sound of the breaking twig, and the growing conviction that they were being watched.

"I've never been scared of the dark, you know that."

"I do," Krister agreed.

"But now I am."

He looked at her, his expression grave.

"What is it that's scaring you?"

"The thought that someone I can't see is standing out there in the darkness, watching me. Someone who is out to get us."

It sounded theatrical, but it was true. Irene wasn't really scared of the dark, but she was terrified of the person who was hiding in the darkness.

Krister nodded to show that he understood. He went into the kitchen and came back with two glasses of whiskey.

"Here. You look as if you could do with this. It's all been a bit too much."

"You don't say," Irene said sarcastically.

"So what are we going to do? You have to be able to feel safe in your own home," Krister went on.

Irene tasted the whiskey and felt its warmth spreading through her body. Deep down she knew what they ought to do. There was one place where she did feel safe.

"Mom's apartment. We move to Guldheden right now," she said firmly.

Krister took a sip of the amber-colored liquid, then he put down the glass with a bang.

"Let's do it."

THEY HAD TO act fast so that Angelika wouldn't realize what was happening if she was keeping the house under surveillance. Irene packed a case with towels and bed linen, and they pushed pillows and the quilt in a black garbage sack. Egon's basket and his toys went in another sack—the poor little soul was on the move again.

Krister went down to the storeroom and fetched the two folding beds and chairs, then started emptying the refrigerator while Irene took Egon into the front yard for a few minutes. The dog didn't know what was going on. Hadn't they just been for a walk? Feeling anxious, he stuck close to Irene's feet as she patrolled the yard. The street lamps and the external lights provided some illumination, but it was dark and chilly. Her plan was to prevent Angelika from coming up to the windows to see what they were doing. Then they would simply disappear.

Irene hoped her colleagues would pick Angelika up within the next few days, but until then hiding from her seemed like a good idea, and that was exactly what they were planning to do.

Irene went back indoors and packed some clothes, laying Angelika's blog on top of the pile. It was time to get to know her enemy. Krister fetched his car and drove up to the gate. Irene thanked the Lord that the battered old Volvo was a station wagon. They loaded everything in the back as quickly as possible.

They had left the interior lights on a timer so that they would stay on until midnight. The security lights at the front and back of the house worked on sensors, while the other lamps would switch themselves off at daybreak.

• • •

KRISTER DIDN'T DRIVE straight to Guldheden but took a detour via Vasagatan, Aschebergsgatan and past Chalmers Institute of Technology. The streets were pretty busy, mainly with young people. The bars and restaurants in the Vasastaden area looked both tempting and welcoming, offering a wide range of food and drink. *We'll be within walking distance of all this from now on*, Irene thought. However, at the moment that was irrelevant. The main thing was to get to the apartment on Doktor Bex gata without anyone spotting them.

There was nothing to suggest that they were being followed. After driving around for a couple of minutes they managed to find a parking space not far away. It took several trips to carry everything up the stairs. When Irene opened the door she was greeted by a slightly musty smell, but it felt like home. They were safe. Only then did she allow herself to breathe out. Subconsciously she had been on full alert for the past twenty-four hours, but now she could relax. She sank down in the only armchair in the living room. Fortunately there was also a floor lamp that had belonged to Gerd.

"Shall I help you with one of the chairs so that you can sit down, too?" she asked.

"Please. It's a bit tricky with one hand," Krister said, holding up his bandaged paw.

They set up the chair and sorted out the beds; Egon was there as soon as they had finished. He curled up contentedly and fell asleep immediately.

"Tea?" Irene said.

"No thanks, honey. I'm exhausted. I'm going straight to bed."

I'm not surprised, given everything you've achieved today, Irene thought tenderly. She didn't say anything, just kissed him goodnight.

She picked up the printout of Angelika's blog and settled down. Then she began to read.

2009-04-29

Welcome to Angie's blog. My plan is to write about my bitter experiance of the outragous behavior of the police and other authorities. It's disgusting that the police can do whatever they like, and go unpunished! If they decide to persacute an individual, they can do it, and they can even drive that person to their death! I know this from my own experiance. Both my children are dead, after years of police persacution! There's one cop in particular who decided to hound me and my kids: Irene Huss. She works here in Göteborg. Just writing her name sends shivers down my spine, and I feel terrified! I don't know why she started hounding me and my kids, but maybe it was because my daughter was different. She was kind of quiet, and because of that she was bullied in school. Sophie wasn't diagnosed with Asperger's syndrome until she was twelve years old, although the doctors still weren't sure because she wasn't a typical case. She was quiet and kept to herself when she was little. I knew there was something wrong, and I took her to see lots of different doctors, but none of them knew what it was. Dance was her great passion. When she danced she was like everyone else. She started to dance when she was only four years old, and gradually she got really good. That's not surprising because I have a classical dance background, and am a qualified dance teacher.

This was followed by a lengthy description of Angelika's brilliant dance career, then she finished off with further examples of what Irene had done to Sophie. The final words of this entry were:

I'll carry on tomorrow; I can't write any more now. Grief has me in its iron grip once again. It is tearing my heart to shreds.

Irene could feel her own heart pounding. She put down the blog and took a sip of lukewarm tea before she continued reading.

The entry had attracted several comments, all expressing sympathy for poor Angie. Several of them had personal experience of police harassment; some comments were obviously written by total nut jobs. For example: *Good!!! Keep going!!!!! We'll kill the bastard bastard bastards!!!!! Let's blow all the cops sky high!!!!!*

So according to Angelika, it was the police, in the form of Irene Huss, who had caused the deaths of Sophie and Frej. To anyone reading the blog who was unfamiliar with the details of the case, Irene came across as a malicious persecutor who had hounded two young people to their deaths. *How do I respond to something like this?* Irene thought wearily. *Can I report it as slander?* She had no idea.

After a while she forced herself to read on.

2009-04-30

It all started with a tragic accidant. My beloved husband Magnus had gone for a lie down after lunch, and fell asleep with a cigarette in his hand. He had a bad habit of smoking in bed, and I'd told him over and over again that he shouldn't do it. He'd started minor fires several times, but this time the bed caught fire. He didn't wake up, because as usual he was out cold and the whole house burnt down! Me and the kids were devastated when we found out that our beloved Magnus was dead! The cops started hassling us before we'd even buried him! It was mostly Irene Huss, but also some male cops. I remember one of them, he was a superintendant called Andersson. He yelled at poor Sophie, trying to get her to confess! The cops got the idea that Sophie had started the fire—she was only eleven years old, for God's sake! My little girl couldn't answer their questions, because she was disabled. They got mad and started interrogating her at the station—long interrogations, with poor Sophie facing several cops at the same time, all by herself! She was only eleven years old! They wanted her to confess that she'd started the fire. Irene Huss subjected my little girl to several long and painful interrogations. She didn't stop until the child psych team intervened and told the cops they weren't allowed to treat a kid that way. The experiance affected my little girl for the rest of her life. She suffered from periods of depression. She was lucky that she had her dancing, because otherwise I don't know what would have happened. I'm crying now, the grief is too much for me. I can't write any more today. Thank you for your support, you wonderful people out there! Your Angie.

Irene had very clear memories of her two encounters with eleven-year-old Sophie. She had been tall for her age, but incredibly thin. She hadn't uttered a single word. She had never been interviewed by any officer without the presence of both her mother and the child psych team. There were regulations governing the questioning of minors. Sophie had certainly never been confronted with "several cops at the same time, all by herself."

And Magnus Eriksson was described as "my beloved husband Magnus." Angelika had had several lovers during her marriage to the drunken journalist, and during an interview in connection with Sophie's death fifteen years later, she had admitted to a long and passionate relationship with Marcelo, a young Brazilian. As handsome as a Greek god, and well aware of it. Irene had even been a reluctant witness to a "romantic" encounter between the two of them. Marcelo rented a room from Sophie in her large house in Änggården. Mother and daughter were rivals for the attentions of the young man, but it was Angelika who claimed him. At the same time, she was planning to marry a rich company director who was getting on for sixty years old. Obviously he must have gotten cold feet, as Angelika was back at her former address. What had happened to the house in Änggården? Admittedly it would have been a major renovation project, but it was in a beautiful location, close to the Botanic Gardens in the city. Had she sold it?

And what had happened to all the money Angelika had inherited from her daughter—something in the region of one and a half million kronor?

Perhaps the rest of the blog would provide some clues.

2009-05-05

My body is sticky with the heat. It is coming from inside. My brain is boiling! All these memories make

me want to throw up! Particularly when I think of
that evil bitch Irene Huss! I feel sick when I think
about the way she and those other cops treated my
children. I want vengance! Surely that's a natural
reaction for a mother who has lost her babies. I've
written to the Chief of Police several times telling
him how my kids were treated, but he hasn't even
bothered to answer my letters. Not once! Me and my
kids will never get justice! I want vengance! My
hands are shaking, I can't write any more! Your
Angie.

Vengance. Angelika had spelled vengeance incorrectly
twice in her blog. The same spelling mistake had been on the
note inside the urn that smashed Irene's kitchen window. *YOU
ARE GOING TO DIE! MY VENGANCE IS COMING!* it
had said.

As was the case with the previous entries, all the comments
expressed their sympathy for the blogger and her two dead
children. Irene also felt sympathetic toward Sophie and Frej,
but for completely different reasons. If they'd had a mother
who loved her kids and looked after them, they both would
have been alive today.

She gritted her teeth and carried on reading. She noticed
there was a big gap before the next entry. Had Sara omitted the
intervening entries because they didn't mention Irene, or had
Angelika stopped blogging for a while? Something to check on
tomorrow.

2009-07-15

Sophie also died in a fire in a tragic accident five years
ago. Freja tried to save her, but failed. Irene Huss
turned up and started destroying our lives again! She

spied on both Frej and me, trying to get us to admit that Frej had killed poor Sophie! Frej idolized his sister! Irene Huss hated him and Sophie! They were beautiful and successful, unlike her own kids. She was determined to eradicate Sophie and Frej! As if Frej hadn't suffered enough, losing his beloved father in a fire when he was only eight years old! Irene Huss started hounding him, day and night! Her persacution, together with his grief over the loss of his father and his sister, was all too much for my sensitive, artistic, gifted son, and he developed severe problems with his nerves. He was admitted to a psychiatric unit for treatment several times, but in the end he couldn't cope anymore. The staff found him hanged in the shower. I am living in a black hole, there is no justice! Vengance! I want vengance for my ruined life, for my dead children! Is that so hard to understand? Your utterly broken Angie.

This entry had attracted over fifty comments, once again all sympathizing with poor Angie. They varied between expressing fury at the cops in general and Irene Huss in particular, and they all agreed that it wasn't at all hard to understand why Angie felt so abandoned, so desperate for justice. One person said: *You have to take matters into your own hands! We all know how the cops cover for one another! Kill that bitch Irene Huss! It's the same everywhere in this fucking society—the little man doesn't have a chance!*

People seemed surprisingly willing to accept what was written in the blog as truth. Irene thought that was weird, given that any nut job could start a blog.

It wasn't the first time she had wondered whether the Internet really was a blessing for humanity. It's an El Dorado for pedophiles and other sex offenders, as well as for various financial scammers. Over the years Irene and her colleagues had investigated a number of cases where killers and rapists had made contact with their victims through some website. She also thought the Internet contributed to a general softening and dumbing down when it came to facts and news reporting. Anyone could put false information online, and it was impossible to check whether such information was true or not, unless you knew more than the person who posted it. Which wasn't usually the case . . . And society was becoming more and more dependent on the Internet. *Not least the police*, Irene thought with a sigh.

She went back to the blog. In several places Angelika attacked "the sick psychiatrist Dr. Eskil Itkonen," and wrote about the "banks that con people out of their money to secure their own fat bonuses." She wrote that the worst place was Nordea on Axel Dahlström Square where Tony Barkén, a personal banking advisor, "systematically fleeces people." Irene looked more closely, and realized that Angelika had sued her bank for "poor investments." She was obviously blaming the bank for the fact that her money was gone. Irene knew the truth, and concluded that Angelika had either left a hell of a lot out of her story, or had simply adapted it to suit her own ends.

Irene realized there was nothing she could do. There was no point in trying to counter Angelika's accusations online. The people who read her blog were on her side, and wanted to believe what she wrote. Irene didn't usually look at blogs, but she knew that bloggers survived on the basis that what they wrote needn't necessarily be true, as long as it was sensational and titillating. That was the way to keep the readers coming back for more.

Irene couldn't take in anymore, and put the blog down on the floor. Her name was being sullied, and she was receiving death threats online. *Oh, Mom, what would you have said if you'd read such things about your daughter? And what would Jenny and Katarina say?* They had been around during the investigation into Sophie's death, and knew the truth. Katarina and Felipe had actually met back then, through Frej. All three had been training in capoeira, which was how Katarina had developed an interest in the Brazilian combination of dance and martial arts, moving away from jiujitsu. Irene still felt a little stab of pain in her heart when she thought about it, but Katarina had been right when she said: "Jiujitsu was your thing, not mine."

Children grow up and go their own way. We stay put, wanting everything to remain the same. But the truth is that everything changes, all the time. Did she really think life would go back to just how it used to be if she moved back to this apartment, where she had grown up? No, this was simply a new phase in their lives. And it was going to be a positive change for her and Krister. And Egon, she decided as the little dog jumped on her knee. It was definitely time for bed.

Irene lay there for an eternity, staring out into the darkness. Whenever she closed her eyes she could see those words once more: "Kill that bitch Irene Huss!" and "Vengance! I want vengance for my ruined life, for my dead children!"

For God's sake, how do I deal with this? she thought over and over again.

You were so close. We could almost have touched each other. But I can't cope with dogs. I hate animals! They are unclean, the spawn of the devil. Our love is not pure, I realize that. Thou shall not commit adultery. But you are the sinner, not me, because you are tempting me. You are an evil temptress. You are trying to lead me astray, lead me into temptation. You want me to break the holy commandment. My conscience is troubling me. You are a danger to my state of beatitude. My pure love could become tarnished. Your unclean soul must be saved.

You must die.

IRENE WAS WOKEN by the sound of Egon whimpering; he obviously needed to go out. She had no choice but to drag herself out of bed. Krister was fast asleep in the other bed. Every time he moved, it squeaked alarmingly. The aches and pains in Irene's back and shoulders told her that moving their proper beds over here was the number one priority. The mattresses on the folding beds were too thin. However, that would have to wait until Angelika had been tracked down. Irene yawned and stretched her protesting limbs. Her eyelids were fluttering. If she gave in and allowed them to close, she knew she would go straight back to sleep. Resolutely she swung her legs over the side of the bed and headed for the bathroom.

She sloshed her face with cold water and pulled on her clothes. That's one disadvantage of living in the city: you can't stagger out of the door in your robe and slippers when you're walking the dog, not even first thing in the morning. Not that she'd done that very often in the past, but it had been done.

The rain had moved east during the night. The air was still damp and cold, but the sky was clear, with a pale sun shining on the yellow brick walls of the Konsum store across the street. There were lawns between the apartment blocks and plenty of well-established greenery. The odd hill had been left when the area was planned in the 1950s, and at the back of the building the sense of a proximity to nature was even more tangible. There were tall trees growing close together, and the occasional fallen tree that had been left to rot. The paths were asphalt, and Irene didn't feel as if she was in a park because there were no neatly planted flowerbeds or carefully pruned shrubs. But the aroma of rotting leaves and damp earth reinforced the impression of a forest walk.

She turned up her collar against the morning chill and set off toward Doktor Fries Square. In spite of the fact that she had known the area all her life, she felt as if she was seeing it with fresh eyes. Not much had changed since her childhood, apart from the fact that the trees had grown into venerable giants. They had aged several decades, just as she had. The trams down in Wavrinsky Square squealed as they struggled up the hills toward the junction. She had stood there so many times as a teenager when she couldn't be bothered to walk all the way down into town. She decided she was suffering from a bad case of nostalgia.

Suddenly she smelled freshly baked bread. Her nose led her to the convenience store on the corner, and with a copy of the morning paper and warm rolls in a plastic bag in one hand, and Egon trotting along on his leash in the other, Irene slowly made her way back up the hill to the apartment.

The aroma of coffee filled her nostrils as soon as she opened the door. Thank goodness they had remember to pack the percolator, which was bubbling away. She could hear the sound of rushing water from the shower.

After several cups of coffee and two cheese rolls, Irene felt ready to face a new day. She decided to begin by calling her colleagues.

"We put her apartment under surveillance yesterday. She got home at midnight, but she was in such poor shape that we had to take her straight to the emergency psych unit," Sara said calmly, reporting on the latest developments regarding Angelika Malmborg-Eriksson.

"What does 'poor shape' mean?" Irene asked.

"Completely out of it. Close to an overdose of just about anything you can think of, according to the duty doctor. That lady sure doesn't feel too good, let me tell you."

Irene was surprised to hear that Angelika was on drugs. The dancer had been very proud of her beautiful, youthful appearance; it had been a key element in her social career, which had always depended on men. Irene could still remember Tommy's reaction when Angelika had made her entrance in a bright red sweater that reached down to her thighs, teamed with black leggings and black, high-heeled boots. His tongue had been hanging out. At the age of forty-five, Angelika still had her supple dancer's body, and could easily have passed for fifteen years younger. Admittedly she had partied pretty hard during the period when Irene had known her, but heavy substance abuse . . . it sounded as if something had triggered a sea change.

"How long are they keeping her?"

Irene was impatient; she wanted to talk to Angelika, find out exactly what had happened and why.

"I have no idea. I guess it depends on how quickly she recovers. They know her well; she's been in and out several times. Mixed substance abuse and some psychiatric disorder— I don't remember exactly what they said."

"Were you there when she was picked up?"

"No—Mathiesen and Asp took her in."

"Okay. Just one more thing while I remember: there's a gap of over two months between some of her blog entries. Did you skip some of the entries because they didn't involve me, or is that all there was?"

"That was it. She didn't write anything from the beginning of May until the middle of July, when she returned in fine form."

"You got that right." Irene laughed

She was trying to sound more relaxed than she felt. What had happened during Angelika's silent period? Suddenly she was struck by a thought; perhaps the explanation was very simple.

"Sara, do you think she could have been in the psychiatric unit then?"

"That sounds like a strong possibility. I'll check it out."

Irene felt much better when she ended the call. At least Angelika was under lock and key, for the time being at least. She passed on the good news to Krister, who looked relieved, but remained silent for a little while before he spoke.

"That's fantastic, but I still think we should move in here right away. The profit we make on the house will more than cover any renovations to the apartment, and we should have something left over to invest in the summer cottage. We can sell one of the cars, too; we won't make much money on that, but it will be one less thing to worry about."

Irene opened her mouth to protest but thought better of it. This was all happening a little too fast; after all, they had said they would carry out any renovations before moving into the apartment. Then again, it was probably best to stop talking and get on with it. They'd been discussing the issue for twelve months now. It was time to make up their minds.

"Okay, although I would suggest that we handle the bedroom first, so we don't have to sleep with the smell of paint," she said.

"In that case let's go and buy some wallpaper and paint," Krister suggested, getting to his feet.

Egon thought that was a terrific idea, and scampered toward the door, barking enthusiastically.

IRENE FELT PLEASED with herself as she walked into the department on Monday morning. She had managed to fit in plenty of exercise on Saturday, which had relieved her inner tension considerably. In addition, she and Krister had painted the bedroom ceiling and all the woodwork over the weekend. He was still in some pain when he moved his hand but thought it was getting better. They were planning to do the wallpapering over the next few days. Krister couldn't manage it on his own, particularly with only one hand working properly, but they figured they could fit it in during the evenings.

Next weekend they were going to lay laminate flooring. They'd never done it before, but it looked easy in the commercials and the DIY programs on TV. Felipe had promised to help out. He was pretty good at that kind of thing, and had made the once run-down apartment he shared with Katarina look ten times better than they ever would have dreamed possible.

Irene's train of thought was interrupted when she saw Sara coming toward her.

"You were right. Angelika was in the secure psychiatric unit during the period when there were no blog entries," Sara said by way of greeting.

"That explains the silence. Have you heard how she is?"

"She's totally lost it. Insists that you and the mafia have a contract out on her. You're in cahoots and have decided to kill her. She refuses to see any cops, because every cop is controlled by you and the mafia. Talk about paranoid! But according to Mathiesen and Asp, when she was sitting in the car she was babbling about how pleased she was that she'd made life difficult for you and your family. Apparently there was a lot of talk about revenge. She was particularly delighted by how scared you were when she smashed the window. So at least she's admitted that."

It felt good to have confirmation that Angelika had been behind the events of the last few weeks. The harassment had escalated fast. How far had she been prepared to go?

"In that case we can focus on the Package Killer again. What's the situation with Daniel Börjesson?" Irene asked.

"We've had him under surveillance, but he hasn't left his apartment. Creepy guy if you ask me. Unfortunately we can't lock him up for that," Sara said.

MORNING PRAYER WAS led by Tommy. Superintendent Thylqvist had gone to Stockholm for a series of meetings with the National CID, and would be away for a few days. Irene nourished the vain hope that they would keep her this time.

Tommy cleared his throat. "Good morning—hope you've all had a good weekend. Although I believe you've had a few problems, Irene," he said kindly.

Did he really care, or was he just saying that because it was expected of him? Irene immediately regretted her suspicion but couldn't entirely shake it off.

"You could say that. We had to move to my mother's apartment in Guldheden while you were looking for Angelika. It's a little basic, but we've decided to make it a permanent move. We're going to sell the house and become city dwellers."

"Exciting. A new chapter for you and Krister," Tommy said with a smile.

He sounded as if he really meant it, and Irene was slightly ashamed of her earlier thoughts.

"Anyway, Angelika is safely locked away in the secure unit now," Tommy went on. "She's in a pretty bad way, and we won't be able to question her for some time."

He picked up the piece of paper lying on the table in front of him.

"We've just received the autopsy report on Ingela Svensson. It doesn't tell us much that we didn't already know. The cause of death was strangulation with a length of twine, of course. What is slightly surprising is that there are no signs of any kind of sexual interference. No penetration of any orifice. No semen anywhere. The body was washed using dish soap and water, and was carefully wrapped in plastic. No fibers on the body. No traces of skin under the fingernails. However, some of Ingela Svensson's nails were broken: four, to be exact, which could indicate that she tried to scratch the perpetrator. There were also scratch marks on her throat where she tried to loosen the twine; it was deeply embedded in the skin, and the pathologist believes the attacker was very strong. We'll have the report on Elisabeth Lindberg tomorrow."

Tommy put down the sheet of paper and looked at his colleagues over the top of his glasses. He sighed, then continued. "So it's back to square one. All we can prove as far as Daniel Börjesson is concerned is that he's been in the ICA Maxi store in the Frölunda torg mall and has asked Marie Carlsson a couple of weird questions. That's not against the law, and it doesn't make him a killer."

"He's creepy," Sara said.

"That's not a crime either," Tommy said with a little smile.

A fatherly pat on the head, Irene thought crossly.

"I think Sara's right. We have to rely on our gut feeling. Instinct is one of our most important assets when it comes to solving crimes," she said.

"We can't start locking up all the nut jobs we come across during the course of an investigation. Otherwise Angelika would be right when she says we persecute the innocent," Jonny pointed out with a delighted grin.

He never missed an opportunity to fan the flames. Before Irene had time to come up with a suitably cutting response, Tommy jumped in.

"You're both right. We need to proceed with caution. There's nothing to link Daniel Börjesson to the crime scenes, or to either of the victims. However, I suggest that Irene and Sara carry on digging into his background. The rest of us will go through all the case notes and all the witness statements one more time. I want everyone to pay special attention to any vehicles seen in the vicinity of the churchyards at the relevant times."

He got to his feet, signaling that the meeting was over, but Irene hadn't finished.

"There's one more thing we need to prioritize: the premises."

"The premises?" Tommy sat down again.

"Yes. The killer must have access to premises of some kind. We know that he kept the bodies somewhere for several hours before he put them in the churchyards, washed them clean and wrapped them in plastic. That takes time, and it has to be a place where he wouldn't be disturbed. So where is it?"

"You're right, of course. Although if we find the vehicle, we might also find his hideaway," Tommy said.

"Very likely. It's infuriating that we don't have enough on Börjesson to ask for a search warrant," Irene added.

"There's no point in going to the prosecutor until we have something that links him to one of the victims or the scene of one of the crimes," Tommy stated firmly.

Irene knew that perfectly well, but she still felt frustrated. Then again, she hadn't seen anything suspicious in Daniel's apartment. No plastic, no brown tape, no blue twine, no possessions or items of clothing belonging to either of the women who had been murdered. Nothing. The only thing that had seemed a little strange—apart from Daniel himself—was that bottle of soap on the side of the bath, which was hardly evidence that would hold up in court.

Hardly enough to persuade the prosecutor to give them a search warrant.

BY LUNCHTIME THE following day, Irene and Sara had a pretty clear picture of Daniel Börjesson's background. They had gathered their information from various archives in the tax office, and Signe Börjesson's older sister had put more flesh on the bones. Irene managed to track her down because she had never married and still shared Signe's maiden name. There were only two people named Rapp living in Veddige, and Alice was one of them. The other was the widow of Alice and Signe's brother. Signe and Alice had met only once or twice a year, when Signe was visiting her relatives. Alice Rapp had lived in Veddige all her life.

Irene had called her that morning and said something vague about one or two questions regarding who Daniel's father was and the issue of the boy's care. Daniel himself had been unable to provide the answers, so Irene wondered if she could come down and . . .

She was more than welcome, came the response. Irene knew what to expect: an under-stimulated and over-chatty old woman who wanted to chase away the loneliness for an hour or so. Nothing wrong with that. Many crimes had been solved through such conversations over the years.

Irene took the freeway along the Halland coastline and reached Veddige in just over thirty minutes. She had no problem finding Alice Rapp's rented apartment in a small complex in the center of the town. Alice turned out to be a plump lady in her eighties. Her perm was growing out, so she had back-combed her hair to add volume, and the thin white strands stuck out all around her head, not unlike a downy dandelion. A pair of bright blue eyes sparkled behind the thick lenses of her glasses. She welcomed Irene with a surprisingly firm handshake and drew her into the hallway. There was a promising aroma of coffee, and Irene allowed herself to be led into the small, over-furnished living room, which had crocheted mats on every surface. The curtains and cushion covers were crocheted, as was the rug in front of the TV. Irene suspected that Alice was responsible for the bedspread and curtains in the clean, undisturbed bedroom in Daniel Börjesson's apartment.

Alice had set out a plate of buns and cookies on the low coffee table. Next to the fine porcelain cups stood a thermos flask of the type that was known as a TV-thermos during Irene's childhood. An old-fashioned pendulum clock ticked reassuringly on the wall. It was ten-thirty—definitely time for morning coffee.

"Please sit down," Alice said, gesturing toward the sofa before flopping down in an armchair with a wedge-shaped seat. She obviously had a problem with one of her hips; Irene had noticed a limp when she walked.

"I know why you're here. I always buy *Göteborgs-Tidningen* at the weekend, and I saw the drawing. My first thought was that it was Daniel. He looks so much like his grandfather. Signe and Daniel used to come and visit during the summer. I've watched him grow up. Is he suspected of these murders?"

Alice's Halland accent was broad, but easy to understand. Those bright eyes were observing Irene with interest. The old lady's curiosity was palpable, and Irene felt a little uncomfortable. She didn't seem in the least concerned at the thought that a close relative might be a suspect in a criminal investigation.

"No, but we've spoken to him because someone saw him in the vicinity of the scene of one of the murders. We think Daniel could be an important witness, but our interview with him didn't go too well. He's a little . . . different."

Alice gave her a sharp look. "Different? He's crazy. Although Signe always said he was perfectly normal and intelligent, he just couldn't talk. She claimed he was painfully shy. I don't believe a word of it. Have a bun. They've been frozen, but they're homemade," the old lady said with a beaming smile.

I mustn't let myself be fooled by her appearance, Irene thought. But she seems very clearheaded and eager to chat.

"That's the thing, he won't talk . . ." Irene paused to take a tempting cinnamon bun from the proffered plate before she went on. "He wouldn't answer our questions. He refused to tell us his father's surname, for example . . ."

"He couldn't have told you that even if he'd wanted to. Marie never said who his father was. She probably didn't know." Alice snorted.

"But Daniel said his father's name was Per, and that he'd died in a motorcycle . . ."

"Nonsense! He's made that up. Or maybe it's what Signe told him. Marie fell pregnant when she was fifteen, and gave birth to Daniel just after her sixteenth birthday. She stayed at home with her parents for a week or so, then she took off, leaving Daniel behind. Two months later she was found dead in a house where a whole crowd of junkies lived."

"Was Marie an addict?"

"Yes. She started running away from home when she was fourteen. Ivar—her father—was too strict with her. I never liked him. A sanctimonious bully. And Signe was too nice. I have no doubt that Ivar carefully chose a gentle, compliant wife whom he could dominate. Both he and Signe were religious, so that was one thing they had in common. She never stood up to him when he came down too hard on Marie, and

of course the girl rebelled. She played hooky and would disappear for several days. She became one of those hippies with
flowers in her hair, taking all kinds of drugs. Her parents
tried. They locked her in, they beat her, they threatened
her . . . nothing helped. Have some more cake," Alice said.

Irene obediently reached out and took a slice of feather-
light sponge cake.

"The last year before Marie died, Signe said she was feeling
more optimistic about the girl because she'd joined some group
called the Jesus People. Apparently they were hippies who'd
been saved. They lived in a commune outside town. That kind
of thing was trendy back then . . . Marie certainly needed
saving, but it didn't do any good in the long run. After a few
months she turned up at home, heavily pregnant. Daniel was
born in the hospital, and the doctors wanted to send Marie to
a rehab clinic to get clean, but it never happened. She disappeared before then. Signe was inconsolable, but she looked
after Daniel very well. She'd always wanted a big family, but
both she and Marie almost died when the girl was born, so the
doctors told her she couldn't have any more children."

Alice needed several sips of coffee after her lengthy
account, which gave Irene the chance to ask a question.

"What did Marie die of?"

"Sepsis and a heroin overdose. Apparently she hadn't
healed properly after giving birth to Daniel, and had developed some kind of infection. Perhaps she was taking heroin
to ease the pain, but she was out of practice and took too
much. Or maybe she killed herself. It was a few days before
they found her. Signe was devastated, but Ivar was a hard
man. Did I say I never liked him? He said the girl had brought
it all on herself. God's punishment and all that crap. I wonder
what he thought about God's punishment when he got sick.
He died of cancer in the early nineties; it was very quick. At
least Signe and the boy had seventeen or eighteen years

without him," Alice said, making no attempt to hide the satisfaction in her voice.

Alice certainly had a sharp tongue, Irene thought, but she was very informative. Ivar Börjesson had died in 1992, at the age of fifty-eight. He had been seven years older than Signe. Irene also knew that he had been born on the island of Donsö in Göteborg's southern archipelago, the fourth in a family of nine children. The siblings had obviously been raised to fear the Lord. Presumably Ivar had tried to do the same with his daughter, but without success.

"So Daniel's care was handed over to Signe and Ivar," Irene said, hoping that Alice had more to tell her.

"Yes. There wasn't anybody else, and Signe was only thirty-five when Marie died. Ivar was over forty, of course. But sometimes I wondered . . ." Alice fell silent. She seemed to be assessing Irene. Evidently she liked what she saw, because she cleared her throat and continued. "Sometimes I wondered why Marie started running away. Certain things that both Signe and Marie let slip made me think . . . I've never spoken to anyone about my suspicions, but let me put it like this: Daniel is very similar to his grandfather. I think Ivar did things to the girl. Things a father shouldn't do. Things that are wrong."

For the first time during their conversation the expression in the old woman's eyes was deadly serious. Gone was the glint of curiosity.

"I recognized the signs," Alice said quietly. She looked down at her chubby hands, clasped in her lap. Then she took a deep breath. "So much for his hypocritical cant and his doomsday preaching!"

Irene got the distinct impression that Alice might not be talking about Ivar, but she decided not to dig too deep. Instead she changed tack. "Did Daniel have a good relationship with his grandfather?"

"No. Ivar referred to him as a whore's bastard and made sure

Daniel heard, and he never had a kind word for the boy. But I don't know whether it had any effect on Daniel. He was never quite all there, somehow. It was impossible to establish any kind of real contact with him. He never played with other kids. As he got older, Daniel spent a lot of time with Ivar, tinkering with his bicycle and later with his moped. Maybe they got a little closer then. In many ways I think Daniel should have avoided Ivar, but he just took whatever his grandfather threw at him. Needless to say he couldn't cope with school either, but I think they put him in a special class for the last couple of years. He didn't get any qualifications. When he was a little boy Signe hoped he would become a priest, but as time went by even she realized that was never going to happen. She idolized him, though; she protected him and mollycoddled him. Even when he was an adult she waited on him hand and foot. She bought him a car with the insurance payout after Ivar's death, in spite of the fact that she wasn't exactly rich. She said he needed it for work, but he's never had a permanent job, as far as I know."

Alice pursed her lips, disapproval etched in every line of her face. She didn't even try to hide what she thought of Daniel. Before Irene had time to ask another question, Alice continued.

"Neither of them seemed particularly grief stricken when Ivar passed away, but it must have been a blow for Daniel when he lost Signe. As usual he didn't show any emotion, of course."

"Did you see him after Signe's death?"

"Yes, at the funeral. He looked dirty and scruffy, and he hadn't organized any kind of wake. We had to go straight home after the burial."

"Were there many people there?"

"No—Daniel, me and my sister-in-law. She has a car, so we went together. And then there were three of Signe's former colleagues from work."

Alice smiled and offered Irene more cake, but this time Irene declined. Her jeans had been feeling a little tight around the waist, after all.

"Just one more question: What was Ivar's job?" she asked.

"He used to work in one of the shipyards, but when it closed down he started repairing bicycles. He had a little workshop. He was pretty good with bikes and mopeds."

"Wasn't Daniel interested in taking over the business?"

"He wouldn't have been capable of doing that," Alice said dismissively.

"So he wasn't as skilled as his grandfather?"

"No. But he seems to be okay when it comes to gardening. Then again, I guess he's mostly involved in stuff like felling trees. He's had quite a lot of work in the area where he lives— pruning trees and bushes, that kind of thing. I remember Signe saying he uses one of those big sit-down mowers sometimes."

Irene decided it was time to leave. She stood up and thanked Alice for being so helpful.

In the doorway the old lady gripped Irene's hand, looked her straight in the eye and said, "I'm sure you think I'm terrible, talking this way about my own family. But the thing is, little Irene . . . although you're not all that little . . . it's important that the truth comes out. At my age I'm no longer afraid of the truth."

With those words she let go of Irene's hand and closed the door.

ACCORDING TO HER birth certificate Angelika Malmborg-Eriksson had just turned fifty, but in the recently taken photograph she looked like she was well into her sixties. Her hair was greasy and greying, with traces of a darker color on the ends. Her face had lost its contours, there were bags under her eyes and her mouth was sunken. Had her teeth fallen out along the way? She must have put on a lot of weight, too. Angelika had managed to hold onto her youthful beauty for many years, but now age had not only caught up with her, it had overtaken her. Irene stared at the photo. How could she have deteriorated so much in five years?

"I tried to speak to the psychiatrist she attacks in her blog, Dr. Eskil Itkonen. As I expected he referred to patient confidentiality, but he did say that she's had periods of severe illness over the past few years," Sara said.

"Just as we thought. Did you manage to get a hold of the guy at the bank?" Irene asked.

"Yes. He can see you this afternoon. I'm going over to the dance school where she taught. The principal has promised to talk to me. Apparently there were certain incidents that led to Angelika's departure." Sara raised her eyebrows.

"Incidents? What kind of incidents?" Irene couldn't help feeling curious.

"I don't know yet, but hopefully this Gisela Bagge will be able to tell me more."

Irene wanted to be there. She had met Gisela Bagge during the investigation into Sophie's death, although Gisela had had a different title back then, if Irene remembered correctly.

"Listen, I'm going to call the bank and see if I can reschedule the meeting. After all, I know quite a lot about Angelika as a result of Sophie's case; I also met Gisela Bagge back then. It might be a good idea if I come along; judging from this photograph, it looks as if a lot has happened to Angelika over the past five years."

"If you can't change the appointment at the bank, you go to the House of Dance and I'll go and talk to the banker. I'm guessing the personal banking thing didn't work out too well for Angelika," Sara said with a smile.

Irene looked down at the photograph again. What the hell had happened?

NOTHING MUCH HAD changed at the House of Dance. Irene walked into the spacious entrance hall that held a cafeteria and a cloakroom. The students' changing rooms were at the far end of the hall, beyond the locked glass doors leading to the classrooms. Several young people were sitting, chatting and drinking coffee. Most of them looked exactly the way one would expect: tattoos, piercings. In their black clothes they reminded Irene of a flock of crows, huddled around the tables.

Irene realized she was looking for Lina, the little dancer with the long, shocking-pink hair who had taken the role of the princess in *The Fire Dance*. But none of the girls was Lina. She must be at least twenty-four by now. *She must be a hardworking dancer on her way to a brilliant career*, Irene thought.

Without hesitation she headed for the door marked ADMIN-ISTRATION and rang the bell. After a while a metallic voice from the speaker next to the door asked who she was. She was buzzed through, and went up a flight of stairs to reach the admin department.

The room was equipped with a reception desk and several chairs. A slim woman was standing in the middle of the floor. Irene couldn't see her face, because of the light from the tall windows, but she recognized her anyway. Irene remembered thinking there was something ethereal about this tiny woman the first time they had met. Gisela had been the only one among all those they had interviewed who had wept over Sophie's tragic fate. Perhaps she had been right when she said she was Sophie's only friend.

They shook hands and Gisela led the way into the small office where they had sat five years earlier. Irene felt a faint shudder. The past was making its presence felt, and now she was back here to find out what had happened to Angelika.

Gisela was still beautiful. Her blonde hair was cut in a short, flattering style. The lines around the bright blue eyes might possibly be a little deeper, but the years had been kinder to Gisela than to her former colleague Angelika.

Irene briefly outlined why she had asked for the meeting. She got straight to the point and described the incidents that had affected her family lately, and she explained that Angelika was definitely responsible. When she had finished, Gisela sat in silence for a long time before she spoke.

"Harassing you and your family . . . no, that doesn't surprise me. Angelika has become so . . . full of hatred. Everyone is against her. She already felt that way when she resigned. She had plenty to say to me, too." She paused, her expression grave.

"We know she's had mental health issues over the last couple of years. Is that why she stopped working here?" Irene asked.

Gisela gazed at her for a moment. "She might have been sick back then, but she started behaving very oddly. The money . . . she partied hard. Came to work under the influence, and I don't just mean booze. This was after Frej had been diagnosed. According to the doctors he was suffering from a serious personality disorder. Angelika was furious and insisted there was nothing wrong with her son. She had managed to deal with Sophie's death, but the idea that her darling little Frej . . . she couldn't handle that at all."

"When did she resign?"

"Five years ago come Christmas. She came rushing in here on the last day of term, complaining about everything and everybody. No one in this place was worth jack shit. We had never appreciated her work, or realized what an outstanding dancer she was. I was totally incompetent, and . . . well, you get the picture. When she ran out of words she knocked everything off my desk onto the floor, and the contents of my bookshelves went the same way. When she'd finished she simply resigned, and she's never set foot in the place since."

"Could she just do that? Give up work, I mean? I know she inherited quite a lot of money from Sophie, but not enough to enable her to retire. And she had big plans for the house in Änggården."

Gisela nodded. "She was going to marry the guy she was with . . . I can't remember his name. As you say, they were renovating the house in Änggården, but things didn't quite work out the way Angelika had intended. Her rich boyfriend, who wasn't exactly in the first flush of youth, caught her redhanded with Marcelo Alves. He simply turned on his heel and walked away. Marcelo told me himself. He also said that Angelika had started using cocaine in increasingly large quantities and scared him with her outbursts."

"Is Marcelo still here?"

"No. He left, too. I think he's living in England now."

The answer was brief, and Irene remembered her suspicions about Gisela and the handsome Brazilian. Tactfully she moved on.

"So Angelika was left to her own devices with the project in Änggården."

"Yes. As I said, I heard she was partying hard, pretending everything was fine. She carried on with the renovation as long as the money lasted, but when it ran out, that was the end of that. She had great difficulty selling the house because it was far from finished. The rumor was that she sold it at a considerable loss. Frej was in bad shape, and she had reached crisis point . . . it was all too much. She was admitted to a psychiatric unit, and I believe she's been in and out ever since."

"You haven't seen her since she resigned?"

"No."

Without another word Irene took out the photograph of Angelika and placed it on the desk in front of Gisela, who stared at it for some time.

"Oh my God, how terrible! Poor Angelika."

"She's certainly changed."

"Could it be due to her medication?"

"Possibly. I don't know much about that kind of thing, but I do know that certain psychiatric drugs can lead to weight gain. And of course she's been a junkie, which can affect the metabolism. And I'm guessing she used to drink a lot, too."

"Absolutely. The number one calorie bomb. As a dancer you learn to avoid the pitfalls of alcohol at an early stage. It impairs your mental and physical capabilities, but worst of all . . . you get fat. That's a mortal sin for a dancer!"

Gisela managed a little smile. She looked as if she had never drunk anything but fresh spring water in her entire life. Somewhere in the back of Irene's mind her guilty conscience came to life. Was it that bottle of wine on the weekends that was making her jeans feel tight? Immediately she pushed aside the thought.

"Have you had any contact with Frej over the last five years?"

"No. He gave up dancing. He was training to be a photographer, but all that stopped. When Frej realized that the police knew he was the one who had set fire to the cottage where his father died . . . that's when he got really sick. I assume he'd suppressed the whole thing. He sank into a deep depression, and sometimes he was completely manic. Apparently mental illness ran in his father's side of the family. I never noticed anything when he was growing up. He always seemed bright and cheerful when he was here at the House of Dance. But he was carrying it all inside; the poor kid must have been such a mess."

Irene knew that Gisela had known Angelika's children for many years. Both children had starting dancing at a young age, and Gisela had been their teacher. Sophie loved dance and had remained in that world, while Frej had chosen his own path.

Gisela looked at Irene. "But surely you must have been aware of all this? It was Felipe who told me—he must have mentioned it to you?"

"Katarina said a couple of things, but of course she only knew what Felipe told her, and he was only in touch with Frej, not Angelika. I had no idea what had happened to her. Felipe didn't see Frej at all during that last year. Frej refused to have anything to do with him. He made it clear he didn't even want Felipe to call or write. Felipe hasn't said much, but I think he was very worried."

"He was. We spoke quite often . . . Frej was a mutual friend, after all."

For a moment Irene wasn't sure how to proceed. It struck her that she didn't know whether Felipe had attended Frej's funeral. Katarina definitely hadn't been there; she would have said something about it to Irene if she had. But Felipe?

"Did you go to Frej's funeral?" she asked.

"No. Angelika didn't even post a death notice. I'm guessing

she was the only one there. Felipe and a few other old friends from the House of Dance put a little notice in the newspaper: I think it said 'In memory of our friend Frej,' but there was no date of death. I don't think they knew when he died."

Suddenly Irene saw a face before her: sparkling blue eyes, streaked blond hair and a charming smile. Frej had been just twenty-seven years old when he took his own life. She felt a lump in her throat.

"Such a tragedy," she said sadly.

Gisela nodded. "The whole of that family's story is a tragedy."

SARA HELD UP a copy of an article that had been cut out of *Göteborgs-Posten* on May 15, 2004. "Woman goes crazy in bank."

"Do you remember this?" she asked.

"No. Angelika?" Irene guessed.

"Exactly. I think Tony Barkén, the personal banking advisor, had cause to regret his choice of profession that day. He gave the newspaper the whole story because nothing comes under the rule of confidentiality. It's all in the article."

"Tell me. I'm feeling lazy today," Irene said, leaning back in her chair.

Sara glanced at the article once more before beginning her account.

"Angelika Malmborg-Eriksson walked into the branch of the Nordea bank on Axel Dahlström Square. Although it actually says 'a forty-five-year-old woman.' She walked straight past the line and demanded to speak to her personal advisor, who happened to be this poor guy, Tony Barkén. The idea of making an appointment like everyone else didn't occur to her; she wanted to speak to Tony, pronto! In order to keep her quiet, Tony took her into his office, where Angelika informed him that she wanted to borrow three million kronor right away. She was offering the house in Änggården as security. Tony had to tell her this was impossible, as it was already mortgaged to the hilt. At that point she lost it. She started screaming and throwing things around. They had to call the police to get rid of her."

"Was she charged?"

"No. Her mental state was so fragile that she was sent to a secure psychiatric unit. That was the first time, and she's been back there several times since then."

Irene nodded without saying anything. That family really had fallen apart. Would they have survived if she and her colleagues hadn't uncovered the truth about the fire in 1989? Would Frej and Angelika have escaped mental illness? She knew the answer.

It would only have been a matter of time before what really happened caught up with them. It would have festered inside them and sooner or later the abscess would have burst, and the truth would have come pouring out like a stinking river of pus. Irene had witnessed the process many times during her years as a homicide investigator.

The truth. The one thing everyone fears. The one thing people will do anything to hide, even to the point of committing murder. But it doesn't help. The truth always comes out in the end. Only then can the victims gain redress.

You feel safe, two floors up. You think no one can see what you are doing. But I can see. And I am very disappointed in you. I am sitting on the hill opposite with my binoculars, watching over you. The dense cover of the trees and bushes protects me. The darkness is my friend. Even though I walk through the valley of the shadow of death, I shall fear no evil.

I am the one who watcheth in the darkness.

We have an agreement, you and I. But you have broken it. Therefore, you must be ready to accept your punishment.

The punishment is death.

FRESHLY SHOWERED, SURROUNDED by a faint scent of expensive aftershave, those brown eyes bright and sparkling, Matti Berggren looked like the very personification of an ad for some miracle multivitamin. The impression was reinforced by the fact that Irene felt like his polar opposite: someone who needed a powerful shot of vitamins. In the absence of a magic potion, she took a deep swig of coffee instead, which immediately made her feel a little better.

"We found Angelika Malmborg-Eriksson's fingerprints on the sabotaged brakes of the bicycle belonging to Katarina Huss, and on the urn that was thrown through Irene's window. In short, we've nailed fru Malmborg-Eriksson," Matti said cheerfully, with an encouraging nod to Irene.

Irene tried to respond with a smile, but the best she could do was a weary grimace. *There's too much going on at the same time*, she thought. *I can't cope with all this.* In spite of the fact that they had slept in their own beds back at the house last night, she still felt exhausted. Delayed reaction. With a huge effort she dragged herself away from her own thoughts and tried to concentrate on what her colleagues were discussing.

". . . good to know that we've got the person who's been harassing the Huss family. We can't question Angelika this week, according to her doctor, but she's in a secure unit. Which means we can focus on the Package Killer," Tommy said.

Thylqvist was still in Stockholm but would be returning on a late-evening train. *So tomorrow we will be able to enjoy her snippy comments again*, Irene thought.

Suddenly she became aware of her own thoughts. *What the hell am I doing? All these negative emotions when I ought to be happy! New dog, new place to live, better finances in the very near future—everything has worked out perfectly for Krister. And Angelika is safely locked away. Why am I complaining?* She gave herself a mental kick in the butt and told herself to get her act together.

"Any more leads?" Tommy asked Matti. Tommy also looked slightly the worse for wear, sitting next to the young technician who was bursting with energy. *Maybe I'm not the only one who's had a hard time*, Irene thought with a vague feeling of guilt.

". . . not really. The twine is a perfectly ordinary washing line; it's made in Taiwan and imported by Polyplast Sweden in Stenungsund. It's sold all over the world. The killer has made sizable loops at either end so that he can get a better grip, and to stop the twine from slipping out of his hands when he strangles his victims. He didn't do that on his first attempt back in March, and . . . the victim survived."

"Marie Carlsson," Sara quickly supplied.

Matti gave her a grateful smile, and Sara blushed to the very tips of her ears. *Wow, things are looking up*, Irene thought, feeling a warm glow.

"Can you describe these loops?" she asked.

"They're just ordinary granny knots—no fancy sailors' knots or Boy Scout specialties. And the twine is too thin for us to be able to secure any prints. He probably used gloves anyway—we didn't find any prints on the plastic or the tape."

"What about the oil on the outside of the plastic?" Hannu wondered.

"Thin engine oil. We've sent off samples to try to establish the manufacturer, but it could be a while before we get the results," Matti reported in the same optimistic tone of voice.

"And the soap?" Irene asked without much hope.

"Nothing yet," Matti replied as expected.

Irene wished the reality were more like the American CSI series, where people inserted samples into machines and received precise answers right away: place and date of manufacture, sometimes even the name of the person who had made the item. All within minutes. In Göteborg it didn't quite work like that. All they could do was wait patiently for the results from overworked lab technicians. It took a long time—sometimes months.

"Do we actually have any other suspects, apart from that nut job Daniel Börjesson?" Jonny asked.

"Not really. And we have no evidence whatsoever against Daniel. I'm not sure if he is a nut job, as you put it, or just very odd," Irene replied.

"Can you run through what we do have?" Tommy requested.

Irene finished her coffee as she tried to organize her thoughts.

"His name is the only one that's come up in the investigation, but that's because he was the man who asked Marie Carlsson a couple of strange questions at the ICA Maxi store, and because he didn't smell too good. We can't even be one hundred percent certain that was Daniel, to be honest. He's a loner, and he doesn't seem to have much contact with the outside world. His grandmother took care of all the practical stuff. It's clear there's something wrong with him. When his grandmother died he lost his way for a while. I'm guessing that's why he was on sick leave, and now he's claiming benefits. He's a general laborer, and he used to make a living doing temporary gardening jobs. He's physically strong, and as I said, he's very odd."

Tommy and the others seemed to be thinking over what she

had said, and when nobody spoke, Tommy gave her a brief nod and said, "What would suggest that it might not be him?"

"When Jonny and I went to his apartment, he didn't stink. Okay, he didn't exactly smell of roses—more a mixture of sweat and dish soap. I saw a bottle of Yes in the bathroom, which indicates that he probably was the guy who asked Marie Carlsson which brand was best."

"We've sent off samples of the soap used to wash the victims, and we think it could well be dish soap," Matti interrupted her.

"You're right, so maybe that's not a point in his favor. But certain facts remain. The odor Marie Carlsson talked about just isn't there. He doesn't have a cat, and there's nothing in his apartment to suggest he's ever owned one," Irene went on.

"That doesn't let him off the hook. We know that the killer parceled up the bodies in a location where there's grit, oil, swarf and cat hairs on the floor, so the cat could be in that place rather than where he lives."

This time it was Sara's turn to interrupt. The youngsters were certainly on the ball today, Irene thought irritably. However, she had to admit they were right.

"Absolutely. The problem is that we can't prove anything. All we have are the conclusions we've drawn, plus a couple of educated guesses. The fact is that he doesn't have a cat. Nor does he have a car, which is essential for our killer. And he doesn't have a place where he can parcel up the victims undisturbed. In spite of what we said when we issued the facial composite, no one has seen him anywhere near the specific churchyards where the bodies were found, though we know he's worked in others. So we can't ask for a search warrant for his apartment."

Silence fell as everyone considered the situation.

"Does he really need a separate place to wrap up the victims? Couldn't he have done it in his bathroom?" Matti asked.

"No, for two reasons. Firstly, there was nothing to suggest that anything had happened in his bathroom, or anywhere else in his apartment. No trace of the victims' belongings, no plastic, no tape. And secondly, and more importantly, he lives in a huge high-rise block. Hundreds of people live there, if not thousands, and it's surrounded by identical blocks, which means even more people. There's no chance he moved a dead body from a vehicle to his apartment without anyone seeing him. The risk of discovery would have been way too high. Imagine standing in the elevator with a body slung over your shoulder when it stops just before your floor because someone has pressed the button. What do you say when the doors open?" Irene said, raising her eyebrows.

"Hi, how's it hanging?" Jonny suggested.

"My point is it's too risky, and what speaks against Daniel being our killer is that he would have a whole lot of practical problems doing what the Package Killer does."

Silence fell once more, broken eventually by Tommy. "I think we'll put Daniel Börjesson under discreet surveillance for a few days, see what he gets up to. However, we can't invest too many resources in him because the case against him is so weak. We need to keep our options open, look for other possible perpetrators."

"There aren't any," Hannu announced laconically.

Tommy gave him an irritated glance and repeated, "We need to keep our options open, carry on looking for other possible perpetrators. There's a risk that we've focused too much on the facial composite. It could well be Daniel Börjesson, but the problem is, as Irene pointed out, it's not a crime to ask strange questions or to smell bad in an ICA store. And those are the only things we can be sure that the man in question has done. What if he isn't the Package Killer?"

No one said anything, because everyone in the room realized that Tommy was right.

• • •

THEY WENT THROUGH every interview one more time. Hannu volunteered to search every database of possible perpetrators, and to check on old cases. By Friday afternoon it was clear that nothing new had emerged. The investigation had reached a phase where they were merely treading water. During the briefing, Superintendent Thylqvist was informed of the situation.

"So no new ideas. Just that oddball Börjesson."

The displeasure in the superintendent's tone didn't escape anyone in the room.

"What about the surveillance?" she continued.

Tommy had requested the surveillance, so he felt it was up to him to respond.

"Nothing. He hardly ever goes out. On Thursday he went to the Frölunda torg mall and bought groceries. Not to ICA, but to the Co-op, please note. So far he hasn't been out in the evening at all."

"Is it worth wasting any more money on such a pathetic guy?" Thylqvist snapped.

Irene saw the muscles in Tommy's jaw tense. A little vein at his temple started to throb, and she realized this had nothing to do with whether or not to continue the surveillance on Daniel Börjesson. This was about Tommy Persson and Efva Thylqvist.

"As long as we don't have any other names, I think we should keep watching him," Tommy said.

"That's not a valid reason. Names come and go in every investigation. Do we really have grounds to believe he's the Package Killer? Do we have any solid evidence against him?"

After a brief silence Tommy said, "Circumstantial evidence."

"So no solid evidence. Just vague circumstantial evidence,

if that. Call off the surveillance. It's costing money and resources that could be better used elsewhere."

The superintendent's tone made it perfectly clear that there was no point arguing. Finances were always the strongest argument in any discussion.

"I'll be in a meeting for the rest of the afternoon. Have a nice weekend," Thylqvist said as she swept out of the room.

"I think she's wrong," Sara said stubbornly, breaking the silence that had enveloped the room.

I suspect we all do, Irene thought. But none of us was prepared to tell her that.

LATE ON FRIDAY evening they put up the last piece of wallpaper in the bedroom. It looked good, they concluded with satisfaction. The faint lime green stripes on a pale grey background made the room fresh and light. Felipe turned up and inspected the result of their labors and nodded with approval, which pleased them enormously. Methodically he measured the floor in the bedroom and the hallway. The parquet in the living room was in pretty good condition. He would only need to polish and varnish it before they decorated.

"We'll go to the DIY store first thing tomorrow morning; we'll be waiting when they unlock the doors. Laminate flooring here we come!" Krister said.

His cheerful good humor had lasted all week. Sometimes Irene thought he was more excited about the move than she was. Perhaps it had something to do with age: Krister was almost ten years older. It hardly ever crossed her mind. He was pretty handy, but during recent years he had mentioned that maintaining the house was becoming more of a burden. A full-time job and general household tasks took up most of his waking hours.

The enforced absence from work over the past few days seemed to have done him good. He had spent the days with

Egon, strolling around in the beautiful autumn weather and simply enjoying himself. In the evenings Irene and Krister had worked on the decorating, although she had noticed that his hand was causing him pain from time to time, which was why she now said firmly:

"Okay, but I'm going to be Felipe's assistant when we're laying the floor. You need to be careful with your hand. What did the doctor say, by the way?"

Krister had been back to see the hand specialist earlier that day, and Irene had forgotten to ask him how things had gone.

"It's not quite right; he decided not to remove the stitches until Wednesday. As far as work goes, he wants me to finish taking the course of penicillin and to do some physical therapy before I go back, so he's signed me off for the whole of next week, too."

Krister didn't exactly look depressed as he passed on the information.

"Perfect. After that you'll be starting your new job, and you can take Egon with you," Irene said happily.

"Exactly. Since I'm free next weekend, I thought I'd go up to the cottage and turn off the water. Do a couple of little jobs around the place. See if there are any mushrooms left in the forest."

"I doubt it—they've already had frost up there."

Irene knew this because she had looked at the weather report for Värmland a couple of days earlier. The days had been sunny and pretty warm, but the nights had been frosty, which was fairly common at this time of year.

"I'll come with you," she decided. "The cottage needs cleaning, and I don't want you to do that with your hand the way it is."

"Fantastic. Although I might leave on Thursday, go via Säffle and visit my sisters. It's been a while."

"If you two are off to the forest next weekend I can polish

the living room floor," Felipe said. "That will give me time to apply two coats of varnish, which should be enough."

"You're a mother-in-law's dream!" Irene exclaimed, giving him a hug.

Felipe smiled and looked pleased.

JENNY CALLED ON Saturday and told them she was planning on coming home on December 17 and staying until January 8. She had managed to find a cheap flight online and knew her old employer at the Grodden Restaurant would welcome her with open arms whenever she wanted to work. A student has to grab every opportunity to make some extra money. The loan wasn't enough to live on, and Amsterdam was an expensive city.

The Academy in Amsterdam was one of the places that trained gourmet chefs in the field of vegetarian cuisine. There were similar establishments in Sweden and in other European countries, but the Academy was widely regarded as being in a class of its own. The course lasted a year and was highly prestigious.

"Are you staying in that run-down apartment?" Irene asked.

"Yes. And crazy Sharon is still here. She hasn't had one single sober day since she got here! Nineteen years old, but you wouldn't believe how childish she is. She's supposed to be studying photography at the Academy of Arts, but there hasn't been much in the way of studying going on. Not so far, anyway."

Jenny sounded like a responsible adult. Which she was, of course, Irene reminded herself.

"One of the girls on my course is renting a big apartment very close to the Academy; she shares with two others, and one guy is going back to Hamburg at the end of October. I can move in when he leaves if I want to, and I think I probably will. This place is a bit of a dump," Jenny went on.

"Sounds like a good idea," Irene said.

When they had ended the call she sat for a while by the phone. Her daughters really were something else: mature, independent individuals. But somewhere deep inside a treacherous little voice whispered: *"They don't need you anymore!"*

At that moment Egon came padding into the room. He yelped with joy when he saw Irene, and scampered over to her. She picked him up and cuddled with him for a while. It was nice to know that there was someone other than Krister who needed her care and attention.

SHE REALLY NEEDED this exercise session. Twice a week was her absolute minimum. It was important to get all the frustrations of everyday life out of her body. Sweating it out was the only way; lying on a couch talking to some shrink wasn't her thing. Building up the body's physical strength automatically increased mental strength. A healthy mind in a healthy body, as they used to say. There was also another key aspect of exercise: it kept her body youthful. Feeling attractive was important to her. She knew that men—and women, too, to be honest—admired her body. Desired it. And that mattered to her.

Her job wasn't necessarily physically demanding, but it was extremely stressful. She was responsible for the well-being of others. She often had to make snap decisions. If she got them wrong, there could be dire consequences for many people, and in certain cases lives could even be at risk. If that happened, who would take the blame? She would, of course. The top bosses made sure they watched their own backs.

She often felt alone. Passed over. Other women were jealous of her. The men around her calmly climbed the career ladder—almost automatically, while she had to use all her cunning and prove herself. But she would get there. So far things had gone pretty well, although success hadn't come for free. Nothing was free in this life. That was a lesson she had learned during her childhood in the suburbs. None of her colleagues had any idea about her background, and she had never given anything away. She had had to pay, but she had gotten what she wanted. The new apartment, for example.

The area was so quiet. It was almost ten o'clock, and there was hardly a sound to be heard. Darkness had fallen over the quaysides and the buildings. A damp breeze was blowing in off the water, carrying the smells of diesel and the sea. The throbbing engines of an approaching Stena line ferry were growing steadily louder; to her surprise, it was a sound she had quickly gotten used to.

She looked up at her balcony. It wasn't very big, but the view was stunning. There was no denying that the apartment had been a bargain. The financial downturn had its advantages, such as falling house prices and low interest rates.

She pressed the button on the ignition key. The click as all the doors locked themselves echoed in the surrounding silence.

A second later she became aware of his presence. He was standing right behind her. It was that terrible stench. When he put his arm across her chest and pulled her toward him, she dropped her workout bag with the police logo on it. She started struggling furiously, desperate to free herself, while screaming at the top of her voice. She could hear him hissing *"Shut up! Shut up!"* but she carried on yelling. Desperately he put his hands around her neck in a stranglehold, determined to make her stop. Her windpipe was compressed, and she couldn't breathe. *Is this the end? No way in hell!* she thought. She tried to dig her nails into his hands, but she realized he was wearing rubber gloves that were too thick for her to tear. The only result was that her carefully filed nails broke. She tried to scratch his wrists, but failed; the bulky nylon jacket had long, close-fitting knitted cuffs, with the gloves tucked underneath. Rubber gloves. *Fucking dish-washing gloves*, she suddenly thought.

A couple appeared in the pool of light beneath a street lamp, with a little black poodle on a leash.

"Hey, what are you doing? Let go of her! I said let go of her!" the man shouted. He ran toward the parking lot to help her; the woman screamed, and the poodle started barking excitedly.

All at once it was over. Her legs gave way and she sank to the ground. A car started up right next to her; she could smell the exhaust fumes. It screeched away, gravel spraying up around the tires and peppering her face. Strange, she still couldn't breathe. Her throat. There was something wrong with her throat. Then everything went dark.

"OKAY, SO NOW the shit really has hit the fan!" Jonny bellowed down the phone.

Irene had just dropped off to sleep, and was only half awake when she answered. She and Krister had gone to bed early after a hard day at the apartment in Guldheden. Her knees were aching from laying the floor, and her index finger was sore from getting it trapped between two planks earlier. She glanced at the clock: just after ten-thirty.

"What do you want?" she asked with a sigh.

"Thylqvist has been attacked! Attempted homicide! And guess who by?"

Irene was wide awake now. Before she had time to say a word, Jonny was in her ear again:

"The Package Killer!"

"The Package . . . How do you know that?" She had already swung her legs over the side of the bed and her feet were feeling for her slippers.

"We found the twine—it was lying on the ground. Blue washing line, knotted into a loop at either end. He was disturbed, and dropped it. Tried to strangle her with his bare hands."

"Disturbed? So someone saw the whole thing?"

Irene's hopes of a decent witness testimony were crushed by Jonny's reply:

"Kind of—a couple was out walking their dog, but they were too far away. They only saw what we already know: a powerfully built guy dressed in working clothes and a baseball cap. He jumped in a car and shot away. Neither of them noticed the make of the car."

"They might remember when the shock has subsided," Irene said in an attempt to hide her disappointment. All at once she realized she had forgotten the most important question. "How's Efva?" she asked, feeling slightly embarrassed.

"She was unconscious when the ambulance arrived. The guy who saved her knew some First Aid, and gave her CPR until the paramedics could take over. They'd all left by the time I reached the scene."

"Where are you now?"

"Still at the scene of the crime."

"Which is where?"

"Sannegård Harbor. Barken Beatrices gata—that's where Thylqvist lives."

Irene was suddenly struck by a thought: the surveillance on Daniel Börjesson's apartment on Basungatan had been pulled on Friday, on Thylqvist's orders.

"Has anyone checked where Daniel Börjesson is?"

"What? No. We were instructed not to watch him anymore."

"Can we check his cell phone?"

"That weirdo doesn't have a cell! At least he doesn't have a carrier," Jonny said.

"So does he have a landline in his apartment?"

"I've no idea. But we can try it. Then again, if it was him he's probably had time to get home. There isn't much traffic at this hour, and it's been at least forty minutes since the attack."

Irene thought frantically. "Find out Daniel's number and call him right away. I'll drive over to Basungatan and see if he's there. I also want to check and see if I can spot a car he could have used. If he's back home the car should be in the parking lot."

"Okay, but don't go up to his apartment on your own. I'll call the station in Frölunda and get them to contact you. A well-built cop on either side of you should make you feel secure if it is him."

Irene was quite touched by Jonny's concern for her safety.

JONNY CALLED BACK a few minutes later to tell her that Daniel had answered on the eighth ring. Jonny had simply said: "Sorry, wrong number," and hung up.

Fifteen minutes after Jonny's original call, Irene was in the car heading toward Västra Frölunda.

Ten minutes later she pulled up outside Daniel Börjesson's apartment block. She got out and felt the hood of every car in the visitors' lot. None of them was warm; in fact they were all ice cold. If Daniel had driven a vehicle during the course of the evening, it wasn't here. Did he still have the parking space that belonged to the apartment? Presumably not. Why would he carry on paying for it when he didn't own a car? In which case there was probably no point in checking every vehicle for a warm hood; there were hundreds in the residents' lot.

A small lamp glowed in his living room window on the fourth floor, the light seeping out through the half-closed Venetian blinds. The kitchen window was in darkness. Irene walked around the back of the building. There was no light in the bedrooms either. Was he already asleep? As she returned to the front of the block, a patrol car was just arriving. She walked over and introduced herself. The two young colleagues in the car—a man and a woman—were definitely well-built. When the woman got out of the car Irene discovered that her colleague was in fact a couple of inches taller than she was. Her uniform jacket clung to her powerful shoulders; her sculptured features were discreetly made up, and could have belonged to a model. There was an air of calm authority about her that was slightly surprising, in view of her age. *Some people have it from the get-go, while others never manage to acquire it*, Irene thought.

She quickly explained what had happened, then rang the bell next to s. BÖRJESSON. It was a long time before there was any response. Irene was about to try again when the intercom crackled into life. She paused with her finger in the air, inches away from the button.

"Yes?" Daniel rasped.

"Daniel Börjesson? This is Detective Inspector Irene Huss. Could I come in and have a word with you?"

The ensuing silence lasted almost a full minute. Eventually the reply came:

"No."

Click.

Irene felt stupid, and the two young officers were finding it difficult to hide their smiles. She put her finger on the button and kept it there.

"Stop that," Daniel's hoarse voice said at last.

"Let me in. Otherwise I'll call for backup and smash down the door. Just like on TV," Irene said, her voice ice cold.

Her colleagues exchanged a surprised glance, but neither of them said anything. After another long silence, they heard a buzzing noise. Daniel had thought better of his refusal.

No one spoke in the elevator, and Irene's colleagues avoided looking at her. Threatening to smash down the door "just like on TV" might not have been the best idea, but it had worked.

They had to ring the doorbell and wait for a considerable time before Daniel condescended to answer. The door opened a couple of inches; Irene could just see one pale eye in the narrow gap.

"Daniel. I'm here on the orders of the Chief of Police," she said brusquely.

She had to improvise fast. She'd gotten the impression that Daniel reacted to direct orders and prestige-laden words; reasoning was a waste of time. Once again the two uniformed cops exchanged a surprised glance. The Chief of Police?

"Why?"

"Something happened this evening, and he wants me to talk to you."

The door opened a fraction wider.

"Cops," Daniel hissed.

"They drove me over here," Irene said, thinking on her feet.

"Why?"

"Because . . . the Chief of Police decided that was the best thing to do!" She didn't even bother looking at the others. She just added firmly, "Let us in, Daniel—let's get this over and done with!"

Irene heard a door open softly on the floor above, but no footsteps came down the stairs. The neighbors were listening to the loud voices, needless to say.

Slowly Daniel's door opened a few inches; Daniel stood there staring at them with those expressionless eyes. Irene stared right back. She was angry, and she had no intention of backing down. Daniel met her gaze without blinking. *Enough*, Irene thought.

"Okay, let's go inside and talk. The sooner we get in, the sooner we'll be done. Then we'll leave."

"Leave now," Daniel muttered.

It was obvious that he didn't want them in the apartment. Did he have something to hide? On the other hand, perhaps it was understandable that he wasn't too keen on a visit from the cops late on a Sunday evening. Irene simply yanked at the door. Her colleagues walked in, and she followed them. Daniel had no choice but to back away.

Irene went straight to the bathroom. Everything was the same, apart from the bottle of dish soap on the side of the bath.

It was gone, but the smell of Yes still hovered in the air. There was a pair of dirty underpants and several socks on the floor.

They steered Daniel into the living room. On the way Irene took the opportunity to glance into each room as they passed by. The kitchen was still a filthy mess, as was Daniel's bedroom. Nothing had changed in what had presumably been his grand-mother's bedroom, or in the living room.

There was no sign whatsoever of preparations for putting together a new "package." If Daniel had attacked Efva Thylqvist and had planned to kill her, then surely he ought to have had the plastic sheeting and the tape ready in advance, but there was no trace of anything like that in Daniel's apartment.

"Where have you been this evening?" she asked, keeping her tone as neutral as possible.

After a truculent silence, Daniel replied, "Nowhere."

"Nowhere? You haven't been out?"

He shook his head.

"So you've been here all evening?"

A brief nod, and that weird shrug.

"So what have you been doing?" Irene could hear the resig-nation in her voice.

"That," Daniel said, pointing to the coffee table and a half-finished game of solitaire.

Irene asked a few more questions, which Daniel answered with a monosyllable or not at all. He was unshakeable. He had been at home playing solitaire all evening, and Irene couldn't find anything to contradict his assertion.

The three police officers were just as silent in the elevator going down as they had been on the way up.

IRENE TOOK A wrong turn at one of the new traffic islands and had to retrace her route a short distance. The last time she had been in this area that particular island hadn't existed. It wasn't easy finding her way around a part of the city that was constantly growing. However, Norra Älvstranden was no ordinary concrete suburb, but one of Göteborg's most exclusive developments. Above all, it was the newest. Ten years ago there had hardly been a single house around here. The closed-down shipyards and docks stood silent and deserted. Today it was flourishing, with around fifteen thousand inhabitants and plenty of offices, schools, colleges affiliated with the university, shops and restaurants. All these people traveled to and from the city center by car, bus and ferry.

Efva Thylqvist lived at the bottom of Barken Beatrices gata, as close to the water as it was possible to get. Irene parked the car and walked down to the cordoned-off zone. The CSIs were crawling around on the ground, securing any possible evidence. Thylqvist's brand-new silver Audi sparkled in the powerful spotlights. A few neighbors were still standing on their balconies, looking down on the scene of the crime. Jonny emerged from the shadows. He nodded to Irene, and a car screeched to a halt not far away and Tommy Persson leapt out. He ran over to Jonny and Irene.

"Have you got him?" he shouted from several meters away. He sounded out of breath, as if he had covered a long distance.

"No. The first roadblocks went up after around twenty minutes, but he was already gone. And to be honest there were plenty of holes in the net that our Package Killer could have slipped through. It was the changeover from one shift to the next, so it took a while before all the roadblocks were in place," Jonny explained.

Tommy merely nodded. His face looked lined and weary. *We're approaching fifty faster than we like to admit,* Irene thought gloomily. Her only consolation was that Tommy was a year older, and would pass that particular milestone first. She straightened up and said:

"I've been to see Daniel Börjesson. He says he's been playing solitaire all evening, and there was no car with a warm hood in the visitors' parking lot. I went into his apartment with two uniformed colleagues; we couldn't see any indication that he'd been out this evening, or anything to suggest that he was planning to parcel up a new victim."

Tommy nervously jangled his keys in his pocket but seemed unaware that he was doing it. He turned to Jonny. "What do the witnesses say?"

"Nothing that we don't already know. They're an elderly couple who were out walking their dog. The man doesn't see too well, and his wife just remembers that it was a dark-colored car."

"If he doesn't see too well, how did he know Efva was being attacked?" Tommy wondered with a frown.

"She was screaming."

Tommy looked pensive. "Is anyone with Efva at the hospital?"

"At the hospital . . . No, I don't think so."

"In that case I'd like you to get over there right away. Talk to her as soon as she comes round. She might be able to tell you something about the perp."

"Okay," Jonny muttered reluctantly. He ambled over to his car and drove off.

Irene and Tommy stood in silence, watching his taillights disappear in the darkness.

In the glow of the street lamp Irene could see that Tommy was pressing his lips together. He looked tormented, but she sensed that this wasn't just about the vague witness statements. It was obvious that he had been affected on a deeply personal level: another hint that Thylqvist had been more than just his boss.

As if reading her mind, Tommy took out his keys and pulled one from the bunch. "I have a key to Efva's apartment."

Irene turned away a fraction so he couldn't see her expression; she had no idea how to handle this confidence. Tommy and Efva Thylqvist were a couple. They had keys to each other's homes. Did they live together? Probably not, as he had arrived in his car, presumably from his house in Jonsered.

"We ought to go up and see if there are any traces of the Package Killer . . . Check if he's contacted her," Tommy went on. He didn't look at Irene; he just turned on his heel and headed for the door. He unlocked it and chivalrously held it open for her. "Do come in," he said, forcing a smile.

Irene made a brave attempt to return it, but she couldn't manage much more than a grimace. *This is difficult for both of us*, she thought, *and it's brave of him to open up like this. He's showing a great deal of trust in me. There must be something left of our old friendship after all.*

They took the elevator up to the second floor in silence. When they stepped out, both of them stopped dead.

On one of the doors was an engraved silver-colored nameplate that said E. THYLQVIST.

Hanging upside down from the handle was a flower wrapped in newspaper. They could see the petals of a large white chrysanthemum protruding from the bottom. A length of blue twine they both recognized was tied around the newspaper. Both ends were knotted into a loop.

TOMMY IMMEDIATELY CALLED up the CSIs. He told them the outside door hadn't been properly closed, which was how he and Irene had gotten in. They photographed and dusted the door, looking for any possible prints.

"We'll have to leave the apartment until later," Tommy whispered to Irene.

She merely nodded. Her surprise at his sudden decision to confide in her meant that she was finding it hard to come up with the right thing to say. Actually, she didn't have anything to say—just a strong feeling of being completely taken aback.

Irene and Tommy spoke to all the neighbors; none of them had gone to bed yet. There had been far too much going on outside the apartment block this evening, and several of them were terrified.

On the top floor they met an elderly man with a very distinguished appearance, thanks to his thick white hair and his monogrammed dark-blue silk robe. His face was bright red, and he kept wagging his forefinger under Irene's nose. She could smell the whiskey on his breath as he sounded off:

"I've paid a fortune for a quiet, carefree life in the autumn of my years! I find it *very disturbing* that the place is suddenly full of cops asking stupid questions!"

Before Irene could respond, Tommy spoke behind her.

"You should be grateful. If you were living in Hammarkullen, there's every possibility that no one would have turned up."

It was a surprising comment; Tommy was usual pretty servile in his dealings with the public. He was clearly upset. The color of the man's face deepened, but he didn't make a sound. His mouth opened and closed as if he were a fish in an aquarium.

Irene seized the opportunity to take the initiative in the

conversation, asking the same question she had put to everyone else. "As I'm sure you're aware, a woman has been attacked outside this apartment block. We have evidence to suggest the perpetrator has also been inside the building, probably this evening. I'd like to know if you've seen or heard anything that could be connected to what's happened."

The man glared at her with his bloodshot eyes before he answered, "Maybe." He clamped his lips together, seemingly unwilling to expand.

Irene managed to dredge up the minuscule amount of patience she had left. "What was it that you saw or heard?" she asked in a pleasant tone of voice.

The pursed lips softened a fraction. "I heard the bell ring downstairs, and someone said something into the entry phone. I couldn't make out who it was, but I thought it was Carl—my son. So I pressed the button, but Carl never arrived, so I guess it wasn't him."

"No, I guess not. What time was this?"

The man frowned, and seemed to be making a genuine effort. "I was watching the news."

"Which channel?"

"One or two. I never watch any of the other channels. They just show crap, with all these stupid Z-list so-called celebrities and . . ."

"Was it the six o'clock news, or seven-thirty? Or could it have been *Aktuellt* at nine?" Irene broke in.

"Not the six o'clock—I have dinner then. It must have been seven-thirty."

His face brightened as he remembered. *No doubt his blood alcohol level had already been steadily rising by then,* Irene thought.

"Was it at the beginning of the bulletin, or the end?" she asked.

The satisfied expression disappeared, to be replaced by a

frown of concentration once more. After a moment he straightened up and looked Irene in the eye.

"I'd say it was in the middle. Definitely in the middle!"

So around seven forty-five. That could fit. The bag Thylqvist had dropped contained gym clothes. If she got home just before ten, she could have left her apartment at around seven-thirty.

The Package Killer had probably arrived just after that. Had he rung her bell? Unlikely, because he wouldn't want to be seen. The woman was supposed to find the flower hanging on her door when she got back; that's what had happened with his previous victims. But why had he attacked Thylqvist before she had had the chance to go upstairs and discover the flower? Had he been watching the building and seen her set off for the gym? Had he been standing out there under cover of darkness? If so, why?

They went back down to the second floor; forensics had just finished. Åhlén held up a large paper bag containing the wrapped flower.

"I'll drop this off at the lab, then they can open it up tomorrow," he said, his eyes twinkling through those round-framed glasses with lenses like milk-bottle bottoms.

He was a veteran on the forensics team and had worked almost as long as Svante Malm.

"I don't suppose anyone could take a look at it tonight?" Tommy ventured.

"No. We're not quite done out there in the parking lot, and we've just had a call about a body in Kortedala. Apparently it's lying in the bath with slit wrists, so it's probably suicide, but we need to get over there as soon as possible."

His tone made it clear that there was no room for negotiation.

Once the technicians had left, Tommy took out his keys and unlocked the door, giving Irene a quick glance before he entered the apartment. *We shouldn't be doing this*, she thought. But they had done a lot of things together over the years that hadn't been strictly by the book, and after all he was her boss, and therefore responsible for their actions. She followed him inside and closed the door.

The hallway was airy, with an unusually high ceiling and pale grey granite tiles. One wall consisted of closets with mirrored sliding doors. Straight ahead lay the kitchen, and in the other direction a generous living room, which was where Irene headed after slipping off her shoes. The flooring was pale polished oak parquet. Two large oil paintings hung on the white walls. One was abstract: white patches on a dark blue background. The other was a stylized representation of a sailboat on a stormy sea. Various shades of blue dominated both pictures, and the white leather sofa and chairs stood on a beautiful blue rug. There was also an enormous flat-screen TV, several shelves of DVDs and a Bang & Olufsen CD player.

Irene went over and picked out a few of the films. Most were well-loved old comedies and action movies; one or two seemed to be slightly more erotic. The few books were best-selling paperbacks.

She took a good look around the room. Modern. Attractive. Expensive. But a little impersonal. There was nothing that looked like a memento or an heirloom. Nothing that gave the slightest clue about Efva Thylqvist as a person. Or maybe there was, and Irene just couldn't interpret the signs. She went over to the balcony and opened the door. It was a corner apartment; the balcony wasn't large, but the view was magnificent.

The ground floor of the building was occupied by small businesses, which meant that even the apartments on the lower floor were quite high up. The city lights were reflected in the black surface of the water down below in a constantly changing, sparkling display. On the other side of the Göta River Irene could see the silhouette of the city, with the illuminated façade of the Masthugg church dominating the skyline. The long span of Älvsborg Bridge stretched out toward the sea, cutting across her field of vision. However, it wasn't possible to see the end of the bridge on the Hisingen side, because there was a rocky outcrop in the way. It was almost directly in the west, and no doubt provided useful protection from the wind when the storms came rolling in from the sea. It was a shame that it spoiled the view from the balconies on the lower floors, but then you can't have everything. Irene's feet were starting to feel cold, as she didn't have her shoes on. With a last glance out across the water, she went back inside.

The kitchen was ultramodern, with all the appliances in brushed steel. The cupboard doors were solid oak, providing an attractive contrast to the black granite worktops and the pale grey tiled floor. A large dining table and six chairs stood by the tall window. Did Thylqvist often have friends over for dinner? What friends? Irene had never heard her mention anyone.

She found Tommy in Thylqvist's bedroom. The double bed was covered in a white quilt, adorned with several bright pink cushions. The rugs on either side of the bed matched perfectly. Two large framed posters showed a naked woman and a naked man. *Perhaps this is more of a clue to Thylqvist's personality*, Irene thought. Tommy was standing with his back to her, gazing out of the window into the compact darkness.

"Talk to me," Irene said.

He didn't move. Maybe he hadn't heard her. Just as Irene was about to repeat her request, she realized he was crying. She heard a sob and saw his shoulders shaking. Clearly she wasn't the only one who felt lonely sometimes. She went over and placed a hand on his shoulder.

"Tommy. Come and sit down. Let's talk."

He offered no resistance as she guided him into the living room. He slumped down in one of the elegant leather armchairs. Irene found a tissue in one of her pockets and gave it to him.

"Thanks," he mumbled, and blew his nose.

"Can I get you something to drink?"

He shook his head. Irene sat down opposite him and waited for him to start, but he didn't seem to have the strength to say a word. She decided to try to get him going.

"So how close were you and Efva?" she asked, getting straight to the point.

He raised his head and gazed at her, his eyes still shiny with tears. She had never seen him cry, not once in the twenty-six years they had known each other.

"We . . . we've been together since the end of last year."

"So why haven't you gone public?"

He gave her a quick appraising glance, but she gave no indication that she had had her suspicions for a long time.

"Efva . . . Efva didn't want to. She thought it would lead to a lot of unnecessary gossip."

"And what did you think?"

"The same, I guess." He took a deep breath. "I might as well tell you right away: We split up. It's over."

That didn't come as much of a surprise either, but Irene managed to adopt a suitably sympathetic expression. "When?"

"Two weeks ago."

"Are you very upset about that?" she asked tentatively.

"Yes . . . but when it's over, it's over."

The words sounded sensible, but his voice was far from steady. He had obviously taken it very hard. She was so pleased he had decided to confide in her; she hadn't expected it at all. Was it Thylqvist who had ended the relationship? Did he still love her? Two questions she definitely couldn't ask. Instead she said:

"So why did the Package Killer attack Efva? She fits the age profile, but she doesn't live in the western part of the city, and she doesn't have any link with the Frölunda torg mall. Or does she sometimes shop there?"

"Not as far as I know. But he could have seen her on TV—she was on *Most Wanted* back in August. The Hindås homicide."

Irene remembered the case, but she hadn't been involved. A sixty-year-old woman was found murdered in the forest just a few hundred meters from her cottage in Hindås at the end of July. The house was in a pretty remote location, so no one had seen anything. There had been no leads at all, so in the end the police had decided to try an appeal on *Most Wanted* on TV3. There was a chance that some visitor or tourist had seen something. The usual press officer had been on vacation, so Efva Thylqvist had been only too happy to take on the task of informing the public about the murder. Irene had seen the program, and remembered that the superintendent had looked good in her smart uniform, with her recently acquired suntan. None of the calls that had come in had been of any use, and the case remained unsolved.

"She took the press conference after we found Ingela Svensson and Elisabeth Lindberg; she's also been in the papers, and was interviewed for the local news on TV-Four," Tommy went on.

"He might have seen her in the media. He probably collects cuttings about the case and follows the news coverage; they usually do," Irene said, hiding a yawn behind her hand.

Tommy noticed and straightened up.

"Time we went home," he said.

He got to his feet and headed for the hallway. Before he opened the door he turned and looked back at Irene. "Tomorrow's going to be a hell of a day," he said grimly.

THE FOLLOWING MORNING both Irene and Tommy were there when the white chrysanthemum was unwrapped. Matti Berggren quickly took all the samples he needed from the outside of the newspaper and the blue twine. Carefully he removed the pages taken from a copy of *Göteborgs-Posten*, noting that they were from September 20. Just as they had expected, there was an envelope stuck to the stem of the flower with ordinary tape. On the front of the envelope someone had written in thick black felt-tip: *2 Ex. 20:5*.

"Exodus, chapter twenty, verse five." Irene said. Isn't that what it said on the envelope Ingela Svensson received? Something about visiting the sins of the fathers on the children to the third and fourth generations? I'll ask Sara to check it out."

She called Sara's cell and got an answer right away. Irene explained the situation, and Sara promised to call back as soon as she had found the quotation. As Irene ended the call she saw that Matti was removing the tape with a pair of tweezers. *He's very skilled, almost on par with an eye surgeon*, she thought. Personally it was all she could do to balance her coffee mug so that she didn't spill the contents.

"Tape!" Matti said, licking his lips. His brown eyes sparkled as he carefully slid the tape into a sterile container.

Jesus, he's so cheerful you could almost hate him, Irene mused. "I know, you love tape because a whole load of stuff always sticks to it, and the person who put it there has no idea," she said in an attempt to make up for her churlish reaction. She sipped her coffee and tried to wake up. Four hours of sleep had been nowhere near enough. She was exhausted.

Tommy looked as if he hadn't slept at all. He'd swung by the hospital early in the morning to check on Thylqvist, and had been informed that she had undergone surgery during the night. The damage to her windpipe was serious, and she was now on a respirator.

Using the tweezers once again, Matti drew a photograph out of the white envelope.

Suddenly Irene was firing on all cylinders. She hadn't expected this. She glanced at Tommy; all the color had drained from his face. He was ashen, and looked as if he was about to faint. Instinctively she placed a hand on his arm, but he shook it off impatiently. His Adam's apple bobbed up and down several times before he managed to speak:

"Interviewing this guy could be a little embarrassing."

Irene merely nodded. She couldn't take her eyes off the picture on the table, illuminated by the harsh glare of the laboratory lamp.

Efva Thylqvist could be seen in profile. She was lying on the leather sofa, naked from the waist up. A man was sitting beside her facing the window, caressing one of her breasts. It was Chief Superintendent Thomas Englund.

The photograph had been taken with a zoom lens, and was of considerably better quality than those the Package Killer had sent to his previous intended victims. According to the date in the corner, it had been taken four days earlier.

"Last Thursday. She goes to the gym on Thursdays . . . unless she's away," Tommy said in a voice thick with emotion.

Irene could hear Jonny's voice inside her head: *"Well, I suppose it's one form of exercise . . . ha ha."* She was very glad he didn't know about this yet. It was lucky that Tommy had sent him off to the hospital the previous evening, otherwise Tommy probably wouldn't have confided in Irene about his relationship with Efva Thylqvist and the fact that it was now over.

But what had actually happened there? She had only heard Tommy's version. The woman in the picture was definitely Thylqvist, but the guy certainly wasn't Tommy. Thomas Englund was one of the most senior officers on the force.

Tommy had a hell of a lot of explaining to do. There was no getting around the fact that he was a suspect. Jealousy is a powerful and common motive when it came to homicide, and if anyone could carry out a perfect copycat crime, it was an investigating officer.

Right now he was in charge of the whole case.

The photographer had stood on the rocky outcrop and

taken the picture through the window as usual. But was this the Package Killer? The quality didn't fit with the other two shots.

Irene's train of thought was interrupted by a call from Sara, confirming that the Bible reference on Efva Thylqvist's envelope was the same as the one on Ingela Svensson's.

"I am a jealous God, and I will visit the sins of the fathers on the children to the third and fourth generations etcetera etcetera," Tommy said with a sigh.

"She didn't do what he wanted. She had someone else, so she had to be punished," Irene said.

She observed Tommy closely to see if he reacted to the insinuation. He just nodded wearily; he seemed to be totally worn out. Seeing him in this state, she found it difficult to imagine that he could have had anything to do with the attack. Or was he tormented by darker feelings? Was he fretting because he hadn't managed to kill Thylqvist? Was he scared that she would remember something when she regained consciousness? Maybe confiding in Irene had been a smart move, just in case the truth about his relationship with Thylqvist came out?

Irene realized that at the moment she was the only one who knew he had a motive for murder. At this stage she had no intention of sharing her suspicions with anyone, least of all Tommy. If it did turn out to be a copycat attack, that would put things in an entirely different light, and she would have to confront Tommy.

As they left the lab, she said, "I'm happy to have an initial conversation with Thomas Englund. You're needed back in the department; you're in charge while Efva's away."

"Fine—it's probably best if I don't see Englund for a few days. This has come as a real shock." He was speaking so quietly she could barely make out the words.

"You had no idea there was . . . someone else?"

"No. She said she wanted a break. When I asked her why,

she said she felt suffocated. She didn't want a long-term relationship. We . . . we argued for a few days, then we broke up."

Irene could see how much it cost him to talk about this.
Rejected. Humiliated. Jealous. Powerful emotions that could
trigger violence. Even murder. Thinking along those lines
didn't make Irene feel any better. As a professional investigator, she had to keep them in the back of her mind. She had
knowledge that was relevant to the case. Right now, that
seemed like a heavy burden to bear.

She spoke quietly. "Tommy, where were you last night?"

He stopped dead and looked at her in surprise. When he
realized why she had asked the question, his expression hardened. "I was at home. All three kids were with me for Sunday
dinner, but they went back to Agneta's at about eight.
Although Martin went to Johanneberg, of course. After they
left I watched TV until the phone rang, then I drove over to
Sannegård. The rest you know," he replied coldly.

Tommy's eldest son Martin was Irene's godson. She had
hardly seen him over the past few years; he was now in his
second year of a journalism program. He had just moved into a
student apartment in the city center after living in a series of
sublets. Tommy's two daughters were in the first and third years
in high school. *It must be quite a feat to get all three of them
together for dinner*, Irene thought. All at once she knew the
reason for the gathering.

"Of course . . . happy birthday for yesterday," she said, overcome with embarrassment.

They went up to the department in silence.

CHIEF SUPERINTENDENT THOMAS Englund was able
to see Irene after lunch. She knocked on his door at exactly
one o'clock, as arranged. He shouted "Come in!" and she
entered his office to find him on the phone. He waved and
gestured toward a chair on the opposite side of the desk.

As he talked Irene watched him discreetly. She had always thought he was a good-looking guy. He was around fifty years old; he was tall, and gave the impression that he worked out. His short dark hair was peppered with grey, and his face was still tan from a summer spent sailing. The wall behind him was adorned with several framed pictures of large sailboats; Englund was at the helm in at least three of them. One was a close-up, taken in the well of a boat. Englund had both hands on the wheel, and beside him stood a blonde woman and two teenage boys. They were all wearing sailing gear and smiling into the camera, the wind ruffling their hair. The epitome of a happy family.

After a few polite phrases, the chief superintendent ended the call.

"Irene. How can I help you?" he said, smiling warmly.

He leaned forward over the desk, palms flat, supporting himself on his elbows. Irene glanced at his left hand and saw a wide gold band. He obviously wasn't divorced. Not yet, anyway.

"Good afternoon. It's about the investigation into the attack on Superintendent Efva Thylqvist."

The warm smile stiffened and began to look somewhat strained.

"I heard this morning; it's a terrible thing. Everyone's talking about it."

His gaze wasn't quite steady. No doubt he was worried, wondering why Irene wanted to talk to him about Thylqvist.

"Tommy Persson and I went to her apartment after the attack. We found a photograph that I'd like to show you."

Irene opened the folder she was carrying and removed a plastic pocket. She shook out the picture and let it fall onto the desk in front of the chief superintendent.

Instantly every trace of a smile disappeared from his face. He took several deep breaths and stared at the photograph.

"This is a copy of a photo the perpetrator sent to Efva. It's part of his MO; he does this before he attacks his victims. He wants to point out their sins, so they will know why he kills them," Irene explained.

"Is it . . . is it the Package Killer?" Englund's voice was strained.

"Yes. There are several aspects of the attempted murder of Efva Thylqvist that match his previous attacks."

Irene observed the man opposite; he had clasped his hands together to hide the fact that they were shaking.

"Clearly we'd like to know more about your relationship with Efva," she went on calmly.

"Of course. Of course. I do realize that. But . . ."

He broke off, and Irene could see the beads of sweat on his forehead.

"It's . . . it's . . . a sensitive matter."

You should have thought of that before, Irene said to herself. It would be difficult to keep this under wraps. Police HQ leaked like a sieve, and gossip spread like wildfire. Thomas Englund knew that just as well as she did, so there was no need to point it out. Instead she nodded toward the photograph on the desk.

"Does your wife know about this?"

"No . . . no."

He managed to tear his gaze away from the image and looked up at Irene.

"I'm sure you understand . . . this meant nothing. We only . . . it was just . . . once or twice . . ."

The word GUILTY was written in capital letters above his head. He was a terrible liar, which suggested he didn't do this kind of thing on a regular basis. That made Irene feel slightly more kindly disposed toward him; his wife might well take a different view.

"How long have you and Efva been in a relationship?"

Englund buried his head in his hands and sighed. "Oh

God . . . a relationship! What a word . . . Since August. After my vacation. We were at a seminar, and . . . it just happened."

"You embarked on a sexual relationship."

Englund nodded, still with his head in his hands. Slowly he looked up at Irene. "I'm not proud of this, but I realize I'm in trouble. I'll be as honest as possible."

"Thank you," Irene replied with an encouraging nod.

The chief superintendent took a deep breath. "It was a two-day seminar. There was a special dinner on the first night, and I ended up sitting next to Efva. We . . . There was a spark. We've been seeing each other ever since. Not very often, because . . . my family . . . but Thursdays suit us both. Late in the evening. I play tennis, and Efva goes to the gym. My wife plays bridge on Thursdays, and she doesn't get home until midnight. We met at Efva's apartment, of course. Which is when that bastard took the photograph."

"When was this seminar?"

He checked his desk diary.

"August twelfth and thirteenth."

Six weeks ago. Had Tommy suspected anything? According to him, he and Thylqvist had split up two weeks ago, which meant she had had two lovers for a whole month.

"Where were you last night?" Irene asked.

He recoiled and gave her a sharp look. "What's that got to do with . . . Surely you don't have to ask me . . . ! Do you really think I had anything to do with the attack on Efva?" His tanned cheeks flushed red; he was indignation personified, but his hands were still shaking.

"You know just as well as I do that we always look at those who are close to the victim. The main suspects are always those with whom the victim is having, or has had, a sexual relationship. From a purely statistical point of view, that's where we find the killer in ninety percent of cases. I wouldn't be doing my job if I didn't ask the question," Irene replied.

Englund looked at her for a long time, then shifted his gaze to the window. The sun was shining between the wispy clouds, and you could easily be fooled into thinking it was a warm summer's day out there. But the thermometer was showing nine degrees, and there was a biting wind. However, it seemed unlikely that he was thinking about the weather.

Eventually he said, "The boys and I were sailing in the last heat of the September Cup. We finished at five-oh-eight. We came in second overall; you can check the results table online—it's on the Göteborg Royal Sailing Club's homepage. By the time we'd sorted out the boat, it was almost eight o'clock. We went home and had dinner, and celebrated, of course. We went to bed around eleven."

Playing happy family, in other words. But you're ready to smash all that to pieces. Perhaps those photographs on the wall show nothing more than a façade, Irene thought.

Englund tried to force a smile, then adopted a more intimate tone. "Listen, Irene, I'd really appreciate it if you could lie low with this photograph for the time being. There's always so much talk, and that wouldn't do either of us any good—me or Efva."

At least he had the grace to look embarrassed. Irene wasn't exactly surprised, but she was a little disappointed. *Just as pathetic as the rest of them*, she thought.

"That's not possible, I'm afraid. There were several officers at the scene when the photograph was discovered, so it's already been seen by a number of people. We'll keep it from the media, of course, as we've managed to do with the previous photographs of the victims. However, I do have to share it with the rest of the investigating team," she said firmly.

Englund nodded. "But you will do your best to make sure it doesn't leak out? I didn't have anything to do with the attack. On the contrary, I . . ." His voice betrayed the fact that he didn't have much hope of his relationship remaining a secret. *Nice try*, as Irene's girls would have said.

The chief superintendent slumped back in his chair. His tan complexion had taken on a noticeably greyer tone. Irene took her leave; he didn't respond, but continued to stare blankly at the photograph on the desk in front of him. He still hadn't touched it.

Matti Berggren turned up just in time for coffee on Tuesday afternoon. He sat down and accepted a cup and a cookie. Irene could see that he had something to tell them.

"Have you found anything interesting, Matti?" Tommy asked. He still looked as if he hadn't slept a wink since Sunday.

"Absolutely! We found two cat hairs on Thylqvist's jacket—the same type as we found on the plastic sheeting. We also found blue fibers from a fleece top or something similar. The hairs and the fibers were on the back of the jacket, so they got there when the perp attacked Thylqvist from behind and pulled her toward him. There's also a small stain that could well be engine oil—we haven't quite finished the analysis yet."

Irene felt a great wave of relief. This indicated that they weren't looking at a copycat. She could remove both Tommy Persson and Thomas Englund from her list of suspects. They could quite easily have arranged the oil and the nylon fibers, but exactly the same cat hairs as forensics had found on the tape securing the plastic wrapped around the two homicide victims . . . no.

"And the noose?" Tommy asked.

"The same type as in the previous attacks. Blue twine, a loop at either end, same knots. I'm guessing he didn't have time to slip it around her neck before she started screaming, because it doesn't look as if it's been used. It was lying on the ground, so presumably he dropped it."

"Any news on what kind of dish soap was used in the previous cases?" Irene asked

"No, but we should hear very soon. I sent a sample of Yes to the lab so they can make a direct comparison, see if it's the same product."

Smart guy, Irene thought.

According to the hospital, Efva Thylqvist's condition was improving, but she was still on a respirator. She hadn't regained consciousness, and the doctors had refused to allow visitors or any attempt to communicate with her.

ON THURSDAY THYLQVIST was taken off the respirator for a few hours. She was now fully conscious, and the doctors had said a brief visit was permissible. Tommy decided it would be best if Irene and Sara went to see her.

They were equipped with protective gowns, along with shoe protectors and masks. Through the glass Irene could see various monitors and drips, and the outline of Thylqvist's body beneath a yellow blanket. The smell of disinfectant struck them as they opened the door and went in. Only then did Irene see Thylqvist's face.

She was lying with her eyes closed. To be honest, she could have been dead. Her lips were as colorless as her pale skin. She looked fragile and vulnerable. The respirator was at the side of the bed, and a large dressing covered the cannula in her throat.

A nurse moved across to the bed and said quietly, "Efva. Some of your colleagues would like to speak to you."

Efva Thylqvist opened her eyes and stared at Irene and Sara. To her relief, Irene saw that the blue gaze was just as intense as ever.

"Hi Efva—it's Irene and Sara hiding behind these masks!

Good to see you're feeling better. We'd like to talk to you about the attack. Do you remember anything?" Irene began.

A brief nod from Thylqvist made Irene's heart beat faster with anticipation. The nurse helped to block the cannula so that Thylqvist could speak.

"Smell . . . smell . . ."

"You mean the man who attacked you smelled?"

Another nod.

"Did he smell good?"

A shake of the head.

"Did he smell bad?"

Nod.

"Was it the same smell as Marie Carlsson described? A revolting stench?"

Nod.

It had to be the same man. The Package Killer.

Thylqvist gesticulated to the nurse, who covered the cannula with a practiced hand once more.

"Old . . . oil."

Old oil. He smelled of old, presumably rancid oil. There had been oil on Thylqvist's jacket. The Package Killer had oil on his clothes, which could have transferred to his victims' clothing. Was that why he had stripped the two women he had killed? There was no oil on the actual bodies, although of course he had washed them thoroughly, perhaps to dissolve any possible traces.

"Did you see him?" Irene asked.

A shake of the head. This was disappointing, but not entirely unexpected; after all, he had attacked her from behind.

"Did you see his car?"

Another shake.

The nurse cleared her throat. "I think that's enough for now. Efva's tired."

The look Thylqvist gave the nurse was poisonous, but Irene realized she was right. Thylqvist was even paler than when they had arrived, and there were blue-black shadows under her eyes. Rather ineptly, Irene patted her boss's hand, which was lying on top of the covers.

"Get well soon. Everyone sends their love. We weren't allowed to bring flowers, but as soon as they move you to the regular ward . . ."

Irene broke off, overcome with embarrassment. Thylqvist's eyes were filled with tears.

AFTER A RESTLESS night, Irene had made up her mind. Before morning prayer she knocked on Tommy's door and walked straight in.

"Hi. You look like shit," she said.

"Thanks. Right back at you."

They both knew the other person was right. Suddenly Irene started to giggle, and soon they were both laughing. For a moment it felt just like before, when they were the best of friends and supported each other in everything. It was high time they tried to restore that friendship, but it was probably best to proceed with caution under the circumstances, Irene thought.

"Tommy, I've been thinking all night. We need to get the investigation out of this deadlock. Right now."

"I couldn't agree more. Do you have any constructive suggestions?"

"I think so. I feel as if we've missed something important, something hiding in plain sight. Something to do with Daniel Börjesson."

"But we've checked him out so many times—there's no concrete proof. He doesn't have a car. He was at home when Jonny called him after the attack on Efva. There's no sign of a cat in his apartment, etcetera etcetera. The facial composite could be him, but the only thing it proves is that he asked Marie Carlsson a couple of strange questions, and . . ."

"I know, I know—we've gone over it again and again. But somewhere . . . it's something I heard, although I can't quite get a hold of it. I want to spend the day digging into Daniel's life. Drive to Basungatan, sound out the terrain. Efva told us to drop him, but now you're in charge—it's your decision."

She smiled, but Tommy didn't smile back. The silence went on and on, but Irene was determined not to break it.

At long last Tommy spoke. "Okay. I respect your gut feeling, but you only have today."

"Thanks. That's enough."

"You should take someone with you."

"There's no need. I have no intention of talking to Daniel. This is something else."

IRENE WAS THE first customer of the morning in the convenience store. Theo Papadopoulos was busy setting out packed boxes of fruit when she arrived. He greeted her with pleasure, as if she was a loyal and valued customer.

"Hello again—can you spare a few minutes?" she asked.

"Of course. It's quiet at this time of day."

He showed her into the break room, where there was a wonderful aroma of fresh coffee. Theo went back into the store and picked up two cinnamon buns, still warm from the oven.

"I'm not surprised you've come back," he said as he poured the coffee.

"No?"

"No. Both my daughter Melina and I think Daniel has been behaving even more oddly since Signe died. Melina's scared. She says he has the evil eye. That comes from her Greek background. People believe in the evil eye in my former homeland. You must avoid those who give you the evil eye, and if worst comes to the worst, you must kill them!" The last comment was accompanied by a big smile.

"In what way has he been behaving more oddly?"

"He's always been a loner, of course—he's never really had any friends. But these days we hardly ever see him. Occasionally he comes in just as we're about to close, and he doesn't even say hi. He used to work, but he doesn't seem to do that anymore. When he didn't have anything else he would help out by pruning the trees and shrubs around here, and he did a good job, but according to Kenneth, who's in charge of the maintenance service, nowadays Daniel just says no if he asks him. Daniel claims he's on sick leave. I don't know if that's true, but Kenneth says that's been the case ever since Signe died. So how can he afford that apartment?"

Theo ran his hands over his cardigan pockets. He fished out a packet of Marlboros and put it on the table, then took a yellow plastic lighter out of another pocket.

"Are the rents high around here?" Irene asked.

"Maybe not as high as they are in the city center, but he's paying for a three-room apartment on his own."

Theo got up and offered Irene a cigarette. She smiled and shook her head. As he moved toward the back door, Melina came in and said hello to Irene.

"Good. You can talk to Irene while I go for a smoke," Theo said.

Melina didn't look too keen, but she took off her jacket and sat down at the old Formica table. She yawned and poured herself a cup of coffee, then looked at Irene. Melina's sea-green eyes were heavily made up, accentuating their unusual color.

"Is this about Daniel?" she asked.

"What makes you think that?" Irene replied, keeping her tone neutral.

"You asked about him last time. And he's kind of . . . creepy," Melina said with a shudder.

"Is that why you called and left an anonymous message about the picture in the newspaper?"

Melina gave a start. Her eyes appeared unnaturally large

in her pretty face as they widened. She pushed back a honey-colored strand of hair and attempted to tuck it behind her ear, but it was too thick and immediately fell forward once more.

"How . . . how do you know it was me?"

"I worked it out. Has something happened recently to make you feel he's even stranger than he was before?"

Melina twirled the strand of hair nervously around her finger.

"I don't know . . . It's just a feeling, really. He . . . stares. Even Mom has noticed. She doesn't want to be alone with him in the store."

"Has he said anything, made any kind of approach?"

"No, never. But it's just horrible. I don't even walk past the garage anymore, even though it's the shortest route to the tram."

Irene pricked up her ears. "The garage?"

"An old place. It's over there," Melina said, pointing.

"That must be . . . west. Do you mean in Ruddalen?"

"Yes. He sometimes hangs out there."

"Doing what?"

Melina shrugged as her father returned from his cigarette break, carrying with him the smell of fruit and tobacco. He smiled, showing his nicotine-yellowed teeth.

"What are you two talking about?"

"Daniel. Melina's just told me he sometimes hangs out in an old garage not far from here," Irene explained.

"Yes, he used to spend a lot of time at the garage, but I don't think he goes there nowadays."

"What did he do there?"

"It was his grandfather's bicycle repair shop; Daniel used to help out."

"But it's been a long time since his grandfather died—eighteen years. Are you saying that Daniel carried on renting the place after his death?" Irene asked.

Theo frowned, thinking hard, then he said slowly, "Daniel used to tinker with his own bikes, then with his moped. When his grandfather died, an old friend took over the repair business, but I don't know how well it worked out. His name was Stig; he was a drinker. People said he lived in the garage with his cats for the last year before he died. I saw Daniel with him occasionally. Daniel used to have an old car, and he would go over and work on it with Stig. But Stig died a year or so ago. I don't think anyone uses the garage now."

Irene thought he was wrong, and by way of confirmation, Melina jumped in.

"I saw Daniel there in the summer. That's when I stopped taking that route with Lukas."

"Lukas is our dog—an old golden retriever. He's so sweet some people might describe him as stupid," Theo explained.

"Dad!"

Theo laughed and winked at Irene. She smiled back, and couldn't help saying:

"I've got a dog, too, a little dachshund."

"He's probably a better guard dog than Lukas—he loves everybody. Even Daniel." Theo chuckled.

"It's true." Melina sighed.

"So where exactly is this garage?"

"Go along Basungatan," Theo said. "You'll come to a small parking lot. Go straight across it, and in the far left-hand corner there's a narrow path leading into the forest. I guess it was asphalt once upon a time, but it's a mess these days. The garage is twenty or thirty meters down the path, but you can't see it from the parking lot. It's hidden by the trees."

IT TOOK NO more than a minute to walk from the convenience store to the dilapidated garage. Theo was right: it couldn't be seen from the parking lot. It was a small grey concrete building with a rusty corrugated metal roof. The windows were barred, and the door looked solid. A painted sign hung above the door, and it was just about possible to work out that the faded letters said BÖRJESSON'S CYCLE REPAIR SHOP. Trees and bushes were growing right up against the walls. Only the area in front of the door was accessible, mainly because it had been paved at some point in the past. Small trees and weeds had sprung up through the cracks, tangible proof of the power of nature. There was garbage everywhere, left behind by generations of teenagers. This wasn't a nice place, but for kids who wanted to hide out, it was perfect.

Irene walked over to the metal sliding door. She grabbed the handle and tried to open it, but it was locked. A long piece of wood lay in the grass, painted the same color as the door, which made her think it served as an additional security measure. There were heavy metal sockets on either side of the door into which the beam could be inserted. It was obviously meant to be fastened with a padlock, but there was no sign of anything like that in the grass. There was dog crap everywhere.

Irene picked her way over to the window. The glass was filthy with years of ingrained dirt, and the thick iron bars meant she couldn't get right up to the window itself. She shaded her eyes with her hand and tried to peer in. It was a while before she realized it was boarded up on the inside. She walked around the garage. Same story with the window on the opposite side. Her heart flipped over as something touched her leg. The cat that had brushed against her was equally scared when Irene let out a scream; it slipped into the undergrowth and disappeared.

Irene made her way back to the front, and spotted fresh tire tracks. She hadn't noticed them when she first took a look around. Was the workshop used as a garage for a car? She turned and looked back at the apartment blocks. Daniel's place was about a two-minute walk away. She took out her cell phone and called Tommy. He answered almost right away, and she quickly explained what she had found.

"We're on our way," Tommy said.

Irene could hear a hint of excitement in his voice. His instincts had kicked in, too. If there really was a car in the garage, and they could prove it belonged to Daniel, the investigation would take a completely new turn.

"Do you know if Daniel's home?" he asked.

"I have no idea. I've avoided being seen from his apartment."

"Perhaps you should keep an eye on the place, just in case he goes out."

"Okay," Irene said with a sigh, "but there are rear exits from the building. I'll have to try to find a strategic position."

"Do your best. Backup will be with you very soon. I'll try to get some help with surveillance, too. Hannu and Sara are out on a suspected homicide in Hisings Backa, but Jonny and I will be there. I'll contact CSI so they can come out to Frölunda as soon as they've finished in Hisings Backa."

"Sounds good. Let me know when you're approaching Basungatan."

Irene ended the call, but almost dropped her phone when she heard a man's voice behind her

"What the hell are you doing here?"

She spun around and saw a man with a shaved head with a huge Leonberger on a leash. The dog's tail was wagging, but its master looked deeply suspicious. He was around sixty years old, short and squat with leathery skin. The dog's head was on a level with his hip. He was wearing heavy boots that seemed to match his heavy-duty blue nylon work clothes.

Irene quickly produced her police ID. "Detective Inspector Irene Huss."

"What the hell is a cop doing here?"

Irene felt a sudden spurt of anger. She couldn't be bothered to waste time on this idiot.

"Police business. If you'll excuse me I'll get on with my job," she said coldly.

As she looked at his clothing, she was struck by a sudden thought.

"Who are you, anyway?"

The man gave her a nasty look. "Kenneth Svensson. I'm in charge of the maintenance service for this area," he muttered.

"Excellent, in that case I have a question for you. Who's using this garage?" she said, nodding in the direction of the grey concrete structure.

Svensson raised his eyebrows. He seemed genuinely surprised.

"Using . . . What are you talking about?"

"Just answer the question, please."

The poisonous expression was back.

"No one is *using* this dump. It's scheduled to be demolished. They're supposed to be building some kind of wellness center here, whatever that is."

"There seems to be a car inside."

"Could be. I don't know anything about that, but if there is, it will have to go, too. The old drunk who used to rent this place died last year, so I guess it's his car."

Kenneth Svensson glared at her before firing off his final shot. "So it's my job to make sure nobody *uses* this shithole before it's knocked down. Which will be in three weeks' time."

He turned and headed back through the trees, with the dog ambling at his heels. Irene followed him, wondering where was the best place to position herself in order to keep an eye on Daniel. She looked up at his windows and balcony, but could see no sign of movement behind the curtains. What does this guy do during the day? Eventually she decided to drive to the visitors' parking lot in front of his apartment block. At least that way she could cover one side of the building.

• • •

TOMMY CALLED TEN minutes later, and Irene directed him to the parking lot next to the narrow path leading to the workshop. They arrived at the same time. Jonny got out of the car and retrieved a large cloth bag from the backseat. Good—tools that could be used to break in would be very handy.

"Hi. I guess you're not a prospective buyer for the place you found," Tommy said with a big smile.

He looks excited; let's hope he's not going to be disappointed, Irene thought.

"Hardly. It's due to be pulled down in three weeks."

They headed along the path toward the grey concrete building. With just a few meters to go, Irene suddenly stopped. Jonny almost ran right into her.

"Oops! What's wrong?" he asked.

"The barricade."

"What about it?"

"It's across the door."

"Well, that's where I'd expect to find a barricade," Jonny said, sighing demonstratively.

"When I left here twenty minutes ago, it was lying on the ground. In the grass just there."

"In which case someone must have slid it into place while you were gone," Tommy said, somewhat unnecessarily.

"Daniel. I didn't see any sign of him, although he could have gone out when I went to pick up my car and move it to the visitors' parking lot, so I could keep an eye on his apartment. Or he could have left by the exit at the rear of the building," Irene said.

Tommy gazed pensively at the securely barricaded door. "Or he was inside when you were here."

Irene's whole body was covered in goosebumps. If Kenneth Svensson hadn't come along with his dog, things could have turned out very differently. In order to hide how she was feeling, she pointed to the barely visible marks on the ground.

"Watch out for the tire tracks," she said.

They walked around the tracks in a wide semicircle and stood by the door.

"It's padlocked," Irene said.

"Not for long." Jonny opened his bag and triumphantly brandished a pair of powerful bolt cutters. A second later there was a loud click and the padlock landed in the plastic bag Tommy was holding out.

"In case of prints," Jonny said with satisfaction.

The lock on the door itself was perfectly ordinary and didn't cause Jonny any problems at all.

The door squeaked in protest as they slid it open. Irene switched on the light, and a flickering glow from several ancient fluorescent tubes illuminated the interior.

As expected, there was no car, but fresh patches of oil on the cement floor gave away the fact that a vehicle had been there very recently.

"A car was started up in here not very long ago—breathe in," Tommy ordered.

Obediently Irene and Tommy sniffed the air: dampness, dirt, mold and exhaust fumes.

"There are mice in here," Jonny informed his colleagues.

Irene could also smell mouse droppings. There were so many different odors that her sense of smell became blunted after a while. They started to look around. The old workshop wasn't very big. There might have been room for three cars back in the day, but it was more than adequate for bicycles. The workbenches along the walls were overflowing with all kinds of crap, as were the shelves above. In one corner several rakes and pruning shears were propped up, but it was the pit that immediately attracted Irene's attention. She went across and looked down.

"Over here," she said, more sharply than she had intended.

The bottom of the shallow pit was covered with a large

sheet of builder's plastic. Then Irene saw the tape, the knife and the bottle of Yes. There was a hose hanging on the wall above the pit.

"The bastard was ready to make a new package," Jonny said.

"I'm guessing this was meant for Efva," Tommy mumbled.

It was a horrific thought, but he was probably right.

Jonny went and took a closer look at the gardening tools. "They've got DB on the handles."

"Daniel Börjesson. Right, we bring him in, and this time we don't let him go until he . . ."

Tommy didn't finish the sentence, but Irene noticed his clenched fists.

"There has to be more," she said.

She went over to a door at the back of the workshop. There was a broken window next to it, partially boarded up. She tried the handle, and the door opened. The room was tiny and stank like a garbage dump. She saw an old camp bed by the wall, piled high with plastic bags containing empty pizza boxes, clothes and God knows what else.

"Clothes . . . women's clothes. And Elisabeth's purse—the one we saw on the CCTV film from the ICA store," Irene said.

"Ingela Svensson's and Elisabeth Lindberg's stuff. And look at the board," Jonny said.

The sheet of plywood was covered in photographs, all of women, all taken through their windows or outdoors. Marie Carlsson . . . Ingela Svensson . . . Elisabeth Lindberg—and two women Irene had never seen before. They appeared to be middle-aged and were going about their lives oblivious to any danger. One was tall, her long blonde hair loose down her back. She was in her living room in an embroidered pale green tunic and looked as if she was whistling. The other woman had short dark hair. In one picture she was getting into a small white car, in another she was watering potted plants on her kitchen windowsill.

"We need to try to identify those two. And there's Efva," Irene said.

Above the camp bed was a newspaper cutting with a picture from the press conference about the Package Killer's two victims. The superintendent was smiling, and looked fantastic in her white blouse and dark uniform jacket. There were also a number of smaller photographs of Thylqvist taken with Daniel's camera: Thylqvist taking bags of groceries out of the trunk of her car, Thylqvist coming out of the front door of the apartment block in her uniform. Tommy and Jonny moved closer. They didn't notice as Irene quickly removed two photographs right at the bottom, nearly hidden by a cluster of empty bottles on the table.

It was obvious that the first in the series of three had been sent to Thylqvist along with the chrysanthemum. These two showed what followed. At the moment she didn't quite know what to do with them, but she would deal with that later. At the moment her main concern was that Tommy didn't need to see them—and nor did Jonny! She slipped them in her pocket, and nearly jumped out of her skin when Jonny suddenly yelled:

"Irene!"

He was pointing to a picture low down on the board.

"That's you."

Her heart pounding, Irene took a closer look. The photograph had been taken outside her house at dusk. In the background the living room window glowed invitingly. Egon was sniffing around the edge of the grass, and Irene was walking along, lost in thought.

She knew exactly when it had been taken: two weeks ago, when the realtor had come to see the house. She had taken Egon for a little walk, and she remembered the sound of something moving in the bushes. The snap of a dry twig. Egon had reacted, wanted to go back home. He had sensed danger lurking in the twilight.

Irene cleared her throat to make sure her voice would hold up. "I just realized that Daniel actually met Efva."

"When?" Tommy asked.

"I was interviewing Daniel at the station, and she came in to ask Jonny for the car keys."

"That's right—they were in my pocket," Jonny confirmed.

"Hmm. This guy makes up his mind pretty fast," Tommy said.

"I wonder why he likes them a little older?" Jonny mused.

Irene had asked herself the same question several times during the investigation, and was fairly sure she had come up with the answer.

"Marie. His mother. I think it's got something to do with her. She'd just turned sixteen when she had him, and she died two months later. She would have been forty-nine now."

"Possibly. Anyway, the shrinks can get to the bottom of that once we've got him. They should have enough material for an entire conference by the time they've finished with that guy. I'll put out a call for him. Pity we don't know what car he's driving. Then again, it's probably stolen," Tommy said.

"Or it's the deregistered Renault Express with false plates; that heap of trash has been bothering me all along," Jonny muttered.

Irene's glance fell back on the clothing hanging on two strong hooks on the back of the door, and she suddenly realized what they were and was there in a second. An extremely scruffy jacket with matching pants in thick dark-blue nylon, and a dark-blue baseball cap. The jacket had a matted fleece collar and fraying elasticized cuffs. Dark oil stains were visible in several places. There was a reflective band around the sleeves and the legs of the pants. One sleeve carried the words BÖRJESSON'S CYCLE REPAIR SHOP in white. An unbelievably filthy flannel shirt that had once been blue-and-white checked hung beneath the jacket. A pair of heavy, scuffed leather work boots lay on the floor.

These were Ivar Börjesson's work clothes, without a shadow of a doubt. Daniel's grandfather, who had been dead for eighteen years, had worn these clothes.

The stench was indescribable.

THE THREE DETECTIVES went outside to wait for the CSIs. The slanting rays of the afternoon sun filtered down through the trees, and the air was beginning to feel a little chillier.

"Half past four. Aren't you supposed to be driving up to Värmland today?" Tommy asked.

"Yes—Krister's already there."

"Why don't you go? We can take care of this. You've worked hard all week—you've got plenty of time due."

Irene protested, but mostly for form's sake. She couldn't deny that it would be good to cover at least some of the three hundred kilometers in daylight.

BEFORE LEAVING HOME, Irene went into the bathroom. Methodically she tore the photographs she had smuggled out of the garage into tiny pieces, and flushed them down the toilet. Nobody would ever see them, especially not Tommy. Things were bad enough already.

She had wisely packed her bag the previous evening. A glass of milk and a banana would suffice to raise her blood sugar level for the time being, and she would stop for coffee and a snack at Riks Rasta in Brålanda. She was sure Krister would have a delicious meal waiting by the time she got to Sunne: perhaps a creamy chanterelle soup with fresh thyme to start, with game to follow. Saddle of venison in a red wine sauce, served with a leek and potato gratin flavored with garlic would be perfect. Krister's childhood friend Per-Erik was in charge of a local hunt, and often turned up with venison, hare or moose. Krister was a dedicated forager, and an interest in fungi seemed to be something that he and Egon shared. Perhaps they could train Egon to track down chanterelles? But dachshunds were originally bred to dig. Could little Egon dig a badger out of its sett? Unlikely—he wasn't inclined that way, Irene decided.

DUSK WAS FALLING fast by the time she passed Åmål. The coffee stop had done her good, and for the first time in several weeks she was feeling positive. She took out her cell to call Krister and tell him where she was, but the phone was dead. Irene swore. She had forgotten to charge the battery—and of course the charger was in Krister's car. If she'd known that she would have called from a payphone at Riks Rasta. Then again, trying to contact someone at the cottage was always a risky business: the only place they had any network coverage at all was in one of the bedrooms, the one on the eastern side. Over the years they had often talked about whether they should install a landline, but they put it off because it was too expensive. *At least we have electricity and our own water supply*, she thought contentedly. And an electric toilet, which was very useful. The old dry privy had done its job, but it had been pretty disgusting sometimes.

IT WAS DARK as she drove past Kil. There was still quite a lot of traffic on the E-45, but it was thinning out. It was Friday night, and the Swedish public was getting ready to vote for this year's winner of *Idol*, or whatever people were doing inside the brightly lit houses flashing by. She couldn't wait to see Krister. And Egon, of course. A good dinner, followed by coffee in front of the fire. An early night . . .

Before too much longer she reached Sunne, with the Selma Hotel and Spa on the left. In the darkness the building's illuminated pointed-gable roof reminded her of an Alpine village. All the rooms had windows facing Lake Fryken, although the view wasn't particularly striking right now, as dark clouds covered the moon and stars. The surface of the water lay black and silent. On the right lay the Selma Lagerlöf Hotel, with its elegance, class and style.

There were hardly any cars at all on the road now, and Irene could go for several minutes without meeting a single vehicle. The car immediately behind her had been there ever since Grums. She recognized it because the right headlamp was a little fainter, and occasionally flickered. Maybe someone who commuted to Karlstad and was heading home to Torsby. She knew that several people traveled the hundred and ten kilometers in each direction every day. Many used the Frykdal railway, which was regarded as one of the most beautiful stretches in Sweden, but for those who worked inconvenient hours, driving was the only option.

She flicked on the turn signal and turned onto the road leading to the Norwegian border; the car behind followed suit. Must be a Norwegian going home to Kongsvinger. Or maybe the driver lived in Charlottenberg. Irene turned up the radio as Paul McCartney's voice came over the airways singing "Yesterday." According to an article she had read, The Beatles' old songs had been remixed and reissued. Not that she could hear any difference, but that was probably due to her car stereo. It wasn't exactly top quality. There was no point in putting an expensive music system in a car in the city; it would just get stolen.

Irene hummed along as she slowed down to turn off onto the dirt road to Kymmen. After a kilometer or so she would take the forest track down to the cottage. It was in a remote spot, but that was one of its main attractions. As Katarina had said when she was little, it was so quiet it hurt your ears.

Suddenly a moose came crashing out of the undergrowth at the side of the road. Irene slammed on the brakes, her tires squealing. Reflexively she glanced in the mirror to see how far away the other car was. At first she couldn't see any lights and assumed it must have stopped somewhere farther back. Then she became aware of something blacker than the surrounding darkness, moving toward her: a car. Someone had killed the headlights. *Why?* The car came closer and closer; there was a grinding noise as the driver attempted to stop. In the red glow of Irene's brake lights, the driver's face was clearly visible in her rearview mirror.

Daniel Börjesson.

You are trying to flee from me. You will not succeed. The sanctity of my soul is under threat, and I feel a weight in my breast. Temptation burrows into me, tears at me . . . The Lord is testing me. I must save both you and myself from evil. There is only one way.

You must die.

Only then will I find peace in my soul.

And I will not be alone. The other beloved women are still there, waiting for me. They will never break our bond. I will never need to punish them. But if any one of them should transgress against me, I know what I must do to save their souls. I must cleanse them from sin. They will become a sacrifice. A sacrifice to the Lord to atone for their sins.

I am simply one of the Lord's chosen tools.

I am the Redeemer.

IRENE MISSED THE moose by a millimeter, and automatically completed the turn onto the narrow road. Her brain was completely frozen. She couldn't formulate a single clear thought. Panic overwhelmed her, and her heart was pounding. She had passed the last farm a kilometer before the turn-off, and now she was on a road that rarely saw traffic of any kind, not even during the day. At this time of night, it was deserted. The only houses along here were summer cottages, and Irene's heart sank as she realized there wasn't a single light showing. That was hardly surprising; it was the first weekend in October, and pretty cold for the time of year. The forecast had promised night frosts all over Värmland. She and Krister were the only visitors.

Irene realized that heading for the cottage would lead Daniel straight to their home. He probably wouldn't attack her as long as she and Krister were together, but he would be there, hidden close by. He was used to watching his victims; he would bide his time, and sooner or later he would strike. What should she do? She didn't dare rely on her Värmland colleagues to track him down in the darkness.

She tightened her grip on the wheel, and the anger began to burn inside her.

Enough! She had had enough of being persecuted. First Angelika Crazy Malmborg-Eriksson, and now Daniel "Even

Crazier" Börjesson. Enough! She didn't want to feel as if she was being watched, constantly wondering if he was out there. Enough!

Without slowing down, she drove past the turnoff for the cottage. If you knew it was there you could just make out the lights in the windows, but otherwise it didn't stand out. She put her foot down; she knew this route like the back of her hand, and Daniel didn't. At first she just kept on going as fast as she could, but gradually a plan began to crystallize. She had to lead him astray, make sure he had no idea where he was, and couldn't find his way back. There was a network of narrow dirt roads she could use, but a quick glance at the gas gauge told her she couldn't drive too much farther. The arrow was already in the red zone. She cursed herself. Why hadn't she filled up in Brålanda? The last thing she needed was to run out of gas in the middle of the forest with that lunatic on her heels!

Plan B would have to be a confrontation. Irene didn't want to fight Börjesson. She might be a black belt and a former European champion in jiujitsu, but that wasn't enough to risk taking on a strong man who could well be armed. She wouldn't have a chance against a knife or a length of iron piping, plus it was pitch dark out here. The street lighting along the E-45 covered only the more densely populated areas, and neither the moon nor the stars penetrated the blackness outside the car. She could use that to her advantage; once again she would have to rely on her local knowledge.

Irene drove toward Björnmyren, a place she and Krister visited several times every summer. It was one of the largest and most treacherous bogs in northern Sunne, but it was also where the best cloudberries could be found. The bog was renowned for its rich animal life, attracting many nature enthusiasts during the spring and summer. Twenty years ago a German couple had taken a wrong turn, and they had both drowned in the bog. Following the tragedy, the local history association and the Sunne ornithological society had raised the funds to build a U-shaped footpath that covered a large part of the bog. Irene knew it well. But Daniel didn't.

She glanced in the rearview mirror but couldn't see him. The idiot was still driving without lights. Did he think she hadn't spotted him? At that moment the lights came on behind her; it must have become difficult for him to follow her in the darkness.

She suddenly felt utterly calm. She knew exactly what to do. Without taking her eyes off the road, she opened the glove compartment and fumbled around until she found the small, powerful flashlight she kept in there. As her fingers closed around it, she allowed herself a triumphant smile.

She floored the accelerator as the road wound its way down to Björnmyren, dense coniferous forest on either side. It was impossible for anyone who wasn't familiar with the area to know what was waiting around the next bend, but Irene knew. Daniel had no chance of keeping up with her at this speed. As the road leveled out, following the edge of the bog, she slowed down. There! She spun the wheel and drove a short distance along a forest track where she and Krister usually parked, making the car invisible from the road. She leapt out and ran back out onto the road, toward the track leading to the footpath over the bog. She bent down, switched on the flashlight, and with trembling fingers picked out a fist-sized rock lying in the undergrowth. She switched off the flashlight. All she had to do now was get ready. When she heard the engine of Daniel's car approaching, Irene stepped out and took careful aim before she let it fly. She heard a dull crunch as the rock hit the windshield, by which time Irene was hiding behind the trunk of a tall pine tree. Daniel slammed on the brakes, and the car skidded into the shallow ditch. Irene remained where she was, forcing herself to breathe evenly. This was it.

After a few seconds the driver's door opened and Daniel

scrambled out. He staggered up onto the dirt road, about twenty-five meters from where Irene stood. She switched on the flashlight once more and shone it straight at him. Reflexively he held up his hands, shielding his eyes from the bright light. Irene was counting on the fact that he would be totally dazzled after staring out into the darkness for so long. The beam of the flashlight bounced off the heavy wrench he was holding in one hand.

"So, Daniel. You've decided it's my turn. But you'll have to catch me first," she said, determined to challenge him.

She turned away, shielding the beam with her hand. She needed to see where she was going; if she stumbled, the consequences would be disastrous. When she reached the path over the bog, she stopped and listened. She could hear the sound of footsteps and heavy breathing. Daniel had taken the bait and was following her. Irene set off across the bog. She knew that the exact length of the path, which was made of wide wooden planks laid side by side in pairs, was 1.1 kilometers. It was a challenge in broad daylight, let alone in the pitch dark. Daniel wouldn't be able to keep up with her, because that meant running the risk of stepping off the path. At the edge of the bog his boots would get a bit damp and muddy, but farther out there were deep holes filled with water. He didn't know about those.

Irene was able to make good progress thanks to the flashlight. She didn't want to get too far ahead, otherwise he might give up. Occasionally she let out a little cry as if she had gone wrong and got her feet wet in the icy water—which did in fact happen once or twice. They were getting farther and farther out onto the bog.

The night was damp and bitterly cold. Veils of mist danced around, trailing their chilly fingers over her face. She shivered in her woolen sweater; she had left her coat in the car, so it wouldn't impede her mobility. She was surrounded by a strong smell of bog myrtle and peaty water. Coarse sedge whipped against her shins, soaking the legs of her pants. From time to time the screech of a bird or the cry of an animal sliced through the silence. She could hear a large creature moving around out on the bog. Wolves were wary and didn't make a sound when they crept up on their prey; they preferred to stay in the forest, deep among the trees. This was probably a moose, but it could be a bear. There was a reason why this place was known as Björnmyren—the Bear Bog.

It seemed remarkable that she was able to register so much of what was going on around her. In some strange way she felt at home, safe in the dense darkness. She was constantly aware of the footpath shaking as Daniel lumbered along behind her. He hadn't said a word, merely set off in pursuit, which was exactly what Irene had expected. From his point of view the situation was ideal: a defenseless woman all on her own, running for her life through the night. He thought he was the hunter.

But he had underestimated this particular quarry.

They had passed the first water-filled hole. The holes were invisible, but Irene knew they were there, right next to the path, dark and cold. Bottomless, according to a tale her mother-in-law had once told her.

Irene estimated that they had covered approximately eight hundred meters, which meant she had roughly one hundred meters left before she reached the spot where she intended to carry out her plan. The planks were still shuddering under Daniel's weight; he wasn't about to give up. Irene started moving faster; she needed to increase the distance between them if this was going to work. She sent up a silent prayer that the path by the hole hadn't been repaired. Her heart started to flutter as she grew closer, and she briefly allowed the beam of the flashlight to play a few meters ahead of her. There they were! The loose planks.

They had suffered badly over the years; the span of the hole was too great, and the planks needed replacing with something considerably more substantial. When she and Krister had been out here picking cloudberries in the summer, they had noticed that the nails at either end had gradually come loose with the vibration of people walking across; they had often said how dangerous it was, an accident just waiting to happen.

Irene tiptoed to the other side, then she turned and kicked first at one plank, then the other. Pain surged through her foot, but after a couple more hard kicks the planks gave way and lay floating on the dark surface of the water. Daniel would have a real problem getting across the hole. Jumping wasn't an option; the distance was too great. If he did manage to balance on the planks he would have to edge his way over.

By that time Irene should be at least halfway back to the car. Daniel would probably turn around, but without a flashlight it was impossible to move fast. Irene would be safe in the cottage when he got to his car; and she could use Krister's cell to call her colleagues in Torsby to come out and take care of Daniel Börjesson.

With a surge of relief she set off at speed.

The splash made her halt. Daniel had fallen in. He wasn't yelling, but she could hear him snorting and struggling in the icy water. Through the splashing she heard him gasping: "can't . . . swim . . . can't. . ." The withered sedge simply snapped off when he managed to grab a tuft hanging over the hole. His arms flailed desperately, and a series of guttural roars rose into the blackness of the night sky. No words, just anguished cries. Irene listened for what felt like an eternity.

She ought to go back and help him.

She ought to go back.

But she doesn't go back.

He is drowning.

Her feet feel like lumps of ice. They have frozen to the

planks, and she cannot move them. The rancid breath of the bog finds its way beneath her sweater. The eyes of the night are watching her. All the restless souls that dwell in this desolate place are clawing at her, tugging at her ankles, trying to drag her down into the water. If she moves, they will succeed.

She stands motionless.

Suddenly everything falls silent once more. It is as if all the creatures of the bog have stopped to listen. The only sound she can hear is the beating of her own heart, throbbing against her eardrums.

The paralysis is gone. She can move her feet. She flies along the path as fast as she can. But she does not run toward the hole, where the loose planks are floating on the surface along with a baseball cap.

She runs in the opposite direction.

"Sweetheart! You're soaking wet! Where have you been? I was starting to get worried."

Irene sank down at the bottom of the stairs and took off her sodden shoes and socks without replying.

"I called your cell, but I couldn't get through. Has something happened?"

"The battery's dead."

Her voice was thick with suppressed tears. Suddenly her whole body began to shake.

"Hold me," she sobbed.

Author's Note

I WOULD LIKE to thank my niece Karin for lending me Hanko, her German shepherd. He's every bit as wonderful and obedient in reality as he is in this novel.

For those of you who might be wondering, I can tell you that Egon is a little sweetheart who I met briefly in Berlin last year. His name probably wasn't Egon at all, but I thought it was a bold name for an unusually small dachshund.

The events in my books are always fictional, as are the characters who appear in them. As usual I have taken considerable liberties with geographical facts. I claim the artistic freedom to adapt reality to fit the story where necessary. No doubt many of the residents of Västra Frölunda and northern Värmland have raised their eyebrows while reading this book.

Helene Tursten